T0146567

BROKEN LIES

ROGER WILLIAMS

WESTBOW
PRESS®
A DIVISION OF THOMAS NELSON
& ZONDERVAN

WestBow Press books may be ordered through booksellers or by contacting:

WestBow Press
A Division of Thomas Nelson & Zondervan
1663 Liberty Drive
Bloomington, IN 47403
www.westbowpress.com
1 (866) 928-1240

Because of the dynamic nature of the Internet, any web addresses or links contained in this book may have changed since publication and may no longer be valid. The views expressed in this work are solely those of the author and do not necessarily reflect the views of the publisher, and the publisher hereby disclaims any responsibility for them.

Any people depicted in stock imagery provided by Thinkstock are models, and such images are being used for illustrative purposes only.
Certain stock imagery © Thinkstock.

ISBN: 978-1-5127-4349-4 (sc)
ISBN: 978-1-5127-4350-0 (hc)
ISBN: 978-1-5127-4348-7 (e)

Library of Congress Control Number: 2016908214

Print information available on the last page.

WestBow Press rev. date: 12/19/2016

ACKNOWLEDGMENTS

What a wonderful journey it has been to place transformational events on paper for others to read, absorb, and process. Although *Broken Lies* is deeply personal, the main character, Chase Macklin, represents each and every one of us as we venture through life's failures and successes, defeats and victories, sorrows and joys, and are able to discover a new way of living once truth prevails over the lies we've believed and accepted about ourselves.

Let me first say thank you to my wife, Tricia, who has patiently tolerated the countless hours I have spent writing and re-writing. You have been so encouraging throughout the entire process, and I'm thankful for the many years we've had together and the many we will continue to have.

Thanks also go to Stephen Zoradi, a gifted marriage and family therapist who, as my friend, took the time to peruse the counseling sessions throughout this novel. Thanks for much for your help and advice.

And thank you, Westbow Press, for your expertise and diligence. Your staff and editors have been amazing.

CHAPTER 1

Upstate New York, 1987

The stillness of the woods screamed danger as he hid behind an old pine. He dared not move, not even to brush the sweat dripping down his nose. Minutes crawled by, the anxious pounding in his chest increasing. Despite growing worry, he would give his buyer, unexpectedly late, just a few more moments. Suddenly he heard footsteps and whispers. His eyes searched the darkness, his body motionless. The sounds drew nearer. Quickly calculating his options, Chase felt for his handgun, pushed himself away from the tree, and exploded down the slope toward an open meadow. Several cops shouted, "Macklin!" He kept running.

The canvas bag slung over his shoulder bounced awkwardly against his side as he wove through the tall grass and the rough terrain with youthful energy. To his left, he saw his one chance to escape. Darting toward the railroad bridge, he glanced behind him. Plenty of time. When his feet hit the tracks, Chase deftly matched the distance between each rail tie. Headlights struck him from the other side of the bridge. He stopped cold, hand on his gun. A pistol shot rang out in warning with cries for him to freeze. He looked down at the river fifty feet below. Then without a second thought, he pulled out his gun and fired into the air. The next shot left him crumpled on the ground.

Chase grabbed his left shoulder and crawled to the edge of the bridge. Cops scurried toward him as he hoisted himself up and over the steel railing and fell into the river.

His face hit the water first, the impact nearly knocking him unconscious. The powerful current pushed him down and away. He reached for the bag. Gone. Frantically searching for it with his feet, one good arm flailing, he reluctantly surrendered to the unforgiving waters.

Chase surfaced, floating swiftly downriver, gasping and choking, desperate to find a way out. He groped for passing rocks that cut at his hands. Finally, with his last bit of strength, he slammed his body into a large rock and held on. Somehow he managed to quiet his breath long enough to listen for sounds of pursuit. Satisfied, he dragged himself to shore, held his shoulder, and prepared for what lay ahead.

As he made his way gingerly to Murphy's house, barefoot after having lost one of his shoes in the river and tossing away the other, Chase wiped his bloodied nose onto his wet, torn T-shirt.

Murphy's home, built in the 1920s, was guarded by four towering maples in the front yard. Their leaves obscured the top half of the house, and thick ivy clung to its brick façade. Brown and white pebbles on the driveway embedded themselves in the bottoms of Chase's feet before he stepped up to the small porch. With only the entry-hall light visible, he hesitated before tapping softly on the front door. He knocked again more firmly, peeking through the small window until a face appeared, forehead touching the glass.

"What are ya doin' here?" bellowed the familiar voice as the door swung open. Murphy towered in the entryway, his bulky frame covered by a black silk robe. His unshaven, deeply lined face revealed a seasoned hardness, and his piercing blue eyes, offset with closely cropped gray hair, matched his imperious nature. Murphy held the door handle with one wizened hand and stretched out the other in front of Chase as if to prevent entry. His speech advertised his Brooklyn upbringing.

"What's goin' on, kid?" Murphy glanced suspiciously into the dark street before pulling Chase inside. "What happened?"

"I need help."

"Ya look terrible. Sit down."

Chase slumped in the chair by the door. Above his head hung a painting of a European nobleman, ax in hand with a menacing look in his eyes, defending his home against a band of raiders.

"Parker!" Murphy shouted. "Parker, get in here! Bring me some water! And a towel! Two of 'em! Hurry up!" He turned back to Chase with a frown. "All right, Mack, I'm gonna clean ya up, but talk fast and tell it to me straight. Parker! What's takin' so long?"

"I'm comin'." A grizzled man soon appeared and quickly placed a bowl of water and two towels next to Murphy. Parker's eyes were dark and blank, the deep lines on his nose extending downward past his mouth. He took a step back, glancing inquisitively back and forth between Murphy and Mack, the nickname given Chase a few years earlier.

"Okay, Mack, talk to me. Parker, gimme a smoke." A Camel instantly appeared. Murphy lit it, placing it clumsily between his wrinkled lips and yellowed teeth. He tore off Chase's T-shirt, picked up one of the towels, and began to wipe the blood.

Chase winced and struggled to sit up a little straighter before answering his boss. "I don't know, Murphy. I took the quarter pound into the—hey, not so hard!"

"This was a bullet, right?"

"Yeah."

"Well, you're lucky. Coulda been worse."

Chase took his first opportunity to look at the wound, relieved that the bullet had apparently just grazed him. He glanced up at Murphy with a grimace, wondering if the luck he mentioned would continue.

"Go on with your story, Mack ... Wait a minute! Where's the blow?" Murphy stopped cleaning the wound, lowering himself onto one knee to look Chase in the eye.

3

"Gone. I lost it."

"Lost it! How do ya lose a quarter pound of coke? Are ya stupid or what?"

"I went to the woods for the drop, but the guy didn't show for twenty, twenty-five minutes or so. Somebody set me up. Cops were all over the place. I nearly got killed and ended up in the river."

"Where's the blow, Mack? Ya better not be lyin' to me!"

"I almost got wasted, and you're askin' me where the blow is?"

"Yeah, I am! Where is it?" Murphy demanded even more loudly.

Chase swallowed an angry retort. He was in far too much pain to argue. He had never lashed out at Murphy, but he felt cornered and mistrusted. He didn't like the feeling. "Look, it got away from me when I fell into the river. I tried to get it back, but there was no way. I can't believe you don't believe me! Like I'm gonna lie to you for seven grand? That makes a lot of sense."

"None of it makes any sense," Murphy snarled, rising from his knee. "Now get outta here. I don't ever wanna see ya again. And if I get word that you're lyin' to me, that'll be the last time ya ever see anybody. Know what I'm sayin'?"

Chase glared at his boss and formed a fist with his right hand. Murphy noticed. "So ya wanna fight me?"

"Yeah, maybe I do. I may lie to everybody else but not to you. I just don't get it. One mistake and all of a—"

"You're too hot," Murphy cut in.

"What?"

"You're too hot, kid. Can't have ya around. I don't know if I believe ya or not, but it don't matter. It's over. Can't take the chance. Parker, give him a shirt."

"What shirt?"

"Any shirt! I don't care!"

Parker quickly nodded and headed for his room upstairs.

Bending over again, Murphy took a towel, dipped it into the bowl, and took a few more swipes at Chase's shoulder. When Parker reappeared, Murphy grabbed the dress shirt he had fetched, draped it over Chase, and stuffed a fresh towel inside. "Here ya go, Mack. This should do for a while. I dunno, maybe we can do somethin' down the road a ways, just not now. I'll talk to Jacobs about it, but he ain't gonna believe me. I dunno, kid. It's just one of those things that—"

"I'm done, Murphy."

"Done with what?"

"Done with drugs, done with sellin', done with this whole kind of life."

Murphy laughed mockingly at Chase.

"No, I'm serious. It's just not worth it anymore. I'm only twenty-two. Got a lot ahead of me. You can do what you have to do, but I'm done."

"Get outta here!" Murphy growled. "I don't need that kinda talk! Ya got some nerve comin' here askin' for help and then throwin' insults at me. Just get outta here! Don't even think about showin' your face around me again."

Yanking Chase from the chair, Murphy shoved him toward the door. Then he stopped, pulled Chase close to his chest, and whispered, "Listen, kid, on second thought, I'll do ya one more favor. I don't know why, but I will. Walk up the street, go left on Jackson, and wait at the next street. I'll send a cab to pick ya up. Tell 'em where ya wanna go. Sorry it had to come down like this. You've always been my favorite, different from the rest. Anyhow, nice knowin' ya."

"Yeah, okay," Chase said, sensing finality in Murphy's words.

"And one more thing. You're not really who ya think ya are."

"What are you talking about?"

"Mack, this business is who ya are. Always will be. So just quit lyin' to yourself."

Chase shook his head and walked backward from the house, dazed from the whirlwind of the last few hours. He couldn't tell which throbbed harder, his confused mind or his wounded shoulder. Turning from the driveway, he walked cautiously toward Jackson Street, knowing all too well Murphy's malicious treatment of others in similar situations. Chase knew he had to be careful. At the same time, however, he saw the significance of this night. A major shift had quickly taken place, and Chase sensed that his entire future pivoted on this single evening. Life would be different now that he had broken with Murphy, who, despite his gruff demeanor and his illegal dealings, had become a father figure to him in the past several years.

Another pivotal moment in Chase's life had come eight years earlier when his father moved permanently out of the house. For as long as Chase had remembered, his dad had gotten up at five in the morning, driven to Syracuse, put in his eight hours, driven home, eaten dinner in front of the TV, and fallen asleep in his favorite chair. He had spent weekends in the local bars, often not returning home at night.

Chase couldn't recall the first time his father cheated on his mom. His father said it never happened, but all the kids knew better. Mom would cry, and Dad would yell. Dad even hit Mom once. After that, Chase vowed never to be like his father. Finally, his mom had had enough.

"You're leaving us, Robert!" she commanded one night in desperation and anger.

"I'm not leavin'!" he roared in return. "This is my house! These are my kids! There's no way I'm leavin'!"

"Either you leave, or I file for divorce. Take your pick."

His dad moved out two weeks later. His mother couldn't stop weeping for days, apparently still in love with the man but unable to tolerate his drinking and cheating. Chase missed his father's presence but despised him even more. Still, the loss gnawed at him for several years until he discovered that getting high eased his pain and calmed his anger. One time after that unforgettable day, he may have seen his dad at an intersection, a blonde seated next to him, but Chase couldn't be certain. Later that year, he met Murphy through a friend.

Nearing his destination, Chase considered the sudden and radical change in his relationship with Murphy. It made no sense. Murphy had always spoken of his team as a family and had said he would never turn his back on any member, especially his right-hand man Mack. Chase had made both of them lots of money. He guessed that didn't matter anymore. But what would he do now? He couldn't go to his mom's. He couldn't go to his place. *Okay,* he thought, *that's it. Maybe that'll work.*

6

Chase noticed a yellow cab pulling up to the sidewalk. Must be his. He waved it down and climbed inside. Before he could give the driver an address, fear gripped him and his mind began racing. *This doesn't seem right*, he told himself. *It has to be a set-up. Murphy said something about doing me one more favor. Why? And what did he mean by 'nice knowin' ya?'*

"Where to, bud?"

As soon as the driver turned his head, Chase bolted from the cab and ran. He heard the squeal of tires and looked back to see the cab turning around in pursuit. Ducking between two houses and vaulting over a short wooden fence, he found the backyard barrier much higher. The towel on his shoulder slipped down to his waist, and blood came through his shirt as he pulled himself over five or six more fences, clawing his way out of the neighborhood.

Sprawled out behind a liquor store, Chase felt exhausted, confused, and angry. He worked to reposition the towel over his wound. Slowly he pulled himself over to the store wall, close to a trash bin, his indignation increasing as he considered ways to go after Murphy. No, he had to stick to his plan and see Frank first. Maybe after that he'd figure out how to retaliate. Still conflicted, Chase reached for his gun. Lost in the river, he remembered. Annoyed that vengeance would have to wait for a more opportune time, he resolved that getting safely to Frank's had to be his priority at this point. Frank and Allie were the only ones he could trust, the only ones who wouldn't judge him, and perhaps the only ones who would help him.

Chase stared at the stars. *God, why did you do this to me? I don't deserve it*, he thought. *But maybe I do. Maybe it's some sort of payback.* Everything seemed to be crashing in upon his life. No, he wouldn't let that happen. He'd win in the end, no matter what.

Spotting the cab drive slowly down the street and then back again, he waited for about ten minutes before stumbling down the dimly lit sidewalk, his eyes carefully trained in all directions.

CHAPTER 2

C hase didn't reach Frank's place until nearly one in the morning. He stood at the door, hesitated, and then rapped firmly with his knuckles. His brother was the middle son, three years older than Chase, married with no children. His wife, Allie, loquacious and full of energy, worked alongside Frank in their accounting business.

Chase knocked again and heard Allie's muffled voice through the locked door. "Who is it?"

"It's me, Chase."

The door opened. Allie took a look at Chase and her gentle features registered alarm. "Chase! You're hurt! Here, let's get your shirt off. Sit down first."

Slumping onto the sofa, Chase closed his eyes and let Allie work on the buttons of his borrowed shirt. He drank in the subtle aroma of her perfume as she questioned him, but her words didn't register. Entranced by the fragrance, Chase found himself drifting in and out of consciousness, his head tilted back in a stupor and his eyes shut.

A deep voice startled him. "Chase, what happened? Chase!"

He opened his eyes and saw Frank squatting in his boxers, staring wide-eyed. Frank was a little bigger than Chase and had a square jaw with a sloping nose. While Chase never let a whisker remain on his face, his older brother had sported a closely cropped beard for the last few years.

"I'll be okay," Chase said unconvincingly.

Ignoring the reply, Frank looked at Allie. "He's going to need some bandaging. Do you mind getting some from upstairs?"

"That's where I was headed. Be right back."

"And bring that bottle of Johnnie Red as well. Chase, who got you? Was it Murphy?"

"Not really."

"I've never trusted Murphy. Looks like he got you good."

"Well it wasn't him. The cops got me."

"The cops?"

"Yeah. It all came after a drug deal gone bad. So then I went to Murphy's, and he didn't believe what happened. Thinks I stole from him. So now he's out to get me too. He actually tried to kill me."

"What?!"

"Yeah, what a night."

"Well that's just great. Both Murphy and the cops. How'd you get away?"

"I jumped off the bridge, and the next thing I know I'm floating downriver thinking I might die."

Frank nodded. "Looks like it could have been a lot worse, though. So Murphy didn't patch you up? Just gave you a towel?"

"Pretty much."

"Wow, this is nuts. I don't get it."

"Well, it's the last time, Frank."

"Good." Frank stood up. "Thanks, Allie. Here, Chase. Take a couple shots of this."

"So what happened?" Allie asked with concern.

Frank knew his wife's need for details, so he explained the events as best he could.

Allie looked at Chase. "What are you going to do? The police? And Murphy? I can't imagine what's going on in your head right now!"

"Yeah, really," Frank added.

Chase emptied the first small glass. Allie cleaned the wound and prepared the bandages, looking back and forth from Chase to Frank, searching for answers. Frank poured another shot and wanted to hear more. "You said something about this being the last time. What do you mean?"

"Forget it."

Allie tucked a strand of black hair behind her ear, leaned forward, and looked tenderly into Chase's eyes. "You know you can trust us, Chase. It doesn't matter what you've done or what you're going to do. We love you, and we always will. You know that."

"Yeah, I know."

"So then talk to us," Allie said, gently probing.

"I don't know. It's just that something happened to me tonight. I guess it's everything together, getting shot, falling in the river, a set-up by Murphy. I, um, I honestly don't know. Just that things are going to be different now. I can't really explain it. I just know it inside."

"Sounds like you need some answers," Frank said.

"Yeah, but maybe I should tell you why I got into this whole thing in the first place. I've never really said much about it all."

"We can do that tomorrow. Right now you need sleep. Crash here tonight and we'll figure out what to do in the morning. Allie, could you bring out some blankets?"

"No, don't do that." Chase slowly sat up, trying to regain his strength. "Now listen, I know it's late and we're all tired, but I think I need to talk since I have no idea what's going to happen. I may not have this chance again. Somebody needs to know everything. I just feel that. You guys are the closest people I have. I mean Sadie's all right, but it's not the same. So let's talk, then I'll go get Sadie and leave the area."

Frank eased into a nearby chair, curious about his brother's intentions. Allie stayed next to Chase, adjusting the bandages. Chase waited until she finished. After a minute or so she stood. "There you go. You're okay for now. Would you like some coffee first?

"Yeah, sounds good."

"Frank?"

"Sure, thanks."

"Now don't tell your story till I get back!"

As Chase's eyes moved slowly around the room, the family photos on the wall caught his attention. He looked at his mother and father on their wedding day, about the only time he could remember seeing his dad with a smile. His mom looked beautiful in her wedding dress, her dark Italian skin presenting a lovely contrast with her white gown. Everyone looked so rich in suits and fine new dresses. St. Thomas's Church, constructed a century ago, looked even more resplendent than he recalled. Though the building was fairly modest for a Catholic church, its statues, crosses, flowers, and incense clearly identified it with the faith.

Chase glanced at a photo of six-year-old Frank in a brand-new uniform, poised to hit a T-ball. Their dad insisted they play baseball, though neither demonstrated the necessary talent or showed any desire to acquire it. After a season of watching his sons' uncoordinated play and listening to their complaints, their dad gave up, though not without insults.

"If you can't play ball, what good are you?" he would ask. That attitude surely characterized his father. He was critical of everyone but himself, at least outwardly. Chase wondered how he could have found much happiness in choosing the bottle over his family. Had his father attempted to cover his emptiness with an unsatisfying replacement? For the first time, he considered that this was what he himself had been doing, hiding his pain through drugs and dealing, escaping so he wouldn't have to face the rejection he felt. Murphy said something about him not being who he thought he was and about lying to himself, whatever that meant. He'd think about it later.

Chase noticed his brothers' graduation pictures, filled with smiling people wearing their Sunday best. This was strange from his jaded perspective. Why celebrate twelve years of educational boredom? Never did make much sense. But maybe others were not like him. He knew Frank and Allie were different from him in so many ways. They were a stable, career-minded, goal-oriented couple. The two finished high school with honors, earned bachelor's degrees, married a year later, and started their own business just months ago.

Chase saw a picture of Lane, the oldest, sitting on his brand-new motorcycle. His smile always seemed to proclaim confidence. Outgoing, adventurous, and full of energy, Lane typically appeared to be unworried about the challenges of life.

The last photo remained Chase's favorite. He looked affectionately at Nattie, a name the family gave his grandmother. Chase spent hours with her after school as she recounted stories of her past. He didn't care all that much for her advice, but he treasured their time alone. On several occasions, some of the money he made from dealing found its way into her purse, though he hoped she never knew the source. Nattie had been so proud of Chase. He cried for days after she died four years ago, shortly before he dropped out of school.

"Nattie was something else, wasn't she?" Chase softly observed.

"Yes she was," Frank agreed, looking up at the wall. "You know she always liked you the most."

"C'mon, Frank. That's not true."

"Yes it is! I'm sure of it because you're the youngest. She loved to spoil you."

Chase smiled broadly. "Wow! I think you're jealous!"

"Probably," said Frank with a grin.

Chase stared at the ceiling. "Seems like a long time ago. I mean not only since Nattie died but since Dad left us, the old high school days, growing up next door to the Ericsons. Where's it all gone, Frank?"

"I don't know." Frank seemed a bit annoyed. "I guess I don't think about it much. I've got a life ahead of me, a good job, a decent place to live. We're trying to have a baby. Did you hear?"

"Really? That's great."

"Yeah," Frank said, smiling. "We thought it was about time."

"Yeah? No kidding."

"Well, what do you think?"

"About what?"

"About us having a baby?"

"Oh, Frank," Allie said with rolled eyes as she entered the living room. "Did you tell Chase what I think you did?"

"Yeah, he did," Chase responded, taking the cup of coffee she handed him. "I think it's cool. What do you want, boy or girl?"

At the same time Frank said "girl," Allie said "boy." Chase shook his head with a smirk. "It's nice to see you still both agree on everything."

They all laughed. Chase grimaced in pain, reaching for his shoulder. "You remember when Dad took off?"

"Yeah," Frank answered, staring into his coffee.

"Well I know we all hate him, but I think what he did messed everything up for me most of all. You and Lane were able to get on with your lives, but I obviously went in another direction. I told you before that when Mom had to go back to work, selling drugs seemed to be the only way I could help out. Maybe I could've done something else, but it's the life I chose, a life that Dad forced on me. Why are you rolling your eyes?"

Frank shrugged. "Because you're blaming Dad for your own decisions and lifestyle."

"Of course I am! Things would've been different had he stayed. We'd have been a normal family. I would've been able to finish high school and get a regular job. I wouldn't be in this situation tonight had he not left us."

"All right. Go on."

"Well anyway, you guys know the kind of people I've been around these past few years. They're all like Dad. It's unbelievable. They draw you in, take care of you for a while, talk about how important loyalty is, and then they stab you in the back when things get tough. I saw it happen all the time, but now I'm the one getting stabbed."

"And shot," Frank added glibly.

"Yeah, right. I know you've warned me for a long time, but once you're in, it's nearly impossible to get out. And listen, maybe I did make some wrong choices early on, but this could just be who I am, or who I was. I don't know. The only thing I'm sure of, the thing I'll be glad to leave behind, is the hunger that was never satisfied. The users were always hungry. They never had enough. The dealers were always demanding more users, and the richer they got, the greater their hunger for even more. My appetite was no different. It drove me on and on, deeper and deeper. I don't think the hunger ever would've left. But it's gone now."

Allie reacted as soon as Chase took a breath. "Are you trying to tell us you're done with Murphy? And the rest of it too? No more drugs?"

Chase shifted his position. "Not sure. I'd like to get even with Murphy, but it's probably too dangerous—you know, with the cops and all. Just take care of myself. That's always been my motto."

"And the drugs?" asked Allie.

"At least no more dealing. In fact, I remember the day Nattie told me that God wouldn't let me die without accomplishing something good. Maybe this is the time. I've got money, but if they'd killed me tonight, money wouldn't have mattered. I think my only option is to take Sadie and leave."

"Where to?" Frank asked.

"Somewhere far away. I've been stashing money in the bank for a long time, so we can pretty much go anywhere."

"How much do you have?"

"Doesn't matter. You've seen the place where I live, the clothes I wear. Sadie and I have only the one car. I guess it all just added up. Maybe saving a chunk of money is the only good thing I've done so far."

"Does Sadie know about it?" Frank asked.

"What, are you crazy?"

Allie jumped in. "So you think she'll leave with you?"

"Yeah. She depends on me."

"I guess this is it then," Allie said with obvious sadness.

"Guess so. Don't have a choice, do I?"

"Doesn't sound like it." She rose to get the coffee pot. "So you're sure the police know who you are?"

Chase thought for a moment. "Yeah. They yelled out my name tonight." He rubbed his eyes with both hands. "What should we do? I'll have to meet Sadie somewhere. Let's see. We could meet at the Midway

Motel. Frank, why don't you take me over to … no, that won't work. Um, okay, I've got it. I'm thinking that Murphy may try to grab Sadie in order to find me, so Frank, you should go right to my place, pick her up, and head for the Midway. Allie, you and I will go straight to the motel and wait for them. From there, Sadie and I will take a cab to the airport."

"Why don't we all just go together?" Allie suggested.

"No, too risky. It's better if Frank goes alone. That way nobody will suspect anything. But be careful, Frank. I'll call Sadie first and let her know you're coming."

Frank stood. "All right. Go ahead and call her, and we'll get ready to go. I'll grab you another shirt." He glanced at his brother's bare feet. "Looks like you need to borrow a pair of shoes too."

"Cool. Thanks."

Chase dragged himself into the kitchen toward the phone. As he dialed, his thoughts jumped ahead to California, the only place he knew that would be far enough away from all his troubles. He had an aunt living out there in Riverside, wherever that was. Maybe they could go see her and try to start over. But what would happen after they arrived? What then? He knew that even if they were fortunate enough to make it to the airport, he could never return to New York. California had to be the answer. But would he bring Sadie along after all? How could she possibly assist him? How could her addict's lifestyle help him make the change he desired?

Sadie answered after the first ring, her voice drifty, her words slurred.

"Sadie. … Yeah, it's me. Listen, something's come up … What? Murphy called you? … What kind of questions? … All right. Don't worry. … I know you need a line. Calm down. I'll see you soon. … Quit whining. I said soon! Now pay attention to me. Frank is coming to pick you up, so pack a couple of bags and go with him to the Midway Motel. Sadie, are you listening to me?"

Chase shook his head, annoyed at having to repeat himself. "You know I don't have my car. Frank is coming. This is serious, Sadie. Grab whatever things you need. Make sure … are you hearing me? … Good. Make sure you bring all the papers in my top drawer. There's a little brown envelope underneath them. Don't forget it, okay? … Sadie, I can't talk any longer.

I'll explain it all when I see you. Just put some clothes in a couple of bags and wait for Frank. But listen, more than anything, don't forget my papers and the brown envelope. Got it? … What? … Well I didn't ask you to like it. I don't like it either. See you soon."

Chase hung up and saw Frank and Allie waiting for him by the door, Allie clutching a package of bandages and a partial roll of athletic tape. "Let's bring these with us," she said. "You'll need them later."

"Good idea," Chase said with a wince, taking her by the arm. "Let's go."

CHAPTER 3

F rank took a circuitous route on side streets to Chase's apartment in case he was being followed. He drove an '82 Seville, deep metallic blue with light blue interior, Frank's proclamation of success. And though he felt thoroughly proud of his prize, spending his weekends washing, waxing, and polishing it, his friends and neighbors accused him of vanity.

Turning the Seville onto Walnut Street, Frank studied the rearview mirror, watching for tails. He mulled over his little brother's predicament. As bleak as things appeared, perhaps this could become Chase's opportunity for a better future, maybe his first break in life. He didn't fully understand his brother's dilemma, but Frank knew that if Chase could break free of the chains that had bound him for years, he'd never turn back. Frank recalled the day Chase had quit smoking when they were both teenagers.

"Frank, I'm not gonna smoke anymore," he flatly stated one night in the bedroom they shared.

"What?"

"I said I'm not gonna smoke anymore."

"Big deal. What are you telling me for?"

"Just wanted somebody to know. That's all."

"Chase, what are you doing something stupid like that for?"

"I don't think it's stupid. I think you're stupid! Dad's been smokin' for years and look at the way he turned out."

"Oh, so you figure cigarettes made Dad the way he is."

"Course I don't. I just don't like 'em anymore. I don't like Dad anymore either, so I'm gonna quit."

"What about drinking?"

"I like drinking."

"You're crazy."

Regardless of his logic, Chase never put another cigarette to his lips. Frank respected him for that. And though his brother was obviously trapped in a much more dangerous addiction, Frank believed in Chase's ability to conquer this as well.

Frank pulled up slowly to the small apartment complex, which had once been a hotel, its tenants contributing to the growing deterioration of the old building. Frank couldn't figure out why Chase liked the place, but his brother never did care much about impressing people. Or maybe his choice of living quarters had more to do with keeping a low profile.

Two busted streetlights made the area a bit darker than normal. Frank turned off the engine and looked in all directions. He stepped out of his car and walked briskly to the glass door, which creaked loudly when he pulled it open. Frank mechanically wiped sweat from his mustache and beard onto his pants. He barely glanced at the overly worn sofas in the lobby as he hurried toward the stairwell.

"Hey, nose-candy king! Where you going?"

Just as Frank turned, he felt the full force of a fist in his side. Another punch followed, sending him reeling to the floor. A hand grabbed him by the neck, pounded his head against the carpet, and held him there. Frank struggled to turn his head and to focus on the assailant, who sported a two-day growth of beard and a scarred left cheek. Out of the corner of his eye, he could just make out a slightly built black man standing in the shadows, watching without expression.

The man with the scar tightened his grip, flattening Frank's face. "I said, where you going, Macklin?"

"I, uh, uh …" Frank coughed, struggling for an answer. He coughed again, saliva flowing from his mouth. "I'm not Chase. I'm his brother! I'm looking for him too!"

The next punch to his side knocked the wind out of him. Frank tried to breathe. Suddenly he felt his right arm being twisted forcefully behind his back. "Listen, Chase!" the man yelled. "You want us to be easy on you? All you have to do is tell us your contact. I'll make sure you get off with minimum time."

"Who are you guys? I said I'm not Chase."

The man took him by the hair, pulling his head back. "Listen, punk—"

"Wait a minute, Scott," interrupted the black man, wiping his brow. "Macklin was hit tonight. The report said his left shoulder. Remember?"

Scott swung him around. "Take your shirt off."

Frank groaned as he lifted his T-shirt over his battered head. Seeing no wound and apparently satisfied, Scott backed away as the black man stepped up. "Where's your brother?"

Frank's anger overtook him, and he fiercely shouted, "If you guys are cops, you're in a lot of trouble!"

Upstairs in the apartment, Sadie heard the commotion. Without hesitating, she snatched up the bags, tore a picture off of the wall, crawled inside a long-unused dumbwaiter shaft, and slowly let herself down to the ground floor.

Entering the abandoned kitchen, Sadie rushed over to the window, pushed out the screen, tossed her bags into the alley, forced herself through the window, and raced out the side gate. She ran all the way to Roselyn Avenue, hid a few steps away from the sidewalk, and tried to catch her breath while she waited for a taxi.

Fifteen minutes later a cabbie saw her waving and rolled down his window partway. "Where ya headed?"

"Um, the Midway Motel."

"Over on Second Street?"

"Yeah."

"Okay, hop in."

Sadie climbed into the back, setting her bag on the floor and Chase's next to her. She started to shake from adrenaline and the need for cocaine. Setting her eyes straight ahead, she tried not to think about it.

The cab driver peered at her from his rearview mirror. "Workin' tonight?"

"No."

"Didn't think so, with the luggage and all. Kinda warm this early mornin', don't ya think?"

Sadie didn't answer, so the cabbie went on. "Yeah well, warm, cold, it don't really matter if ya know what I mean. Did ya hear the news about the earthquake they had over in Africa or Asia somewhere?"

"No."

"Yeah! It was somethin' else. Killed a buncha those people over there, but the way I figure it, they got plenty to spare. I seen the pictures. Swear to God, kids got bellies down to their knees. I don't know what you think, but the way I figure it, we oughta forget spendin' money over here on abortions and start givin' it to people like that who really need it since they got all those unwanted babies and all."

Sadie had no interest in conversation, but the cabbie proved too annoying to ignore. "What makes you think they're unwanted?"

She saw his wrinkled brow in the mirror. "Don't tell me. You're not one a those, uh … hey, you movin' into this motel or somethin'?"

"What?"

"The Midway. You movin' in?"

"Don't know." Sadie didn't care. Her thoughts centered only on the need to stop shaking.

"You don't know?" The cabbie turned and frowned at his passenger. "Well that beats the livin' daylights outta me! Can I ask how old ya are?"

"Don't matter. Just get me there."

"Oh, I know it don't matter. I'm just wonderin' what a young, pretty girl is doin' out at this time in the mornin' with travelin' bags, goin' to a motel. Not my business a course. Just wonderin'. I seen it all."

Sadie's silence did not deter him.

"You from 'round here?"

"No," she lied.

"Well, I just want ya to know, the way I figure it, life is too short to throw it away. Not that ya are. I just know ya probably use drugs, probably wanna make it big somewhere. Just be careful, girl. People are mean. They'll love ya and then keep ya and use ya and step on ya. That's just the way the world is, ya know. Everybody's out to make it. Some try with their good looks. Others try with their sharp minds. Some use the connections they have. Legal or illegal, don't matter no more. If it's illegal, they just call it unethical and try their luck. And what are they tryin' to make? Money. Hah! Ya love it but ya hate it. Ya gotta have it, but the more ya gotta have, the more it has you."

The cabbie cleared his throat and continued, glancing periodically at his captive audience from his rearview mirror. "I know what you're thinkin'. I drive a cab, so who am I? Well I'll tell ya. I'm nothin'. I'm a nobody. I'll never make it. But ya know what? It's okay. Don't think I didn't give it a shot when I was young. Ya better believe I did. Why sure. I had my day. But the way I figure it, my days had me more than I had them, if ya know what I mean. Maybe ya don't. It don't matter. You're young. I betcha you even have a good head on your shoulders. But you're bein' controlled, maybe even lied to. That's what I think. Just my opinion."

Sadie kept to herself, trembling anxiously, attempting to focus on anything other than the mindless chatter. She speculated on what could have happened to Chase and how the scuffle in the hallway figured into it all. Though concerned, she cared more about her next fix. The ride went on, as did the cabbie, for another five minutes or so.

"Okay, girl," he said with a smile, "here we are. Lemme help ya with your bags."

"No, I got 'em."

"Okay, but do me a favor, will ya?"

"What?"

"Try to remember what I told ya. All the fightin' and scratchin' and strivin' and pushin' for more and more of whatever's out there isn't worth it. Believe me, when ya get there, wherever there is, ya probably won't even know it. And if ya do, it won't mean nothin' 'cause you'll just want more and you'll go to any lengths to get it, and once you get it … well, ya know what I mean."

Sadie got out, handed him some money, and without a word, shrugged and walked away.

She found Chase and Allie waiting for her as she opened the door to the small, dank motel lobby. Allie immediately jumped to her feet. "Where's Frank?"

"I don't know what happened." She set the bags down and looked pleadingly at Chase. "I'm needin' somethin' bad, babe."

Allie frantically grabbed her arms. "Sadie, I asked you where Frank is!"

"Well Chase said Frank was pickin' me up, so I guess he gets there and I hear some noises. I don't know, like fightin' or somethin'—"

"What?" Allie cried out. "Did you see him?"

"No, just heard his voice. I don't know who was down there with him. I just grabbed my stuff and took off."

"I gotta go!" Allie shouted as she ran out the door.

"Allie, wait!" Chase called out, shaking his head in disbelief.

"Sorry, Chase," Sadie whined. "What's goin' on?"

"I got a room. Come on."

He led her into the dark hallway. Sadie began to tremble again. "I need a line," she whispered.

Chase ignored her plea, searched for the room number, and unlocked the door. When he flipped on the lights, they revealed a well-used double bed, a small nightstand, a nondescript dresser, and two straight-backed chairs. The heavy drapes, drawn closed, reeked from years of cigarette smoke. Dropping their bags on the floor, Chase glanced into the tiny bathroom. Just a shower, a sink, and a toilet.

"Chase, I need a line. You have some, right?"

Without a word or even an expression, Chase worked his right hand into the left pocket of his jeans, slowly producing a piece of glossy magazine paper folded over several times into a four-inch square.

"There you go," he said, tossing it onto the dresser.

Sadie quickly leaned over to unfold it. "What's this? It's all caked up! Looks like it got wet!"

"Yeah, probably did. Hey, don't worry so much. Just work with it a little bit. It's dry enough. Wait a minute."

Chase again reached gingerly into his pocket, this time producing an inkless pen. Sadie had already formed her line. He watched her head move back and forth, inches from the top of the dresser. She finished the line and then raised her head, sniffling, eyes watering.

"Go ahead, babe," she said, offering him the tube.

Chase felt fatigued, disoriented, and completely unprepared for this temptation. His shoulder throbbed as he looked at Sadie waiting for him to take his share. He stared at the blow; he could almost taste it, feeling the sensation wash over him. For the past year and a half, ever since he had met Sadie, he'd rarely missed a day. Though he wasn't a heavy user compared with others, he felt the addiction. Suddenly he jerked himself away, frustrated and angry. "You toot it all," he said forcefully, pushing Sadie between him and the coke. "I don't want any."

"Whatever," she said indifferently. Chase plopped on the bed and within minutes fell asleep. He thought he remembered Sadie trying to wake him, prodding and kissing him, but he wasn't sure.

**

Allie burst through the front door of their home, saw her husband resting in his chair, and rushed to his side. "Frank! Are you all right?"

"Not really. I think my rib's broken. It's really painful, hard to breathe. Maybe I should see a doctor."

Allie gently touched his shoulder. "Yes, definitely. Who did this to you? Sadie mentioned a fight. What happened?"

"They were looking for Chase, thought I was him, and beat me up."

"That's horrible! Who were they?"

"I have no idea. They acted like cops, but maybe Murphy's guys."

"Do they know where we live?"

"Don't know," Frank said, wincing. "I don't think we're a target if that's what you're worrying about. They're looking for Chase, not us. Anyway, hopefully they believed me that I didn't know anything. How are Chase and Sadie?"

"They're okay. We met her at the motel, and then I ran to the car as soon as I heard about you."

"Good."

"We need to get you to emergency. Here, let me help you up. Hold on. Take it slowly."

"Sure. Listen, Allie, don't worry. We'll be fine."

**

Chase finally awoke, the room still dark, Sadie asleep at his side. Quietly, so as not to wake her, he scooted off the bed, went to the window, moved the drapes slightly, and peeked outside. A sliver of daylight fell across the bed. He quickly closed the drapes. Checking on Sadie, Chase noticed a dimly lit alarm clock on the nightstand. Ten o'clock in the morning.

He stealthily crossed the room and unzipped his bag, stealing another look at Sadie before searching through the stack of papers. Relieved when he touched the rough fibers of the brown envelope, he opened it and stared at his bank book. Last deposit, June 3, $1,500. Balance, $29,200. Chase smiled. He found a sheet of paper and without another thought, sat down to write a letter.

Sadie,

None of what I'm about to write will make much sense to you, but it has to be this way, at least for now. It shouldn't be hard for you to figure out that the cops are after me and Murphy too. If I'm caught, I either go to jail or get killed, so I have to leave. I'm done with dealing and need to start all over again. I can't take you with me. I don't even think you'd want to go, not if you knew the options. I'm going to fly to Miami and then on to somewhere else. I hate to do this to you, but I gotta take a different road and live a different life. If anything changes, I'll be in contact. Sadie, try to understand. I wouldn't do anything to hurt you, but I know this will. Take care of yourself. I'll miss you.

Chase

Not at all pleased with his lie about Miami, he nevertheless understood the necessity of protecting himself. Chase stood and placed the letter on the dresser along with three crumpled hundred-dollar bills. Reaching for his bag, he glanced once more at Sadie and gently closed the door behind him.

Walking as briskly down the hallway as his body allowed, Chase had no idea what his future held. Right now he had to take one step at a time and get to the bank and then to the airport. A tall reception counter nearly hid the disheveled man reading a magazine behind it.

"Hey, can you call me a cab?"

"Sure," the man answered, obviously annoyed by the interruption.

The taxi ride proved uneventful, as did Chase's large cash withdrawal at the bank. There were no questions or comments; it was surprisingly easy. Chase tucked the envelopes filled with hundreds into his small duffle bag and nodded thanks to the teller.

When he stepped back into the cab, his confidence grew. "Take me to the Syracuse airport."

Chase wondered what had happened to Frank. It was likely that either Murphy's guys or the cops had accosted him, and Chase hoped his brother hadn't been hurt. He couldn't believe he had gotten Frank and Allie so involved. Everything in him wanted to call them from a pay phone, but he couldn't take the time. He had to leave now. He'd make contact as soon he arrived in California. Chase reached up to touch his shoulder, flinching a bit from the pain. He forced himself to believe that everything would turn out for the better. "So far, so good," he whispered to himself.

The cab driver pulled up to the airport and stopped alongside the curb. "That'll be thirty-four dollars."

Chase handed him one of the hundreds from his pocket. "Just give me fifty."

"Thanks, buddy."

With no one in front of him as he walked up to the ticket counter, Chase managed a meek grin. "I need to take the next flight to Los Angeles, one way only."

"Well let's see. Hmm. It's going to depart in three-and-a-half hours with one connection."

"That's fine."

"Any bags to check in?"

"No. I've just got this one here."

CHAPTER 4

Glendora, California, 2000

C hase sat alone in a meticulously decorated waiting room, sinking wearily into one of four high-backed leather chairs, clammy hands moving nervously up and down his khaki slacks while he stared blankly at two framed Ansel Adams photographs. He struggled with the idea that a successful, happily married thirty-five-year-old man found himself seeking answers from a psychologist chosen randomly from the Yellow Pages.

Two nights before, Chase couldn't sleep, tortured with an unidentifiable knot in his stomach. A little after two in the morning, he got up and went to the bathroom. "This is messed up," he told the baggy-eyed guy in the mirror. "Something's going on."

Back in bed, sleep still evading him, Chase looked over at his wife, studying her face, examining her breathing patterns, hoping he could somehow find a solution in her peaceful slumber. But was it really peaceful? What if his concerns proved to be true? Chase could no longer ignore the jealousy that had intermittently gripped him over the last few weeks.

Though he felt guilty for having such emotions, Linda's behavior seemed highly unusual. Frustrated with his inability to pinpoint anything, and not wanting to bring up the subject and look like a suspicious fool, Chase felt trapped in the nightmare of possibilities.

Closing his eyes in a futile attempt to sleep, he soon found himself leaning on his elbow, staring at his wife for help, knowing his search was hopeless but searching nevertheless.

When Linda rose with the morning alarm, Chase observed every hurried move. She would often drop off their children at school and then meet her girlfriends at a coffee shop. Chase lay in bed, wondering if she had made such plans today. He thought about driving past the shop to check on her car. Or maybe he could call her and listen for background noises. He hated feeling so suspicious; it reminded him too much of the past.

Out of desperation, he made his way to the kitchen, thumbed through the phone book, and noticed a listing for Dr. Wesley Rhinegold, a psychologist in Pasadena, about twenty minutes away. Chase quickly dialed the number before he could change his mind. The woman who answered told him the doctor could see him on Wednesday at three-thirty.

The next night proved even more torturous. Chase carefully analyzed every word Linda spoke, every inflection in her voice, every gesture, as if he were building a case against her. During dinner, the two said little to each other but kept the conversation centered on their children. Amy, a very bright girl, recently turned nine. The tiny curls in her light-brown hair matched her mother's. She loved school, playing dress-up, and dolls—everything most parents would deem normal for a daughter her age. Ryan, two years younger, typically kept to himself and was content to stay in his room for long periods, his collection of video games apparently providing enough entertainment.

Watching his children, Chase looked for signs that they were bothered by or even curious about the chill between Linda and him, but they seemed oblivious. He wondered if they appeared unruffled because they were accustomed to their parents' disconnect. He hoped they sensed nothing wrong. Perhaps no chill existed. Maybe his imagination had simply conquered his sanity.

After putting Amy and Ryan to bed, Linda retreated to their room while Chase languished in his chair, deflated and melancholic as he stared at the Lakers gliding almost effortlessly across the basketball court. A classic film, *The Godfather*, followed the game—a good excuse to stay up even longer since he knew sleep would be impossible.

But this wasn't like him, Chase mused. Never easily overcome by depression, he had always demonstrated a carefree, playful, unpredictable, and even somewhat reckless nature, qualities that attracted Linda to him in the first place, and he to her. Though much more predictable and never reckless, Linda too was carefree and playful. He loved her sense of humor, her stable nature, her compassionate heart. What had happened?

Chase quietly wept. He knew his wife to be a wonderful mother—nurturing, thoughtful, considerate. Everything she did exemplified a caring heart for Amy and Ryan. Himself? He was probably much too selfish. *Maybe that's it*, he thought wearily, brushing away the tears. *Maybe I've become far too self-centered in this relationship. Perhaps Linda has had enough of me and my attitude.* Chase moved restlessly in his chair, frustrated at such a possibility and having no idea what to do if this proved to be true. Finally he fell asleep.

"Hello. You must be Chase." The voice interrupted Chase's wall-gazing, arresting his thoughts. "I'm Doctor Rhinegold." His tone was quite businesslike and his physique rather imposing, six foot two or three, large jaw, with eyebrows sinking over his eyes. He wore a well-pressed shirt with a striped tie that hung a bit too long over his brown slacks.

"Nice to meet you." Chase stood and extended his hand. A moment later, he followed the doctor into the most well-appointed office he had ever seen. He admired the plush teal carpet, the dark walnut desk, the shelves filled with expensive-looking books, and a sofa flanked by two oversize armchairs. Chase sat tentatively in one of the chairs, feeling the soft crinkle of leather giving way and peering at the impressive gold-leaf credentials hanging just above eye level.

"So, Chase, tell me why you're here."

"Oh. Well, I'm not exactly sure. I guess I didn't know where else to turn. I'm not sleeping. I'm suspicious of my wife. I don't know if I'm going crazy or what. I just … I just thought I could use some help."

"I understand. So continue on with your feelings. And try to relax. Whatever you say will be held in strict confidence."

Chase gripped the arms of the chair as if he were riding on the upward arc of a roller coaster and preparing to barrel downward. He released his grip, but his hands tightened again when he heard the words *strict confidence.*

What am I doing here? Chase asked himself. *How deep do I want to go with this guy? Is this a big mistake?* But he could only manage what sounded like a flippant reply. "That's nice," he said.

"Good. Like I said, relax. Even though this is the first time we've met, just talk with me like you would one of your close friends."

"I don't know anybody I'd want to talk to."

"You don't want to be here, do you?"

"No." The abruptness of his answer shocked Chase.

"Well that's all right. No one enjoys coming to a shrink!" the doctor said with a grin. "Why don't you start by sharing what caused you to pick up the phone to make this appointment?"

Chase hesitated. He moved nervously in the armchair and then blurted out, "I think my wife's having an affair." Relief swept over him as he took a deep breath. He felt better having finally said aloud the words that had haunted him for weeks.

"What would cause you to feel this way?"

Chase retreated from the question. "Oh, I don't know. Maybe I'm being overly suspicious. Maybe it's nothing."

"Tell me what you mean."

"About what? Feeling suspicious?" Chase shifted uncomfortably.

"Well yes, but also what behavior you've noticed in your wife. What is her name, by the way?"

"Linda."

"What behavior have you noticed in Linda that would prompt your suspicion? But first let me ask you how long you've felt this way."

"Two or three weeks."

"So what has Linda done in the last couple of weeks that caught your attention?"

"She's acting peculiar; she's unresponsive in bed, out of the house longer than usual. I don't know. It's just weird."

"When you say she's out of the house for unusually long durations, what do you think is happening?"

"Beats me," Chase said wearily. "She has these girlfriends she hangs out with, but recently she's been away for two or three hours instead of just one or so. She also goes into L.A. a lot more often and will call me to say she's running late."

"What does Linda do in the city?"

"She works for a marketing firm but doesn't always have a regular schedule."

"So this recent behavior is not typical?"

"Yeah. I mean, in some ways not, but something's different. Every aspect of our marriage feels strange."

The doctor nodded as he jotted on his notepad. Chase arched his neck ever so slightly, trying to see the notes. Unable to make them out, he nevertheless felt himself relaxing little by little. Talk therapy appeared not to be as bad as he'd thought—until the doctor's next question. "How do you think that you have contributed to the strangeness you mentioned?"

"What do you mean?" Chase asked with a frown.

"You said that your marriage feels strange and that you've noticed this only recently. In what way has your own behavior been a contributing factor to this strangeness?"

"Well, just last night I considered the possibility that I am the selfish one in our relationship and that perhaps Linda is tired of my attitude. I mean, she's a generous and giving person. I don't know what's happening, but I guess if something is going on, maybe it's due to my own thoughtlessness."

"Okay, that could definitely be an issue. Now when you say Linda has been unresponsive in bed, is this new?"

"Yeah. Well maybe not totally, but it's definitely different from how she's acted in the past, if you understand what I mean."

"Tell me."

"All right. She's been going to our room by herself these past few weeks, and by the time I get there, she's asleep."

"So this is new behavior."

"Right."

"And have you been reaching out to her, asking if everything's okay, touching her, speaking words of love?"

Chase smiled. "Well, I'm not the greatest at that! I know I've done those things in the past, maybe just not recently."

Rhinegold nodded again and leaned slightly forward. "Have you considered asking her if she's seeing someone else?"

"No way!"

"Why not?"

"Are you telling me that's what I need to do?"

"No. I'm asking you why you haven't done it."

"Because if it's not true I'll look like a fool, like the suspicious husband who's been through this before."

"You were previously married?"

Chase eyed the door, completely uncomfortable with further vulnerability. Seconds passed. He let out an exasperated breath. "Yes," he conceded. "I was twenty-two, my wife twenty going on sixteen. It lasted about six months. She had an affair with one of my friends. I really don't want to go into the details."

"No, you don't have to," the doctor said.

"It's all so cliché," Chase continued as if Rhinegold never said a word. "Beautiful wife. Best friend at the time. I suspected something for a while, but I never knew for sure until I caught them in the act. I don't need to explain that, do I?"

"Not at all. I get the picture."

"There's no way I want to go through that kind of stuff a second time. I don't deserve it. Nobody does."

"I agree. So you want to discover the truth, but you're afraid to ask the difficult question."

"Well yeah! Of course I am! Even though finding out the hard way is worse by far, I'm just hoping nothing is going on. But hey, I can't just come straight out and ask Linda if she's seeing someone else."

"All right. Then would you be open to allowing me to pose the question?"

"What are you talking about?"

"Is your goal to have Linda join us at some point to work through these issues together?"

"Definitely."

"Okay, so let me make a suggestion to assist in that endeavor. You can tell her you met with a psychologist since you feel your marriage needs help. Let her know that it went well and that you'd like her to join you next week. If your wife is not having an affair, she'll probably love the fact that you're making an effort without her prodding you. And if she doesn't, if she fights the idea of coming here, you can pursue the issue a bit further by asking something like, 'What's wrong? Why can't we work on this together?'

"Of course you have to be ready to handle the potential blowout if she's completely resistant and repeatedly challenges your unusual interest in improving your marriage. At that point you'll need to decide how to proceed. Chase? Chase, are you with me?"

"Yeah, I'm sorry. I just faded out for a moment."

"At what part?"

"I guess where I'm speaking with Linda."

"Chase, I see you're extremely ill at ease. And you absolutely don't have to do any of this, but let me ask you something. How long are you willing to live tormented by suspicion?"

"Not long, Doc. I can't do that. That's why I'm here."

"Okay, then give some thought to what I've suggested. I'm here to help, but we will make much quicker progress if Linda is willing to be part of the process. And I hope she will be excited at the prospect of working on your relationship. Most wives don't have husbands who initiate intervention or counseling. If she is merely going through some personal changes, then she will more than likely be pleased with your efforts. She may initially question what you're doing, but if you explain that you'd like to improve your marriage, hopefully she'll agree to come."

"And if she does, you're going to ask her flat out if she's having an affair?"

"Perhaps. Perhaps not. I'll have to feel things out, see how she responds, look for cues. The point is that you two cannot go on as you are. Rather than continuing to be driven by suspicion, rightly or wrongly, you've got to find relief to maintain your sanity. If your suspicions are accurate, we've got a long road ahead. If inaccurate, then we can proceed with helpful tools to enhance your marriage." Rhinegold hesitated. "Are you okay with all of this?"

"Hey, I just want this to work. I love my wife and my children. I'll do anything to keep them."

"That's great, Chase. And I don't expect this to be easy for you, but don't you want to do something to end any and all mistrust one way or another?"

"Yes."

"Then the next step is up to you. I'm sure you made the right decision by coming in today, so let's go ahead and schedule you for another appointment next Wednesday, same time, hopefully with Linda by your side."

"That's it?"

"For the moment, yes." Rhinegold stood, thick eyebrows moving up and down.

Chase rose and shook the doctor's outstretched hand. "Okay. I think I can do this. We'll see how it goes."

He walked slowly to his BMW, his head spinning with ideas about what to say when he returned home. Chase hoped Linda would be there. He stopped at all the lights, but it didn't feel as if he were driving. His mind was in a fog. He noticed the one-hour cleaners, a corner liquor store, a new Starbucks, but all of it blurred together. He heard the Rolling Stones on the oldies station as he merged westward on the 210 freeway, and though he felt himself accelerating to the speed limit, everything seemed to be moving in slow motion.

Chase considered his limited options. He could continue on with the hope that this was merely a passing difficulty without consequence, or he could try to persuade Linda to meet with the doctor next week. Convinced that he would be unable to solve his troubling issue alone, the latter seemed the only feasible path. He reached for his head, scratching an itch that wasn't there, and allowed his mind to wander back to the day he arrived on that L.A.-bound plane thirteen years earlier, feeling nearly as confused and alone as he did now.

CHAPTER 5

When he walked into the arrival area of LAX, mentally exhausted, badly bruised, and feeling anxious and agitated from cocaine withdrawal, Chase quickly searched for an information booth, figuring someone might be able to tell him how to get to Riverside. A smartly dressed woman instructed him to take a taxi to the bus station and said it would be about five hours from there.

Numerous stops, loud destination announcements, and increasing muscle pains prevented Chase from sleeping. As soon as the bus pulled up to the station, Chase stepped out, thinking he would vomit. He didn't. Slowly he headed to a phone booth inside.

"Let's see," he muttered to himself, thumbing through the pages. "Betty Forester. Shouldn't be too hard." He glanced through the Fs and found two Foresters, Ron and Stephen. He vaguely remembered Ron since he and Betty had visited New York when Chase was around five. He put a quarter in the slot and dialed the number.

"Hello?"

"Aunt Betty?"

"This is Betty. Who is this?"

"It's Chase, your nephew. How are you doing?"

"Chase! My Lord! I'm fine. What about you?"

"Well I'm at the bus station here in Riverside."

"At the bus station? In town? Chase, what on earth are you doing here?"

"It's a long story, but I was hoping that, um, I was hoping I could come and see you. I know it's last minute and all—"

"No, that'd be great! You need a ride?"

"Yes. Is that a problem?"

"No, not at all. Are you alone?"

"Yeah."

"Okay, give me about twenty minutes. Are you hungry? We've already eaten, of course, but I'd be happy to fix—"

"That's okay, thanks. I'm just tired."

"All right, honey, just stay there and I'll pick you up shortly."

"Sure. Thanks a lot."

Chase slouched wearily on a nearby bench and observed the people at the station. A woman stood anxiously with three children—an infant in her arms, a girl around two, and a five-year-old boy whom the mother repeatedly warned to stay close. Chase couldn't tell if they were arriving or waiting for someone on the next bus, but he couldn't miss the stress on the woman's tightly drawn face. He felt sorry for her and wondered if she was alone or if her husband would soon come to rescue her.

A transient walked past them, slowly heading toward the bench next to Chase's. The man abruptly turned and plopped down across from him. Chase immediately smelled a disgusting odor of urine and dirty clothes emanating from the man. His hair appeared greasy, his shirt noticeably wrinkled. He stared at the floor and the ceiling, avoiding eye contact with passersby. Chase could hear him mumbling something about himself or about how he wanted something, but the words were far too difficult to make out.

As the muttering continued, a teenager caught Chase's attention. The young man, about seventeen with a slight build and scraggly hair, glanced suspiciously back and forth. As he walked by Chase, their eyes met. Chase immediately recognized the signs of an addict. He had grown up with kids like this. But whom was he kidding? He was one of them until just yesterday! Would he stay strong? Would seeing himself in teenagers such as this encourage him never to return to such a life? Suffering the effects of withdrawal and painfully aware of his addiction, Chase had resolved on the bus ride to remain resolute. He was determined to take this opportunity to start over again. What that meant, he had no idea.

**

As he continued his reflections, weaving his way homeward toward Glendora, Chase realized how far he had come since those early days on the lam. But he wondered if he could claim real progress. He felt isolated again, just as he did all those years ago. Putting aside his current circumstances, Chase let his thoughts return to his aunt's arrival at the station.

Betty was a small-framed woman with facial features remarkably like his father's, her thick hair put up in a bun with something resembling a crochet needle holding it all together. Chase kept his eyes on the surroundings as she talked and he answered questions about the family. He didn't tell her about his situation, saying something about coming out for a visit, maybe even staying awhile and looking for a job.

The Foresters' small, simple house nestled on Selma Court, a cul-de-sac next to the freeway. After Chase convinced his aunt and uncle that he needed sleep more than conversation, they led him to the first room down the hallway.

"I hope this will be comfortable enough," said Betty.

Chase expressed his gratitude, closed the door, and fell into a deep sleep moments after crawling into the bed underneath a window overlooking the front yard.

He awoke late the next morning and gazed around the room as he massaged his hurting legs. It felt strange to wake up in a new bed in a new home in a new state. Chase had left the window open all night as he normally did, but the air wasn't hot and sticky like in New York. He didn't care, merely noting the difference. He stared at the walls for a few more minutes, listening for any sounds in the house. Hearing nothing but chirping birds, he slowly dressed himself and meandered down the hall toward the kitchen. A note from Aunt Betty on the table in the small adjacent dining room said that he could help himself to coffee, toast, cereal, or whatever else he wanted and that she and Ron would return home at five-thirty.

Chase quickly grabbed a cup of coffee, finished off a few pieces of toast, and headed out the door, still wearing Frank's shirt and shoes. Finding himself on a freeway frontage road that led to the back of a shopping center, Chase remembered that he could use some more bandages for his shoulder since Allie's supply was nearly gone. It took him awhile to locate the first-aid section in the grocery store, but finally he walked out with his small package and returned to Aunt Betty's place. Simple, quiet, and normal. He liked that.

However, he didn't like the agonizing withdrawal symptoms, coupled with the throbbing of his shoulder. He gently rubbed it. Knowing that a distraction would help, Chase decided to call his brother.

"Hello?" came the familiar voice.

"Frank, it's me. How are you? What happened back at my place? I heard there was a fight or something."

Frank reported that he had suffered a broken rib and several bruises but that his doctor said he'd be fine. "But that's enough about me. What about you? Where'd you go?"

"I'm far enough away. Just trying to heal and to get my head together."

"Are you close enough for a visit?"

"Not really. And listen, I'd rather not say over the phone where I'm at."

"Got it."

"I just need to figure out my next step, how I'm going to live and all."

"Well that may be quite a challenge for the two of you."

"Sadie's not with me."

"No?"

"Yeah, I decided at the last minute that I'm better off alone. Hey, have you heard anything about Murphy?"

"Well that's another story. I guess Murphy knew or somehow found out where we lived since a couple of guys came knocking at our door asking about you."

"Oh, great."

"Yeah, that's what I thought, but the strange thing is they first apologized for mistaking my identity. The two who beat me up must have been cops since they mentioned something about a police report of you being shot. So the two at my house had to be Murphy's guys, don't you think?"

"What'd they look like?"

"One was tall, the other ... I don't know, Chase. I can't remember."

"That's okay. Probably all Murphy's guys."

"Yeah. Well anyway, I told them I didn't know anything. Said I just went to your place to hang out."

"Cool. Anything else?"

"No, that's about it. I don't think they'll be back. Don't worry about us. Allie's still troubled by it all, but I told her I didn't think they'd bother us again."

"I hope not. Sorry you had to go through it, though."

"That's okay. I'm more concerned about you. Any idea what you'll do?"

"Just make the best of things. Try to get situated and start my life over."

"Without drugs, I hope."

"I'll try."

"Just do it, Chase. You shouldn't want anything to do with that stuff anymore."

"I know."

"Well don't be a stranger. Stay in touch, okay?"

"Sure. Take it easy. And say hi to Allie."

Chase rubbed his shoulder again, thinking long about whether he should go ahead with his next call. Under orders from Murphy, he had taken a young man called Zeke under his wing during the past few months. Though they became instant friends, could Zeke be trusted under the current circumstances? Did he possess the fortitude to carry out such a request? And should Chase take the chance of placing himself in danger again? He ran his fingers through his long hair. He considered that Murphy might already have tapped Zeke's phone. But what would that matter since Chase planned to leave Riverside immediately? He decided to take the risk and pulled out Zeke's number from his wallet.

"Yeah," came the short answer.

"Hey, Zeke, it's me, Chase."

"Chase! What are you doin', man?"

"Just checkin' in."

"Where are you?"

"Not far. Hey listen, I'm wondering if you can do something for me."

"Like what?"

"I'll give you ten grand to take out Murphy for me."

"Take out Murphy? Why?"

"I'm sure you know what he did to me. Time to get even."

"You're crazy."

"Maybe so. Are you in?"

"No way."

"Not enough?"

"Man, I can't believe you're serious. And no, ten grand is not nearly enough."

"All right, make it twenty, ten now and ten after. That's the best I can do."

"Twenty grand to kill Murphy," Zeke said slowly.

"Yeah."

"No, forget it. Find somebody else."

Chase raised his voice in frustration. "Zeke, I need this done. Come on, man. You're the only one I trust."

"Not anymore. See ya later."

Chase heard a click and stared at the phone before angrily slamming it down. Feeling defeated, he wondered if his vindictiveness toward Murphy could ever be restrained.

When his aunt came home from work, Chase handed her a twenty and told her he had taken the liberty of calling Frank. She tried to hand it back, but he insisted.

At dinner, Betty immediately bombarded Chase with questions. She had a peculiar trait of squinting whenever she posed one. "So Chase, you briefly told me that you're here visiting but that you may look for work. What type of job are you hoping for? And where do you think you'll live?"

"Not sure," he responded, helping himself to another serving of mashed potatoes. "I just need to find something that I enjoy, maybe not even around here. I think … well first I'm going to buy a car over at that auto mall I saw off of the freeway and explore the area. I've never been out here, you know."

"You have money for a car?"

"Yeah, I've got enough." Instantly he felt relief at not having spent it all to get even with Murphy.

Ron chimed in. "What type of work do you do?"

Chase thought for a moment. He decided to deflect the question by telling them about how the cops were looking for him, but he tailored the story to make them believe he suffered unfair treatment simply for hanging around the wrong people and being labeled by the police as one of the town troublemakers.

Betty wanted to know more. "What were you doing for work when this all happened?"

"I, uh, I haven't really done a whole lot since high school. Just some odd jobs here and there."

Betty glanced at Ron and then back at Chase. "So you're here to make a fresh start."

"Yeah, that's about it."

"You may want to consider cutting your hair and buying some new clothes if you're going to look for work."

"Yeah, I've thought about that."

"Well, Chase," said Betty, "why don't you consider coming with us to church on Sunday? I think you'll like it! We have a really nice worship band, and the pastor's a wonderful teacher."

"You mean Mass?"

"Oh no, I'm sorry," she said with a smile. "We're not Catholic. I guess you must be, though."

"Not really. Dad took us to church when we were little. No big deal."

His aunt's eyes widened. "But it is a big deal! You can find some real answers." She squinted and Chase braced himself. "Why don't you come try it out?"

"Thanks a lot, but I really have to get going soon."

"Do you know that Jesus loves you?" Betty asked.

Chase couldn't believe his ears. He had no idea his aunt was so religious. She didn't seem like a hypocrite, but his dad had surely earned the label. His mom went to Mass on occasion, but she rarely spoke about God. He didn't know how to answer.

"Chase," she pressed, "don't you know that Jesus really, really loves you?"

"I don't know. Never thought about it."

"Well he does. He died for your sins, for all of our sins. He rose from the dead to make a way for you to have a relationship with God. Have you ever thought about eternal life?"

Chase rubbed his eyes. "Listen, Aunt Betty, I really appreciate all you've done for me, but I'm not a religious person and I don't want to be. I'm taking a road totally different from my dad."

"Oh, your dad," Betty said, rolling her eyes. "He's never had a personal relationship with Jesus. He simply went to Mass, which is nothing like what I'm talking about. I'm speaking of a real relationship with Jesus Christ. You're young, Chase. Don't you want more out of life than you can see now?"

"Well yeah, of course I do, but that's not me, religion and all." He quickly dodged the increasingly uncomfortable subject. "Hey, can you tell me more about my dad?"

"Well, sure. Because he was my older brother, I always looked up to him. We had a great time growing up in the Bronx, I'm sure you know. After high school we became rather distant, however. He was quite the wild one, and I just wanted to be married. I thought Bobby would finally settle down after meeting your mother, but he was so set in his ways. Very stubborn, that brother of mine. And I was obviously sad and disappointed when he walked out on all of you. Wish I could've been there, but you know it's a long way from here."

"Yeah," Chase agreed quietly. "Ever hear from him?"

"Never. I tried to get hold of him, to write—nothing. I guess I gave up a long time ago. What about you?"

"No. I think he's still around, but I don't really care."

"I believe you're a dreamer, Chase."

"What do you mean?" he asked, startled by the shift in conversation.

"You have dreams with significant messages. Am I right?"

"No, not really. In fact, I never dream."

"Never?" Betty asked with a squint.

"A few here and there, I guess, but no, nothing special."

"Well, you will," she said firmly, folding her arms.

What did she mean by that? Chase wondered, sitting back in his chair and running his fingers through his hair. *She must be a little nuts*, he thought, *a religious wacko of some sort.*

Betty noticed his discomfort and the clean plate before him. "What else can we get for you?"

"Oh, I'm okay. Thanks a lot," Chase answered, rising from the table. "I think I'll buy a car tomorrow and then say my good-byes."

"Well, you know that Ron and I—"

"Hey!" Chase shouted at the car in front of him. His BMW screeched to a halt, and he frantically checked the rearview mirror. "Man, that was close," he said, realizing the potential danger of his deep reflections. "I've got to stay focused."

He never finished his thoughts about that brief visit in Riverside, but the next day he had left a thank-you note for Betty and Ron, visited the auto mall, paid fourteen grand for a new Toyota Celica, and started driving west down the 91 freeway. He wound up living in Orange County. Though he still had plenty of cash, it took him several months to find a steady job. Shortly after, Chase met one of the most gorgeous women he had ever seen, and he and Yvette married a few months later.

When he finally turned the corner to his street, Chase thought the worst, that maybe there would be two vehicles in his driveway, Linda's and … no, he couldn't go there. He wouldn't allow conjecture to rule his mind. But what if two cars indeed sat in front of his house? What would he do then?

CHAPTER 6

His house in Glendora, built in the late 1980s as part of a development near the hills of greater Los Angeles, nestled near enough to the San Gabriel Mountains that Chase had felt satisfyingly isolated. Though located relatively close to the freeway, when he and Linda had purchased their home four years ago, they believed it would be their refuge from the city.

Chase found Linda's SUV sitting alone in the driveway and allowed himself a huge sigh of relief as he pulled up next to it. He scrutinized the off-white and beige-trim home, remembering that he had never cared for the uniformity of those muted colors and that he had long intended to hire a painter to add a distinctive flavor to the place. He sat for another moment with the engine running, musing over the disorderly looking hedges on both sides of the driveway, wondering if they held a relevant message regarding the state of his marriage and of his life.

His eyes made their way toward the porch. Taking a deep breath, Chase shut off the engine and slowly, quietly let the car door close behind him. He took another breath, deeper than the first, his hand trembling on the handle of the front door. Chase's determination overruled his fears as he stepped into the entryway.

He found his wife in the kitchen, browning a pound of hamburger on the stove. A head of lettuce, several tomatoes, a small red onion, and some coarsely grated cheese lay on a cutting board on the counter.

Linda looked up. "Oh hi, hon'. Tacos won't be ready for another twenty minutes or so." She wiped her brow and glanced at the clock on the microwave. "You're home early. Everything good at work?"

"Sure, but um … I need to talk to you about something."

She noticed his sober, expressionless face and the way he slumped against the countertop. "What's up?" she asked with concern.

"Well it's just … can we sit down and talk?"

Linda heard an urgency in his weary voice. "Of course. Just let me finish with the meat first. I'll join you in the living room in a sec."

Chase retreated to his La-Z-Boy and rehearsed his lines under his breath. "Babe, I went to a psychologist this afternoon. I told him that I think we need help in our marriage. We talked for a while, and he said it'd be great if we came in together next week. What do you think?"

About halfway through his third rehearsal, Linda sat down on the sofa next to his chair. She had a curious habit of toying with her curls, a trait Chase found rather endearing.

"So you want to talk," she said. "Anything wrong?"

"What do you mean?"

"Well it isn't every day that you want to talk. Usually I'm the one who pushes for conversations." Linda crossed her legs. "So what's going on?"

"Where are the kids?"

"In their rooms doing homework. Why?"

"Well," he said after a deep sigh, "are you seeing someone else?" The words spilled from Chase's lips before he could pull them back. He was startled by the bluntness of his question. Anger registered immediately on Linda's face, and her body tensed like a cat waiting to pounce on its prey.

"What are you talking about?" she demanded, moving to the edge of the sofa.

"I don't know," Chase said, fidgeting. "I'm just feeling like we're distant, like something's going on."

Linda glared at her husband. "I've been telling you for months that we're growing distant, and now you're accusing me of having an affair? How dare you suggest such a thing!"

Chase felt trapped. He understood the emotional dynamics of accusations and of defense but knew that any attempts to pull himself out of the hole he had just dug would be futile. "I'm sorry. That was the wrong way for me to begin."

"Begin what?" she demanded.

"Well I went to a psychologist today because I'm just … I don't know, just frustrated with the way things have been, and yeah, I'm a little bit suspicious."

Linda shook her head in disbelief. "So you're finally admitting there's a problem, and you're blaming me for it!"

"Well no," Chase meekly replied. "I'm not blaming you for anything. I know I've been messed up, so I went to this doctor to talk about it all."

"And you told him I'm having an affair?"

"Not exactly. I just said that things feel strange, different, not like they used to be. He recommended that you come in with me next week."

"Why would I want to do that?" she asked angrily.

"Well come on, Linda, don't you think we could use some help?"

"I've been trying to get you to see that for I don't know how long, but now you've gone behind my back, painted some dark picture to a psychologist, and want me to come with you so he can try to pick me apart? I'm not going to play that game with you."

"It's not a game, Linda. I'm sorry for the way I started out. I don't mean to accuse you of having—"

"Well you just did!" she interrupted.

"I know. Like I said, I'm sorry. Can we just forget about it and go get some help?"

Linda sat motionless, her eyes appearing to look right through him. Chase remembered Doctor Rhinegold's warning that his wife might resist coming in for counseling. But for what reason? Could she fear something hidden being exposed, or could she simply be defending herself against a false accusation? Feeling overwhelmed and vulnerable, Chase had no idea how the situation would play out. He wanted to escape, to run away, to surrender—anything but face her indignation.

As he attempted to decipher her defiant responses, Linda suddenly stood and said with disgust, "Is that it? Are you finished?"

"I guess so. Will you come with me?"

"Listen, I'm not going anywhere with you if you're going to verbally assault me like this and put all the blame on me! I'm going out." He heard the front door slam behind her.

Bewildered and frustrated, Chase didn't move. What did she mean by "going out"? He shook his head roughly as if to jar loose the cruel images his imagination created of her with another man. Chase dismissed the idea of following her. He'd done that with Yvette, and he wouldn't do it again. Forcing his mind to focus elsewhere, he pulled out a couple of folders and pretended to study a new account.

Chase had worked his way up to a sales trainer and consultant position in the L.A. area. In the late '80s, after holding down odd jobs in Orange County, he had walked into the small office of a company that had been running an ad for a salesman. He knew nothing about sales, but then again he knew very little about anything outside of drugs. He had, however, mastered the art of fast talking, at least on the streets. Could he leverage that art into a real job? Earlier in the week he had made an appointment with a hair stylist, instructing her to cut his shoulder-length hair and to give him a more businesslike look. Then he purchased a pinstriped suit. Maybe he could pull off this ruse.

"Hi, my name's Chase Macklin," he said, offering a hand to the heavy but well-dressed man sitting behind a metal desk. The room was dismal compared with most offices. A few fluorescent bulbs provided dim light, and the mini-blinds were closed as if to hide something. Loud music blasted through the walls from the other side, and the faint scent of what Chase immediately recognized as marijuana crept through the partially closed door. Desperate for work, Chase ignored it all.

"I'm Sam. Have a seat."

The interview, such as it was, lasted perhaps fifteen minutes. The company sold industrial supplies and safety equipment to contractors, truckers, and oilmen all over the United States. He would be trained and could start the next day at four in the morning. Sam saw the expression on Chase's face and explained that the shift began at four since it was seven back East, the perfect time to reach those with work crews. He could ditch the suit, Sam informed him. Jeans and a shirt would be fine. This was good news for an independent youth so recently off the streets.

Chase proved himself a natural. Everyone noticed how quickly he connected with people and closed sales. The main difficulty was adjusting to the boiler-room atmosphere with blaring rock 'n' roll and to young men on telephones raising their voices nearly to a shout to block out the competing noise. Chase eventually managed to ignore most of the racket since he himself needed to stretch his vocal chords so that customers could hear him.

More challenging were the small joints frequently passed around the office. The problem was not so much the temptation but the ribbing from guys who didn't know his history. Chase kept his past to himself until one day after work. Since he had no other friends, Chase would hang out with a few of the guys after their morning shift, sometimes eating lunch at Jeff's house just a half-mile or so away in the heart of Santa Ana. Jeff, recently married and a little older than the rest, pulled out his bong and offered it to Chase.

"Come on, man. It's been a couple of months now and you're still afraid to get a little high with us?"

Chase had grown weary of the taunting. "Listen, Jeff, you guys have no idea where I come from. I dealt coke for five years. You keep thinking I'm afraid to take a few tokes? I've seen more than you guys will see in a lifetime. I've been in jail, fights, shot by the cops. This ain't nothing. I just don't need to go there anymore. I'm just trying to make some money and stay ahead."

"Dude," Jeff said defensively, nodding at the other guys, "we're just havin' fun. You don't have to get on our case. Take it easy, man."

"All right. Hand me the bong. I'm tired of all this."

Chase couldn't be certain why he gave in to the pressure. He knew better. Smoking pot was no big deal. He had already relapsed with cocaine twice, just escaping arrest the second time after a fistfight went from a house into the street. Knowing his temper, he had since vowed that if he used again, he would do so alone.

After the bong had been passed around a few times, the guys got Chase to open up about his past—dealing drugs, the fights he had mentioned, and even the night the police shot him in the shoulder and how he managed to escape. Their admiration became evident as they hooted and howled in approval. After a couple of hours, he dragged himself away and drove home to his apartment. Staring in the bathroom mirror, looking directly into his reddened eyes, Chase spoke to himself. "What are you doing, man? This is not who you are. You're lying to yourself. You can't do this anymore."

Determined to follow through, Chase avoided his coworkers and focused completely on his job. At least the teasing stopped. His history traveled the office, and the others treated him with unusual respect, perhaps concerned about what he might do if pushed too far.

After two years with the company, he became sales manager of the early crew. When the business shut down in 1989, Chase found other sales jobs and evolved into a top producer. After marrying Linda the following year, he began transitioning from salesman to trainer. He loved what he did for a living. When it came to his career, he considered himself a success. When it came to his marriage, that appeared to be an entirely different story, one he wished he could somehow rewrite.

**

Linda felt distraught after she stormed out of the house, and she drove aimlessly through the neighborhood. She thought about the tacos, wondering if Chase would turn off the stove. Tears of frustration and helplessness rushed down her cheeks. How could their relationship work? Would it be a repeat of her parents' failed marriage? Linda had felt it crucial to be strong for her younger sister, who had just turned fourteen when their dad moved out after one last marital fight. She remembered him holding her and Lisa tightly that night, expressing his love for them. He said he wished things were different, but unfortunately he and their mother couldn't work things out. Linda spent countless hours assuring her troubled sister that the three of them would always be together, that life would go on.

She missed her father, more so even now. Would she once again have to be the strong one? Linda didn't want that role. She yearned to crawl into Chase's arms and to be loved. More tears flooded down her face. Chase was certainly not like her father, she told herself, desperately hoping it to be true. He would do anything for his children. But what about for her? Like her father, had Chase become too distant to notice his wife's needs? And would he awaken himself in time to save their fragile marriage?

For the next few days, the two barely spoke. Linda remained angry and silent, waiting for something, anything, that would demonstrate her husband's concern. Chase, utterly frustrated over their impasse, hoped that his wife would simply be honest with him. Linda finally broke the stalemate one night after the children were in bed. "So when's your appointment?" she asked, sounding confrontational.

"With the psychologist?" he responded, completely taken aback by the suddenness of her question.

"Yes. Didn't you say you've got another appointment?"

"I do, at three-thirty on Wednesday."

Linda shrugged. "Well I've been thinking about it, and I'm not happy at all with you, but I guess I'll go. I just don't want to talk to you right now. I'm still upset."

"Okay then. Thank you. I'm glad you're coming." Uncertain if he kept his obvious relief to himself, Chase pursed his lips with a sense of victory, however small.

The momentary victory allowed him, for the first time in weeks, to drift off to sleep instead of anguishing for hours while staring at the ceiling. Chase had positioned himself on his side of the bed. He indeed desired to touch Linda, to comfort her, to express his love for her, but the last thing he needed was to rock the boat and to evoke emotions in her that, once again, he wouldn't know how to handle. He had never learned to understand his own emotions, much less those of the women in his life. Sleeping seemed to him the preferable alternative.

Long after Chase's breathing settled into the rhythmic cadence of slumber, Linda lay awake, tears sliding onto her pillow. She longed to be held, craving love and affection from her husband. She couldn't figure out why he gave her so little attention even then, having fallen asleep so quickly. Why wouldn't he at least reach out to her and tell her everything would be all right? In the past she may have pushed him away at times. But not now. Now she needed assurance that he would fight for her, battle for their marriage, and rescue her from an uncomfortable situation she did not know how to resolve.

When Wednesday finally arrived, Linda wanted to hear more about Chase's conversation with the doctor as they drove to the appointment.

"Well, I just told him that I was a little suspicious, that you were behaving, at least from my perspective, a bit peculiarly. I couldn't point to anything concrete, just weird feelings. He asked me if I understood my own responsibility. I told him I'm probably too selfish. It wasn't a long appointment at all. We spent most of the time talking about you and me coming back together to see him."

Linda fell silent, fingering her curls.

"Is that okay?" Chase asked, hoping he hadn't said anything wrong.

"What do you mean?" she muttered wearily.

"I mean, do you want to know anything else?"

"Is there anything else to know?"

"I don't think so. That's about it. I did tell him about Yvette but just to give him information." Linda didn't respond, so Chase continued. "Now the doctor's a little intimidating, but he's okay. Pretty smart, I think. And listen, babe, all I really want is for us to return to what we had. I love you, and I'll do whatever it takes." He glanced at her with a smile that she perfunctorily returned.

53

Ten minutes later, Chase introduced Linda to Doctor Rhinegold. She sat stiffly on the sofa, toying with her curls, hoping to conceal the worry she felt. Chase settled next to her but not too close. Linda, painfully aware of her husband's body language, slid a little farther away, pressing herself against the arm of the sofa.

Doctor Rhinegold observed the couple for several moments before speaking, his eyes peeking out from behind his eyebrows. "So tell me about this past week."

Chase cleared his throat. "I mostly got the silent treatment."

"Why is that?"

"Well, I told her I wanted her to come here with me, but I first made the mistake of asking if she was seeing someone."

"And?"

"That didn't go over very well. She walked out and we didn't speak for a few days."

"Linda, is that the way you see it?"

She shifted her legs and felt for her curls. "I basically told him that after the last few months of not having my emotional needs met, he's finally seeing that we have a problem, but now he's accusing me of having an affair instead of looking at his own life."

The doctor turned to Chase. "What do you see as the primary issue in your marriage?"

"Probably me. I don't open up all that much, and as I said before, I think I'm too selfish or self-centered. I don't know. Maybe you should ask her."

"I want to hear your own perceptions."

Chase shifted nervously. "I've never thought we had a bad marriage. Obviously it could be better, but I know that's true with everyone. I didn't tell you this the last time, but I was a drug dealer many years ago, somebody who grew up just taking care of himself, always guarded, never trusting, not a guy you'd want to hang out with. I thought everything had changed, but maybe I've never been able to fully shed my past."

"That's a good insight, something we may want to explore later."

"Listen, I really am willing to change, but I need help."

"And of course that is why you're here. Thank you for letting me know you a little better." The doctor turned toward Linda again. "I'm sorry to be so blunt, but why do you think Chase believes you're having an affair?"

Linda took a long, deep breath. "An old friend contacted me a couple of weeks ago."

Chase tensed, his stomach knotted.

"After a few phone calls he wanted to meet me somewhere. I told him I didn't think that would be such a good idea. Sure, I enjoyed our conversations, but I told him I'm married. I just didn't want to go there, and besides, I didn't feel that way about him. I just appreciated having someone to talk to, someone to reminisce with. He apparently wanted more, but for me, it really was just an innocent reconnection with an old flame."

Chase squirmed. He couldn't believe how quickly everything had begun to unfold.

"And are you still having conversations with him?" Rhinegold asked.

"No, not since last week when Chase confronted me. I knew I must be acting suspiciously, but I mean, honestly, it was just an emotional thing. We never met. We never saw each other. He just made me feel good about myself, attractive again, I suppose. When Chase noticed something different about me, I knew that I needed to end the connection, so I emailed him to say that it was over, not to call anymore."

"Okay, Linda, thank you for your honesty. Chase? This has to be painful but perhaps not as bad as you were imagining."

Chase ran his fingers through his hair. "I can't handle this. I mean, I believe her, but I can't believe … oh, I don't know. This is just really frustrating."

"I understand," Rhinegold reassured him, "but this is a good beginning. You've both communicated openly, and Linda has revealed a secret that's been eating her up for a few weeks. It's a great starting place. Now Linda, you have a decision to make with this recent contact, one that I cannot make for you, but you must know that your marriage and your family are at stake."

"I do know that," Linda insisted. "That's why I cut it off."

"I understand. The problem, however, is that this man may not accept your decision so quickly. If he contacts you again, you need to stand firm."

"I can do that."

"Good. And Chase, you need to allow Linda to do this herself, to make her own decisions in this matter. Now our session is obviously a short one, but I'd like to see how you're able to work through these issues and to smooth out this unfortunate situation. Let's meet again on Monday."

Driving home, they kept silent, Linda thinking about what she needed to do and Chase fuming over the entire emotional affair, or whatever it might be called. He hadn't felt this helpless and angry in a long time. Not since that afternoon in 1988 when he opened his bedroom door to find his first wife in bed with another man.

CHAPTER 7

Unfortunately, the man having the affair with Chase's first wife happened to be his best friend, Bill, whom he knew from work. Chase had gotten off early one day, and after grabbing a beer in the kitchen and heading down the hall toward his bedroom, he suddenly stopped when he noticed the door was closed. He and Yvette always left it open, so this seemed peculiar. The door squeaked a little as he eased it open. Just as his lips began to form his wife's name, his jaw dropped in utter disbelief at the scene before him: Yvette and Bill in bed, his bed, together.

Chase hurled his bottle against the wall above them, the glass exploding and beer foaming down over the bedframe. Bill quickly gathered up his clothes while Chase paced the room, shouting expletives. Once Bill hurried into the hallway, mumbling "Sorry, Chase," as he fled, Chase vehemently told Yvette he was done with her. Though they had navigated through many conflicts and arguments, he knew their already feeble marriage could never weather this storm. The divorce became final in just a few months.

A year and a half later he met Linda. They were attending a sales and marketing seminar in Westwood. He was nearly twenty-five; she was two years older. Though Chase had vowed not to date, he had a sudden change of heart and asked Linda out for coffee during a seminar break. They instantly connected. She too had a father who drank and an overly protective mother, and she had lived through a separation that had devastated her and her sister. She too did not want a marriage like her parents'—one of the reasons she remained single.

Linda had beautiful green eyes and a soft demeanor that Chase found attractive. She was tall, just a few inches shy of his own five-foot-nine frame. While Yvette had always been combative and disingenuous, Linda offered sensitivity and honesty. Instead of ridicule, Linda showed appreciation; instead of fear, confidence.

Chase asked her out a second time, hoping to impress her by taking her to his favorite Italian restaurant, not far from his apartment.

"So you say you've never been married?" he asked with a twinkle in his eye.

"What? Oh yeah, I guess I did," Linda answered with a smile. "No, I can't seem to find the nerve."

"But you've had boyfriends."

"Of course," she said with a laugh, "lots of them over the years. Guess I'm simply not the right type, or maybe I've never met the right type. I don't know. Perhaps marriage is not in the cards."

Although they had known each other for only a short time, Chase hoped her luck might change, but he knew he had to be careful. "Yeah, I think that's true of me as well. I was married once before, but it wasn't anything I'd recommend."

"What do you mean?"

Chase let out a sigh. "Well, it's a long story, but let's just say that I married the worst person on earth." He chuckled as soon as he said it.

"Can you tell me about it?" asked Linda, smiling in return.

"I'd much rather hear about your life."

"I know, but this sounds like a big thing. I can understand if you don't want to talk about it."

"All right. Here goes." Chase told her everything. He watched Linda's reactions as he spoke, how her cute lips would widen when he tried to make a joke out of difficult circumstances, her curiously raised brows when he haltingly recalled entering the bedroom that day. He didn't think she moved the entire time.

A waiter approached their table and asked them the typical questions, allowing Chase to take a breath and think through what else Linda might want to know. "I've never shared this with anyone," he finally admitted.

"Well I can see why! Chase, what a horrible experience. So then you, um, divorced her right away?"

"Absolutely. Didn't think I'd ever date again." He couldn't believe he said that.

Linda giggled. "Oh, I guess that's what we're doing, isn't it?"

"Yeah, but this feels a whole lot different from anything I've ever experienced. It's like I've known you forever. Hey! What are you laughing about? That wasn't a line. I'm serious."

"It just struck me as funny." She gently wiped her mouth on the cloth napkin and then reached for her hair with her free hand. "Actually that's very nice. Thank you."

"I like it when you do that, by the way."

"Do what?"

"Play with your curls."

Linda's right hand dropped to her side. "I'm sorry. It's just a habit I've had for a—"

"No, really, it's charming," he assured her with a smile. "Anyway, here's the craziest part of the story, if you can imagine it getting crazier. Yvette gives me a call about three months or so after the divorce. I've already moved up here, so I'm not sure how she located me. This is still pre-cell phone days! So she calls me and says that she met Jesus, that she's sorry for everything she did and wants my forgiveness, that everything was her fault, that I was a great guy, and would I like to see her again. I couldn't believe it. I couldn't believe this was the same person, but there was absolutely no way I could agree to meet up with her. I just told her that I was happy for her but way too busy to get together anytime soon. She begged for my forgiveness, so I gave it and said good-bye."

"That's it?" Linda asked, eyebrows raised.

"Yeah, pretty much."

"She never called you again?"

"Nope."

"What about Jesus?"

"What about him?"

Linda leaned forward with a mischievous look. "Did he ever call you?"

"Oh yeah, you're real funny!"

They laughed, Chase realizing he had never enjoyed someone's presence as much as this.

Linda suddenly turned sober. "Chase, have you ever done anything about religion? I mean, do you believe in God?"

"Of course I do. I'm Catholic."

"Oh."

"What about you?" he asked.

"Do I believe in God? Sure. I mean, I was raised in church. Not Catholic. I was Baptist. I went to Sunday school and all that. I really liked the camps because of all the boys," she remembered with a grin. "So, yeah, I believe in God. I just don't talk about it much."

"Well that's okay with me. I don't like people trying to cram things down my throat like they have something I need. God is God, and that's enough for me."

The two continued to date for the next several months. Since their careers in sales and marketing overlapped, they spent countless hours helping each other, discussing market trends, and brainstorming corporate-sales and management issues. They talked children, dreams, goals, life's joys and pleasures.

Though he was never completely certain at what point they fell in love, Chase felt so free from a life of rejection, failure, and self-inflicted isolation that it seemed as if his other life never existed. He knew and experienced love for the first time, not only because Linda helped heal his wounds but because they were such a perfect match intellectually and emotionally.

Chase had never shared his feelings with anyone before this relationship. He didn't even know that he had long wrestled with his true identity, with deep father issues, or with fear of vulnerability. Somehow Linda made him feel safe enough for self-revelation, and somehow she always had the right words to say, bringing comfort to his soul.

He knew that Linda loved his sense of humor and his easygoing nature. She told him so. One night she surprised him, however, by saying that she trusted him more because of his past, not in spite of it. She quoted someone who once said, "Don't follow anyone who doesn't walk with a limp!"

Since Linda admired all that he had endured over the years, Chase felt ready to limp down the aisle with her as his wife. Their first several years proved marvelous. Each had never met a closer counterpart.

CHAPTER 8

Chase found a nice Dominican—dark, rich wrapper, soft and pliable—in his humidor. Linda had retreated to their bedroom. After agreeing to go to dinner, they each apparently required time to regroup after the revealing session with Doctor Rhinegold. Chase pocketed his lighter and his cutter and headed for the French doors leading to the patio at the back of the house, his favorite place to think and to unwind.

Sitting for a moment on the padded porch swing, he carefully prepared his cigar with a few licks of his tongue. Satisfied, he let the lighter toast the end until it produced a bright red glow. Chase took a couple of puffs, watching thick trails of smoke wisp away in the gentle breeze. He stared thoughtfully at the wrapper, noticing the skillfully woven tobacco leaves. Studying the lines and the folds and the shades of brown, his eyes fastened upon his wedding ring. He quickly shifted his focus.

Becoming reflective, Chase slowly twisted the ring back and forth with his right index finger and his thumb. He sighed deeply, thinking of the how-to marriage books he had faithfully skimmed and of the short-lived alterations he had made to his life. Chase was frustrated at his feeble attempts to be someone he knew he couldn't be. He let go of the ring, took another puff, and rubbed his eyes wearily.

Several crows in a nearby pepper tree seemed to be in turmoil. One of them—probably a female, Chase thought with a smirk—had become territorial with the others, squawking at them as she flew from branch to branch. He felt pity for the rest since they appeared to have no idea what she wanted, or perhaps they knew but didn't care. The apparent leader won its rights as the others fled to the safety of a nearby telephone line on the side of the house.

Chase looked down at the burning cigar in his hand, caressing it with his thumb. His eyes drifted toward the yard. The flower bed needed watering. Two small trees begged for a trim. A little play area for Amy and Ryan held an outdated wooden structure with a plastic ladder and a slide, and three small swings, still dirty from previous rains. Chase knew outside maintenance was his responsibility, but he never seemed to have time. He cared about it. He wanted to provide a neatly manicured lawn. It was just that … His mind drifted. Chase forced himself to concentrate entirely on the flavor of his cigar.

He was staring at the growing ash when he noticed the silky threads of a giant spider web attached to the side of his swing, near his right hip. He sat frozen, mesmerized by the oddity, chills racing down his spine, sensing it to be a three-dimensional vision, yet fearful of moving away from it. Looking upward, he observed the web stretched taut between where he sat and the posts supporting the patio structure.

Chase's head jerked backward in terror when he saw a hideous, man-sized black widow busying herself near the outer edge of the web, her long front legs flying to and fro. Not until she scuttled away after weaving a solid strand of silk and securing it firmly to a post did Chase realize what he'd been watching. Something struggled helplessly at the center of the web, bound by sticky threads, several of which stretched to the perimeter of the web, anchoring the creature securely to it.

The black widow had been wrapping her prey. Staring at the spider's bound victim, Chase realized with a start that the face looking imploringly back at him was none other than his own—drawn, malnourished, and ashen with wide, panic-stricken eyes and a tight mouth attempting to form words.

The spider returned and crouched over her prey. He was trapped. Chase watched in horror as the black widow made her next inevitable move, her victim feeling powerless against such an indomitable enemy. A scream formed in his throat. Nothing came out. His head recoiled, nearly hitting the stucco on the house. Suddenly he was startled by the appearance of huge fingers sweeping through the web to release the spider's prey. Chase looked on in utter amazement as the prodigious hand lifted the victim aloft. He was set free!

As the vision continued, letters of the alphabet rushed furiously toward his face from the spider's web, spinning tauntingly, suddenly disintegrating, then returning full force as complete words, zooming in upon him: *vulnerability, touch, abandonment, anger, pride.* One at a time they came at him with heightened speed and then vanished just as rapidly.

What on earth is going on? he asked himself, sitting as erect as he could in the motionless swing, knowing that he didn't have an answer.

"These are the lies you've always believed about yourself."

Rattled by his own voice, Chase screamed, "What? These are lies about myself?" As soon as he asked, he knew it to be true; four, five, maybe six lifetime lies jumping out of the spider's web were his. Instantly he perceived that he had been ensnared by these untruths exposed before his eyes.

"But what do I do now?"

"Watch me," came his voice in return.

"Watch who? Watch what?" he called out to the tree before him.

Chase snapped out of his state, quickly looking for tangible signs of the event—a spider, a web, anything. He saw nothing.

He studied his hip where the web had formed just inches from him. More chills ran down his back, and perspiration stained the armpits of his shirt. Chase wiped his brow and sat in silence, trembling, his heart still pounding.

Through overhanging trees, he watched the sun sink slowly amid the billowy clouds far beyond. He looked at the pepper tree in front of him. The crow was gone. He could hear every sound—his children playing next door in the neighbors' backyard, birds chirping as they flew overhead, cars pulling into driveways. All his senses were acute as he attempted to understand this enigma, cautiously intrigued by it. Had he gone insane? Had his anxiety and stress finally caught up with him? Had this really happened? He needed to talk with Linda.

Chase noticed his neglected cigar, long out. He tossed it into the ashtray and walked inside, shaking his head, feeling spent.

A little after seven, their children at home with a sitter, Chase and Linda sat across from each other at Giuseppe's.

It wasn't the first time they'd had dinner there, and long-ago memories temporarily displaced images of giant spiders, sticky webs, and flying phrases. Chase looked at his wife, her green eyes beautiful in the candlelight. He suddenly felt shy.

"Bet you don't remember what we ordered the first time we were here."

"Of course I do," she said coyly.

"Oh, come on. Really?"

"You had spaghetti, which I thought rather funny since this restaurant is so nice. And I had, um—wait a minute, Chase. This is nice, the restaurant, the candles, reminiscing and all, but we have some serious issues here."

"I understand that. And I definitely want to find a resolution, but … well, I just think it's important for us to try to enjoy each other in the midst of it. You know me. I'm a fighter, but I definitely don't want to fight you. You've been a wonderful wife, an amazing mother, and I simply don't want to lose what we have."

"Well we can't sweep everything under the carpet!"

Chase nodded. "That's true, and I don't want to. I just know that the person you married is still here and completely in love with you despite my failures at showing it. Babe, I'm committed to us, and I hope you are as well."

"I am."

The waiter stepped up to their table for their drink orders. A short, round man, completely bald except for a few side patches of hair, he wore a simple expression and was extremely courteous and friendly. Chase had known him for years.

"Thanks, Freddie. And could you bring out the asparagus appetizer to start with?"

"Sure."

Freddie left and Chase continued to stare intently into Linda's eyes. He gently took her hand. "You're not going to believe what happened to me when I was outside this afternoon."

"What's that?"

"It's hard to explain, but I was sitting there, thinking about everything we've been going through and hoping that I could change but not knowing how. All of a sudden I saw myself trapped in a spider web, an unnaturally massive one."

"You saw this?"

"I don't know, Linda, maybe it was a vision or something, but it seemed as real as you and me sitting here. But catch this. A menacing black widow was spinning me in this sticky web. And then, out of nowhere, an enormous hand swooped in and plucked me out, pulling me back into myself, and as—"

"What do you mean?" Linda interrupted.

"About what?"

"About an enormous hand."

"I'm not sure. It happened so fast. But when that hand snatched me out of the web, it brought me up toward where I was sitting." Chase saw Linda lean back a little with a puzzled expression, her right hand stroking her curls. "I know. It's a bit uncanny to say the least."

"No, that's okay. I'm sorry. It's weird, but go on."

"Well then I got a picture of a bunch of words being released from the web, moving toward me at lightning speed. They were lies I've believed about myself for a lifetime. I'm not sure where all of this is heading, but I am interested in focusing on them to see if these things can be overcome, at least if that's what I'm supposed to do."

"So you believe some sort of action is necessary?"

"I don't know, but listen to this." Chase sat forward. "The strangest thing took place when I began to ask myself questions and then heard myself respond. The words came from my mouth, but they didn't come from my own thoughts."

"Like quick mental responses?"

"I guess so, but I've never experienced anything at all like it. I told myself, 'Watch me!' I said aloud that the words I saw myself being freed from were lies about myself. It's as if the answers have resided inside of me all along! Isn't that crazy?"

"Are you sure you're okay?" Linda asked, withdrawing her hand from his.

"What do you mean by that?" asked Chase, sitting back in his chair with a scowl.

"Well you've had a history with drugs, and you're in the middle of a very stressful situation. I don't know. It just seems like this could be some sort of a mental breakdown."

"Are you being serious?"

"Of course I am. After all, look at the way you've recently been tormenting yourself. And what about the possibility of your former drug use affecting your mind? I mean, at the very least, maybe it's some sort of subconscious reaction to everything."

"Linda, I told you this was real. You're thinking drugs could be a factor? No way, not after all these years. And yeah, of course I'm struggling right now, but that has nothing to do with what I saw."

"I think maybe it does. It could explain your emotional struggles. Latching on to visions sure seems like an easy way out. You'd do better to try to work on our issues as a couple."

"Unbelievable. You're not getting it. This has everything to do with us. Listen, Linda. All I want is to be the husband you've always needed and obviously longed for. I think I used to be good for you." He said this sincerely.

"You were," she answered flatly. "I just don't know what happened to you."

Chase looked at his still-outstretched hand on the table. "These lies I seem to have believed about myself are probably at the root of our troubles. Don't you see it? Maybe they're to blame for all of my behavior. I'm not using them as a scapegoat, but they may be the real issue behind how I've treated you recently."

"So they were hidden all these years and somehow suddenly manifested themselves today?"

"I have no idea. And I can see you're skeptical, but try to believe me when I say that I think these lies are the key to everything."

"What are they specifically?"

"One is abandonment. This must be an issue with me, though I've never considered it previously. I think Doctor Rhinegold mentioned it, but I can't be certain. Touch is another big deal, or rather not touching. But it's the way I was raised, the way I am."

Linda stared intently at her husband, attempting to reconcile his recent behavior with his new insights.

Chase hesitated and then continued. "What else did I see? Oh yeah, vulnerability. I don't know how to be vulnerable, and I'm not sure I want to. Well maybe I do, but I've got a lot of fears. Yeah, that was another one. Man, that's a lot of lies! And then the word *pride* rushed at me. I don't think of myself as overly proud, but I guess pride must play a part somewhere. What I've been thinking is this: in my attempt at self-preservation, I have slowly assassinated everything good within me. Unfortunately for you, and for us, you became the ultimate victim as I became wrapped up in my own lies." He paused. "So what do you think I'm supposed to do now?"

Linda leaned forward. "I have no idea, but I'm not willing to continue on the same way. Our lives have to change. This can't be some temporary modification. It won't work that way. I don't completely understand this crazy event, but I am willing to work things out if it's real."

Chase grinned broadly. "I'm so happy to hear you say that! And I'm not going to promise you this or that or tell you … Hang on a second. It may be the sitter." He reached for the cell phone hanging at his side and recognized the number.

"Hi, Frank. How's it going? ... What? No way ... Really? ... All right. Yes, I will. I'll check for flights and be out there as soon as I can ... Okay, I understand."

Cell phone still in hand, Chase turned to Linda, ashen and dazed. "My mom's dying. I've got to go back to New York."

"Dying?" Linda leaped out of her chair, rushing to embrace her husband. She knelt in front of him, holding his knees. "I'm so sorry, hon'. Can I do anything to help"?

"I don't know. Can you come with me?"

"Of course, but what about the children and school? I know it's awkward to ask this, but how long do you think we might be away?"

"Who knows? Frank said she's somewhat stable at this point. The doctor guesses she may pass in the next week or so." Chase took Linda's hands with a gentle squeeze. "It's all right, babe. Why don't we do this? I'll go out and see what's happening. If I think you and the kids should follow, we'll make the necessary plans."

"Okay."

Chase dropped off the sitter at her home while Linda read Amy and Ryan to sleep. As they prepared for bed, Chase gently guided his wife toward him. "You know I love you," he said.

"I love you too."

Chase couldn't recall the last time he felt so passionate toward Linda. He held her tightly as if this would be their last night together. Their lovemaking was wonderful for both of them, but Linda needed much more. She thought about her own issues of abandonment, how alone she felt at seventeen when her parents divorced, how she desperately searched for young men to fill the void. Her emptiness remained until she met Chase. He was everything she longed for in a man: handsome, spirited, and ambitious. Though a successful businesswoman, Linda desired someone stronger than she, a motivated, career-minded man who was emotionally present and tender. Despite his moments of anger and passive aggression, Chase had proven to be genuine and caring.

What happened? Could recognition of these lies he said he saw pave the way toward a resolution? Could it be that easy? Had all these things been mysteriously hidden from him for years, or worse, had he intentionally buried them? And if so, who was this man she had married? The one she fell in love with or someone else she shuddered to imagine? Chase said their problems had to do with his selfishness. Maybe so. But what about her own? Could her need for love and attention have been what pushed her husband away? Had Chase given her all he could and simply run dry? Had she been too demanding for more? Whatever the truth might be, Linda was determined to persevere. She knew it would take both of them working together to recover what they had lost.

"You know that this is not good timing for me to be away," Chase whispered in her ear as she cuddled up to him.

"I'm not going to call him, Chase."

"Can you at least look at me when you say that?"

Linda gazed into his eyes. He held her arms. "I'm not going to call him. You need to see your mom. I'll be here with the children. It'll be okay."

"I need you." As soon as he said it, Chase realized he had never spoken those words to anyone, not even to his wife.

"In what ways?"

He rubbed his forehead, her question catching him off guard. "Well, just in the way you're always there, in the way you're strong. Um, I don't know, in the way you encourage me. I really do need you."

"I need you, too." Linda repeated the words. They sounded hollow, however, as if a magic moment had somehow come and gone.

Chase fell quickly and soundly asleep. Linda looked at his arm gently stretched across her stomach. She always desired nights such as this, not merely the intimacy of lovemaking but the heartfelt sincerity of the man she had married. It had been too long. She felt frazzled and confused. Could this be the reason she reached out to someone from the past and naively thought this contact could be innocent? Not that she didn't enjoy it. She loved the conversation, the feeling of freedom to laugh and to be herself, and reminiscing about mutual friends.

Sure, she felt uneasy when he remembered her beauty and her captivating green eyes and told her how much he thought about her every day. The awkwardness became easy to ignore because of the overwhelming sense of acceptance she felt after the compliments. It had been only three weeks. Could she really cut their ties? Linda knew with certainty that she wouldn't call or email, but what about him? Would he pursue her? Had she opened the door a bit too far for him to accept having it so quickly slammed in his face? Would she talk with him if he did call?

Linda tried desperately to sleep, tossing back and forth in bed, taking off the covers, and then putting them back on. An hour later she still lay awake, staring at the ceiling, a few tears finding their way down the side of her face and onto her hair. She stroked her curls.

CHAPTER 9

Chase woke early the following morning and called United for flights to Syracuse on Saturday. The weekend departure would give him the day to wrap up sales consultations before leaving. After securing a 1 p.m. flight, he left a message with Doctor Rhinegold asking to change their scheduled appointment to Friday if possible.

After hurriedly preparing Amy and Ryan for school, Linda rushed past him into the kitchen without a word. Chase noticed her stress. "Hey, babe, I'll make their lunches today and drop them off. Why don't you just take it easy?"

Eyebrows raised in surprise, Linda placed her hands on Chase's face. "That's so sweet, hon', but really I can manage."

"I know you can, but I want to help."

"All right then. Do you know how to make sandwiches?"

"Get out of here!" Chase said playfully, tickling Linda. "Hey kids!" he yelled down the hallway, still holding her waist, "Daddy's taking you to school. Be ready to go in five minutes. By the way, babe," he said as Linda squirmed away, "I found a flight for Saturday."

"Perfect. I'm sure everyone will be glad you're there."

Chase found quite a bit of pleasure in the fifteen-minute drive to school with his children. He knew the names of their teachers and their friends but asked again just for the joy of hearing their surprised responses when he feigned ignorance.

From there he drove to his office in Irwindale. His company sold chemicals to industrial plants all over the nation. Though employed as an independent contractor, Chase felt like part of the firm in every other way. After his first two years, the owners gave him free rein with their other reps. He had demonstrated his uncanny abilities, and company sales had increased by more than 15 percent in twelve months. Chase's office consisted of three fabric dividers with a small desk and a computer, but he didn't mind. He was hired to produce, so salespeople became his primary focus.

The younger of the two brothers who owned the company greeted him first that morning. Tom had a slight build, small, manicured hands, and a belly that protruded over his belt. A receding hairline made him look a little older than a man in his forties. The laugh wrinkles around his eyes matched his affable nature. "Good morning, Chase. How is everything going?"

"Hi, Tom. Not too good actually. I got a call last night that my mother in New York is dying."

"Oh, I am so sorry."

"Thank you."

"Anything we can do?"

"Yes. I need to go see her right away, so I booked a flight for Saturday. I shouldn't be away too long, but I hope this is okay."

"Of course it is! Take whatever time you need."

"Thanks a lot. All I need to do now is contact James about a few clients he's working with and then talk to Alan over in Dallas. I shouldn't be much more than a few hours. Most of the other work I can do on my laptop."

"Sure, no problem. Hey, you look different," Tom said.

"What do you mean?"

"I don't know. Just something about you. You seem quite relaxed considering the circumstances, like you just got a massage or something."

The comment took Chase by surprise. He was unable to recall any time in his life when someone thought of him as relaxed. He considered himself to be more of a fighter, not someone radiating tranquility. *Hmm*, Chase mused, *I wonder what he's noticing.* "Thanks a lot," he answered. "I needed that."

Chase retreated outside that afternoon, cigar in one hand, two cans of Miller in the other. He told Linda that Doctor Rhinegold had rescheduled their appointment for the next afternoon and asked her to join him on the patio when she could. Only one day had passed since his vision, or whatever it was, on this same swing. He chose the same brand of cigar and sat in the same spot, attempting not to appear superstitious. Taking a pensive puff on his dark Partagas, he surveyed the grounds for anything unusual. He closed his eyes for several seconds and reopened them, looking down near his hip for a web. He tried to imagine staring through different dimensions and attempted to use his thoughts to bend objects in the yard. His contorted face must have caught Linda's attention.

"Chase, what on earth are you doing?"

"Wow! You look beautiful!" She wore a spring dress he'd never noticed before. The pink and red flowers adorning it were woven into a maze of teal lines. The hem skimmed her knees, the fabric flowing across her long, graceful legs. Her light-brown hair curled softly down her shoulders, moving gently in the breeze.

"Why thank you! Is this a good time to join you?"

"Totally," he answered, handing her a beer. "Let me just have you sit here, and I'll move to the other side so the smoke won't bother you."

"Okay, thanks. Now tell me what you were doing out here."

"You were watching me?"

"Yes, as I walked out."

"Well I was simply trying to see if the spider web would reappear and if more lies would be flying out of it. I even hoped that voice would speak again."

"I thought you said it was your own."

"Well yeah, of course, but it was weird. That's all I can say. Just didn't seem like me, kind of like someone speaking through me, moving my lips."

Linda shook her head. "I've never heard of such a thing."

"Well anyway," he said with a shrug, "that's what ol' Chase was up to."

"So you told me you wanted to share more about your lies—how did you put it?—the lies you believed about yourself."

"Yes, and I just finished writing a few of them down." Chase reached into the back pocket of his pants. "Here. I hope you can read my scribbling."

Linda opened the twice-folded paper, staring at the title he had placed at the top, "The Spider Web." She glanced at Chase and then began to read with cautious anticipation.

> Something suddenly broke into my world like a huge wave that overpowers and crushes anyone who dares stand in its path. I saw many lies I've accepted as reality all my life. Here are a few that have affected, and infected, my relationship with Linda:
>
> First, this is who I am and I cannot change, and I wouldn't want to change even if I could.
>
> Second, I cannot provide touch to those who need it.
>
> Third, I cannot be open and vulnerable with Linda.
>
> Fourth, I cannot be a good friend to Linda, much less her best friend.
>
> I am not certain where to begin in this battle against lifelong lies, but perhaps for the first time, I desire change. I will fight for my marriage and my family, doing whatever it takes to overcome my misconceptions about who I am.

Linda's hands trembled slightly, her lips quivered, and her tears slowly dropped onto the paper below. She carefully and lovingly handed it back to Chase. "Hon', that is so beautiful. I had no idea what you were going through."

"Neither did I! Writing it down solidified it, but I'm not exactly sure where any of this will lead. I guess just one step at a time, as they say."

"That works for me."

75

Linda told Chase through her tears how she'd already noticed changes in him. He wanted to know specifics. "You're more attentive, more sensitive—you know, the way you treated me last night and this morning. You seem less guarded or something."

"Well, babe, I think this is the real thing. I mean, I've attempted to change my ways in the past whenever you've pointed out various dysfunctions. Behavior modification can certainly be effective for a time, but in my case, it never completely takes root. I can find no comparison with whatever happened to me yesterday. I've held on to more than twenty years of lies! The web I was in and the way I saw myself being spun and then nearly bitten by the black widow … I don't know. I think there was simply no way of getting free without some sort of major miracle."

"So you think that's what happened, a miracle?"

"I guess so. Due to my stubbornness, it apparently took something dramatic like this to bring the needed change."

"It all sounds great, but I don't totally get it yet. Are you saying that you've never noticed any of these behavioral traits before, that they appeared magically out of nowhere?"

"No, I've been aware of them. I just thought that they were part of who I am, that I couldn't do anything about them."

"And your plan at this point, besides taking one step at a time?"

"To discover who I really am."

"Well I'm for that! I just hope it continues," Linda said with raised brows.

"Me too! I don't want to go back to the way I was. I see now that I pushed us apart into our own little worlds. I have no idea why, but it must have been the lies dictating how I treated you. I am so sorry, babe."

Linda tenderly touched his leg. "It's okay. I sure hope this trip is good for you."

The next morning, while Chase was busy packing, Linda checked her emails and stopped cold. Trembling, she opened the dreaded message. He hadn't heard from her in several days. Wondered how she was doing.

Couldn't sleep much after her last email. Missed her greatly. He would call her soon.

Linda deleted the message, her body shaking as she did it. What could she possibly do now? Write him back and tell him once more never to contact her again? Or call him to make sure he was okay or didn't do something dramatic? "I'll wait till Saturday," she concluded, "after Chase is gone."

CHAPTER 10

When they stepped into the waiting room that afternoon, Doctor Rhinegold stood at his office door with a grin. "Come on in! Have a seat," he said cheerfully as the door shut behind them.

Linda sat on the middle of the sofa. Chase rested himself next to her, taking her hand in his. The doctor took mental note. "So, Chase, how have things been going?"

"Actually it's been quite amazing. We've been able to talk, communicate, connect again. I feel positive about everything so far."

"Great. And you?" he asked, peering at Linda through his thick eyebrows.

"I couldn't ask for more. Chase has been very open, sharing deeply with me and going through some incredible changes. I think it's good."

"What type of changes do you mean?"

"Well he had this experience. Honey, you should tell him."

"Sure." Chase shared his spider-web vision in vivid detail. He could see Rhinegold's interest increasing as the doctor scribbled notes on his pad. When Chase mentioned the voice that had spoken to him, the doctor interrupted.

"What do you mean by a different type of voice?"

"Well, it was definitely mine but eerie, like someone else speaking or someone manipulating my voice."

"Have you ever had such an experience before?"

"No. Never."

"Would you say that this was a voice in your head? Or did it seem audible?"

"Definitely audible, as clear as anything I've ever heard."

"And you feel that you yourself spoke the words."

"Yes. I mean, I think so."

The doctor fingered his eyebrows. "Interesting. And what do you think the voice meant by saying to you, 'Watch me'?"

"I have no idea. Does it sound a little crazy?"

"No, not at all. It says to me that all along you've wanted to change but didn't know how. Your own voice is perhaps encouraging you that this is achievable, that this can be done."

"Makes sense."

"Okay, continue."

Chase explained as best he could how the lifetime lies had shot toward his face and had disappeared just as quickly.

The doctor frowned. "Tell me more about these words."

"Well here," Chase said, unfolding his notes. "I wrote a few of them down so I wouldn't forget, mainly the ones I recognized as having affected Linda."

Doctor Rhinegold spent a few minutes studying the paper, thoughtfully rubbing his chin, peeking at Chase once or twice, and then nodding to himself before raising his eyebrows. "Would you like me to give my opinion about this?"

"Absolutely."

The doctor cleared his throat. "First of all, I'm pleased that you've expressed a desire to change, that you're no longer willing to accept the lie that you are who you are and cannot make positive alterations in your life. Is this what you're saying?"

"Yes. I mean, I've never thought like this before. I've always believed that I am who I am and that people just have to accept me for that. I'm beginning to see that this is a lie, that I can be whoever I want to be. I think I've kind of known that all along, but seeing the lies exposed so vividly added much more understanding."

"I'll bet it did," agreed the doctor, leaning back in his chair. "Now what about this issue of touch? Apparently that has been a problem for you?"

Chase and Linda smiled. "Oh yeah. I've been thinking about that a lot. There was actually a whole layer of lies in this area, one built upon the other. It started, I think, with the notion that I'm Irish and British. You know, the stereotype that they don't touch."

The doctor nodded in agreement. Chase continued. "Well once I accepted that, the next layer of lies arose from viewing a model or example of not touching, basically given me by my parents. And even though that was true of them, it led to the lie that because of my heritage and my upbringing, I did not need to be touched by others. Then I concluded that since I didn't need touch, even if I wanted to change and to learn how to be more tactile, I wouldn't enjoy such change. Do you know what I'm saying?"

"I'm with you, Chase, but can I ask you a question at this point?"

"Sure."

"This is an incredible amount of understanding in such a short time. How have you been able to come so quickly to these remarkable conclusions?"

Chase chuckled. "The few times I've been able to write down my thoughts have been amazing. Things I've never thought of or considered seem to pour out of my mind. What you have in your hand is only a summary of what's come to me."

"That's indeed amazing. Please go on with this issue of touch."

"Okay. When I concluded that I didn't need to give or to receive touch, I became completely satisfied with who I was. Then, if others needed touch, well, they'd have to get it from someone else. After all, I couldn't reasonably be expected to supply something that it wasn't in me to provide. Finally, I suppose that I resented anyone trying to change me in this area. My attitude was essentially "Leave me alone because this is who I am.""

Over the years, this attitude evolved into a complicated, confusing layer of lies that formed a web around me."

"A web from which you could not escape."

"Exactly."

"Thank you for sharing this, Chase. And something that may help you in this area is the truth that we all need touch, that to give and to receive it is actually to transfer life from one person to another. It is part of man's basic need to love and to be loved."

Chase looked at Linda with a sparkle in his eye. "Wow! That's awesome!"

"Yes, and you have apparently withheld these basic needs from Linda and from yourself."

"Oh." Chase's enthusiasm suddenly changed to dourness. "Yeah, you're probably right." He squeezed Linda's hand, and tears formed in her eyes.

The doctor stared at the paper again. "Now you also appear to struggle with openness and vulnerability, at least with Linda. Can you tell me about this?"

"Well it's weird since I've always been very direct with people. I couldn't care less what they think of me, so opening up to others is easy. But with Linda, it seems to be a challenge for some reason."

"Do you feel that if you're vulnerable with her, such sharing of yourself will be used against you in the future?"

"Perhaps."

"Has this happened to you before?"

"I don't know. What do you think, babe?"

Linda glanced at Chase, holding his hand more tightly. She looked back at the doctor. "There have been times when I'm sure I've brought up past events and have hurt him."

"Chase, do you remember times like this?"

"I guess so, but doesn't everybody do that?"

"How did they make you feel?"

"Probably pretty guarded."

"Okay. And did you make any sort of inner vow not to open up again?"

"Oh, I see where you're going with all of this. I locked myself up for fear of being exposed again. Is that it?"

"You tell me."

"I think so. I must have believed the lie that I couldn't be totally open with Linda. Or maybe that I could but that I didn't want to be since that might lead to further self-exposure. I don't know, Doctor Rhinegold. All I know right now is that I want Linda to know me better."

"Very good, Chase. Thank you for your honesty." Turning to Linda, the doctor said, "You must be very pleased with all of this."

"As I said, things are a lot better. Chase has definitely changed in a short time. I can't fully comprehend what happened to my husband, but I have never before heard him speak like this. It's as if he's a new person."

"And it may be a long journey, but it appears he is taking the right path. What about your own situation?"

Chase cocked his head slightly. Linda hesitated. "Well, I try not to think about it."

"So there's been no contact with this person?"

"No," she lied, justifying herself with the thought that he, not she, had sent the email the previous night.

"Good. But let me suggest something here." Rhinegold set his pad down and looked intently at Linda. "This guy probably will try to contact you. I'm surprised he hasn't already. I hope he won't, but my hunch is that he will. You have to determine now what your response will be if that happens. You've already asked him not to call or write anymore, correct?"

"Yes."

"But as I said, he more than likely will. He may not be easily convinced that you mean it. You had an emotional connection, and he may not be willing to let it go. Have you thought through what you will say if he does call or write?"

"Not really."

"Well how will you respond if he says how much he misses you, that the two of you had something special going on?"

Chase took a deep breath, shaking his head.

"I'll just say that it wasn't special, that it's over."

"Good. And may I suggest that you keep the conversation or the email brief? You may have to be short and forceful depending upon his reaction."

"I think I can do that."

"Linda, I recommend that you picture yourself being strong in this potential situation. You've admitted that Chase is going through significant changes, and though you two still have a ways to go, you may not progress much further if you allow this other issue to keep hanging over you. I obviously hope this guy doesn't make contact, as I'm sure you do as well, but you must be prepared if he does. Maybe you can write down your response and keep it with you if that will help."

"All right," Linda agreed weakly. Seeking comfort, she peeked at Chase. He gently squeezed her hand.

"Now Chase, how are you doing with all of this?"

"Not too good, actually. We haven't even talked about it. I'm trying to give her space, but it's killing me inside."

"How is that?"

"Well, when I realize how I've not been meeting her needs, that's one thing, but knowing there's someone else out there is just eating me up."

The doctor slowly looked at each of them. "Well I recommend that you begin to work through this issue with deliberation. Chase, you don't need to know all the details of the past few weeks, but it is important for you to relate your feelings to Linda, perhaps a sense of devaluation, hurt, betrayal, whatever creates the angst within. Linda, you can be honest with Chase. It's okay to share how you became drawn into this relationship, how you're perhaps embarrassed by it, how you want to focus on the two of you now. Just be self-disclosing with one another." He glanced slowly back and forth. "And don't rush the process. Is this okay with both of you?"

"Yes," they responded simultaneously, though Chase still felt uncomfortable. "The only problem is that I have to fly back to New York tomorrow since, as I told you in my message, my mother is dying."

"Yes, I'm so sorry, Chase. Are you going alone?"

"Yeah, it's too complicated with our children, Linda's work, and the fact that I have no idea how long I'll be gone."

The doctor rubbed his chin for a moment. "Allow me to be unequivocal. Despite the incredible progress you've made in just two short days, you have to consider the fragility of your marriage. Because of this reality, both of you must be very intentional about communicating every day. You may think such a thing obvious, but trust me in this. Stressful and emotional situations can often distract us from what is most important at the moment, shifting our minds toward admittedly serious but comparatively less significant issues. The illness of a mother and the compromising actions of a spouse, along with all the accompanying emotions, can derail your progress. You must determine that no matter what happens in the weeks ahead, your marriage is the priority. Keep your focus there, okay?"

"Got it," Chase responded.

"It's easier said than done, Chase. You have to work together on this one and be completely accountable to each other."

"All right. I understand," he answered less glibly.

"Thank you, Doctor Rhinegold," added Linda. "You have been a great help to us both."

"Well let's do this. Linda, please don't hesitate to call me for any reason while Chase is away. And Chase, give me a ring when you return and we'll arrange another appointment."

"Sounds good," he said, helping Linda up. "Thank you so much. We really appreciate all you've done."

"Let me ask you one more question," the doctor said as he rose. "Linda, describe Chase for me in one word."

"Um, thoughtful."

"And Chase, what about Linda?"

"She's kind."

"Thoughtful and kind. Those are great attributes. Why don't you try focusing on each other with thoughtfulness and kindness? Despite what has happened, you two are wonderful people. Give yourselves to one another in the days ahead. It'll pay great dividends."

Chase extended his hand. "Will do. Thanks again, Doctor Rhinegold."

The family drove to the airport late Saturday morning. Chase and Linda had processed their appointment the previous night, neither one mentioning the other man. Chase waited until they pulled up to the terminal entrance to attempt a feeble warning. Carefully phrasing his words, he turned to Linda, taking her hand and looking into her eyes. "So we'll stay in touch every day. I have no idea what to expect, but I'm sure I'll have enough time to call or email. You will as well, right?"

"Of course!"

"And nothing out of the ordinary."

Linda knew what he meant. "Hon', please don't worry. I'll keep myself busy enough with work and the children."

"Okay, I just want to make sure that you'll be all right, that nothing weird is going to happen."

She let go of his hand. "Chase, there's nothing going on. Just give my love to your mom and your family. I'll be fine."

"Babe, you know I love you."

"I love you too, hon'."

"And remember," Chase said with a wink, "I am apparently thoughtful, and you are kind."

"Apparently?"

Chase smiled and kissed her, then turned and hugged the children before stepping out to grab his suitcase from the trunk. "I'm going to miss you all!" he shouted as he disappeared into the crowd.

CHAPTER 11

Linda knew what needed to be done that evening. Making certain Amy and Ryan were asleep before closing her bedroom door, she crawled underneath the blankets, cell phone in hand, wrestling with her issue, nearly talking herself out of the formidable decision she had made. "If I call Stan," she argued quietly with herself, "he'll think I'm still interested no matter what I say. But if I don't, I run the risk of him phoning me at a bad time."

Though she believed Doctor Rhinegold would surely not advise such a call, Linda understood the urgency of the matter better than anyone. She again hesitated, toying with her curls. What if Stan was desperate? What if he refused to listen? But the truth was that they were just friends. Or were they? Stan had always wanted something more. Did she, in fact, lead him into all of this? Did she too want something more? She shook her head quickly, not wanting to continue these torturous thoughts.

Cheekbones tightening, Linda stared at the phone in her trembling hand. She recalled the doctor's suggestion about being short and forceful. What sort of advice was that, especially concerning someone who was always so nice to her? Without any further thought, she pushed the buttons, her lips quivering when he answered.

"Hello, Linda?"

"Yes."

"So good to hear your voice! How've you been?"

"I'm fine, but I have to tell you something."

"Sure, great! But hang on to your thoughts 'cause I've been thinking a lot these past several days. I know you wanted some space and I know I emailed you and all, but I honestly can't seem to find any peace without you. I think I've discovered something in you that I've never experienced before. Linda, I know it's complicated, but let's take some time with all of this. We don't have to rush it. We can remain good friends. Nobody has to know, just you and me."

"It's too late for that," she answered dryly.

"What do you mean?"

"Chase knows. Our psychologist knows. It's all out—"

"Chase knows? And a psychologist?! Linda, what are you doing?"

"I'm trying to make my marriage work."

"Did you tell them who I was?"

"No, not yet."

"Then what's going on? There really is something special between us. I'm certain you feel it." Stan spoke as if imploring her to listen to logic.

Linda's agitation increased, the lines in her forehead deepening. "No, I don't, Stan. This was supposed to be a friendship. You're apparently looking for more, something I can't give you."

"But I know you've been looking for more as well. You told me as much."

"Whatever I've said, this has to end, and it has to end now."

"I can't do that."

"What do you mean you can't?" Linda recoiled, feeling the anger she thought impossible beginning to rise within her.

"Well let me be honest. I've fallen in love with you. I can't give up on the idea of us being together. You are the most amazing person, and I—"

"Stop it, Stan!" she cried out vehemently. "I can't listen to this! I told you that I'm ending it. I love Chase, and I'm committed to him and to our marriage and our family. I can't help how you feel or whatever you're going through, but you need to leave me alone. No more calls, okay?"

"I don't think I can do that."

"You can and you better! I don't ever want to hear from you again!" Linda couldn't believe the intensity of her words. Always amicable, she was completely frustrated at having to end a relationship that she thought had begun so innocently.

"And what if I call, not right away, but maybe in a couple of weeks just to check on you?"

"I don't need you to check on me."

"Mommy?" came a small voice from the behind the door. Amy opened it and looked in. "Are you talking to Daddy?"

"Hang on," she said into the phone. "No, honey. I'm just doing some business. It's all right. Go back to bed now."

The door closed and Linda, irritated, put the cell back to her ear. "Listen, Stan," she said sternly, "I have a family, and I'm not going to jeopardize it for you. You found me in a lonely and vulnerable state, and despite the things I've said to you recently, I don't mean them anymore. If you call or write, I will not respond. And don't press the issue, because I might just give Chase your number and let him deal with you. I don't think you'd want that."

"Come on, Linda. This is not you. We've talked for countless hours these past few weeks. I know what you want, and it's certainly not going back to the life you've been living. You don't want to live a lie."

The words felt like a blow to her abdomen, but she steadfastly held her ground. "I'm not living a lie!" she shrieked into the phone, trying to muffle her voice with her other hand. "And no, you don't know me and what I want. How could you after a few phone calls and emails? In any case, don't push this any further. I'm moving on, and you need to do the same. I'm going to hang up now, and believe me this is it. I'm hanging up. Good-bye."

"Wait, Lin—"

She hit "end" before Stan could say anything more. Not quite indignant but deeply hurt, Linda was displeased that she had to cut him off so abruptly and in such a cruel way. Still trembling with confusion and agitation, she curled up in her bed and cried herself to sleep.

**

His plane landed in Syracuse near midnight. Chase trudged to the baggage claim area and waited. "Wouldn't you know mine would be the last one," he muttered when he finally spied his black-and-brown suitcase. As he stepped out of the terminal toward Hertz, the chill surprised him since he didn't expect April to feel so cold, at least back home. Pleased that he had the foresight to bring a light jacket, he wrapped it over his shoulders.

Soon speeding along the freeway, Chase punched in Frank's number on his cell. He would arrive in about an hour. They could leave a key under the mat.

"No way! Just knock and I'll come down. Allie and I can't wait to see you."

"All right. Just checkin'. See you when I get there."

"Sounds good. See you soon."

Frank had called Chase that morning to let him know their mother's condition had grown worse and that she kept asking for him. She wanted to know when she could see him, how long he would stay, and whether the grandchildren would be with him. He called her, promising to visit on Sunday.

Riding the freeway, Chase depended upon Frank's directions. When he fled New York at twenty-two, he had left his hometown only once before, on a family excursion to New York City shortly after he turned five. Chase attempted to recall as much of the trip as possible, not merely because he remembered it as special but mainly to help fight his fatigue.

After ten minutes or so of relative success, his mind turned to his family. Tears fell down his cheeks as he thought about his intense love for Amy and Ryan. Suddenly he sobbed uncontrollably. Chase pulled off at the next exit, wiping the tears with his sleeve as he sat near a gas station. He remembered his vow many years ago never to be like his father. Was that it? Had he emotionally abandoned his own children? He loved them. He cherished them. But did they know it? Did they feel it? Tears again welled up. And Linda? He treasured her beyond words. Chase could not imagine life without her. Whatever it took to preserve his marriage, he would do.

He wiped his nose, looked around him, and shook his head when he realized his concern that others may have seen him crying. This was truly a fight, he told himself, a fight for those dearest to him. With renewed resolve, Chase hopped back onto the freeway.

He finally reached his exit and stopped at the end of the off-ramp. "This is weird," he said half aloud. "I haven't seen this place in ages." Chase rolled down the window, stretched out his arms, and inhaled deeply, thoroughly enjoying the crisp early morning air. *I wonder what it looks like now*, he mused.

Taking a direction opposite from Frank's house, he drove west toward the woods. *So this is where it all began*, he reflected, coming as close as the road allowed and then pulling over to stare at the railroad tracks with the river below. After all these years, nothing had changed. Just him. How would his life have turned out if the drop had gone down as planned? He wondered if he'd still be dealing.

Chase thought about that and considered how often events that appear to be disastrous can turn out well in the end. He mused about the possible role of destiny, a word he surely had never uttered before. Perhaps fate made better sense, whatever that meant. Or maybe simple coincidence defined this phenomenon best. "Oh, whatever," he said flippantly. These events had happened and now he had returned thirteen years later.

As he drove toward Frank and Allie's, Chase felt gratified by the changes he had experienced. He was pleased that upstate New York and all it represented existed in his past, that he had a wonderful family and a good career, and that something new, fresh, and exciting had happened in his life.

He even became mysteriously content with the ambiguity of the event on his patio. Though Chase couldn't explain the hand or the voice, he knew that the lies were too real to deny. That Linda noticed considerable changes in his behavior testified to their reality. She would never accept more of the meaningless and temporary promises he had made in the past. And even if he could never identify the source of his freedom, Chase felt secure enough to leave that question unanswered and to wholeheartedly pursue the revelation that he indeed could become a new person.

By the time Chase pulled up to the house, the one Frank and Allie had lived in for years, exhaustion overwhelmed him. *Man, that was a long trip*, he thought. Clutching his suitcase in one hand and his carry-on in the other, he stepped up to the front door. He tapped lightly several times and knocked more loudly after about a minute.

The door opened and Frank stood in his robe, bleary-eyed but grinning like a little boy. "Chase!" he shouted, reaching out to embrace him. "Great to see you! Come on in."

Allie waited in the entryway with outstretched hands, buoyant and breezy as ever. "It's been so long! How was your flight? Can I get you something? Maybe some coffee?"

He stole a kiss on her cheek. "No, thanks. I'm just whipped. A nice bed sounds better."

"We have one made up in the guest room. I put towels on your bed, so just make yourself at home. How are Linda and the children?"

"Oh, they're great."

"And you?"

Frank stopped her questions. "Allie, I think he needs some shut-eye. Why don't we talk in the morning?" Chase nodded his agreement.

"Okay then," Allie said cheerfully. "I'll have the coffee brewing. Chase, it's so good to see you!"

"Good to see you too, Allie. Seems like forever. And thanks for putting me up. I really love you guys."

"Wow!" Allie exclaimed. "I don't think I've ever heard you say that! We love you too. Anything else you need?"

"I'm good."

"Okay, well, get a good night's sleep, and we'll go see Mom as soon as you're up."

Chase hauled his bags upstairs, plopped on the bed without removing his clothes, and immediately fell into a deep sleep. Five hours later, around seven in the morning, he got up to go to the kitchen for a drink of water. Walking downstairs and into the living room, he saw Linda sitting on the sofa in deep reflection. He didn't question her being at Frank and Allie's but quietly knelt behind her, placed his hands on her shoulders, and tenderly asked if she felt okay.

He immediately sensed a presence. Someone slowly crept toward them from the study. It could be Frank, but somehow Chase knew that wasn't possible and that danger lurked right behind them. Panic seized him as the eerie presence walked past the sofa, glanced over at Linda, and mechanically asked, "What's going on?" Without waiting for a response, the presence continued toward the kitchen.

Chase turned to look and nearly collapsed. It was himself, but he was wrapped in rags like a mummy. Completely dumbfounded, Chase nevertheless instinctively knew this to be his old self, the same desperate, terrified person flailing in the spider web. He rubbed his face with his trembling hands before looking up again. The figure was gone. In disgust Chase resolutely vowed, "I'll never be that person again."

Instantly Chase found himself back in bed. Glancing at the alarm clock, he saw that the green numbers read seven-thirty-three. He wiped the perspiration from his brow and noticed his body shaking. He looked around the room but saw nothing out of place. What had just happened? Did he actually get up and go downstairs? Did he really see what he thought he saw? Linda was there, so it had to be a dream, one of those vivid dreams that seem so real.

No, he couldn't believe that. This was much more substantial than a dream. Didn't he just climb back into bed? Chase stroked his chin. He considered calling Linda but realized the hour on the West Coast. Digging for his laptop, he opened it up on the small antique desk and drafted an email.

> Linda my love,
>
> I hope all is well with you and the children. I arrived at Frank's early this morning and had the strangest experience a few minutes ago. I got out of bed and walked downstairs and then noticed you sitting on Frank and Allie's couch. This was something similar to a dream but much more tangible, even more so than the web, if you can believe that.

Anyway, after I knelt down behind you, I felt someone creeping up behind us. When he came into view I saw that it was me, a walking corpse or something! I was kneeling behind you, trying to give you comfort, but the old me, the man I saw move past us, behaved as I once did, barely recognizing you and walking into the kitchen. We didn't make eye contact since he seemed to look beyond me or through me. I then resolved, out loud, never to be that person again!

What do you think it's all about? I believe that I'm changing, and maybe I simply saw an aspect of myself that treated you so poorly, the part that separated our lives and forced you to make it on your own. I am so sorry, Linda. I've put you through a lot, but I don't want to be that person any longer. I wish you were here. I'm already missing you. Hug the kids for me and call as soon as you can.

Love,
Chase

He hit "send," closed his laptop, and went downstairs.

**

"You're up early!" chirped Allie as Chase made his way into the kitchen. "Did you sleep well?"

"Short but good."

"Coffee?"

"Definitely."

"It'll be ready in a minute. It's so nice to see you again after all these years! We've really missed you. Frank went out to the bakery and should return shortly. Can I get you anything else in the meantime?"

"No, coffee's fine. Hey Allie, how long have you been downstairs?"

"What, you mean this morning?"

"Yeah."

"We just got up maybe ten minutes ago. Why?"

"Oh, just wondering." He checked his cell phone and saw that it was seven-fifty-five. "So how have you been?"

Chase listened, savoring each sip of freshly ground beans as Allie chattered away about Frank, their business, some neighbor down the street who accidentally ran into the back of their parked car last week, and other apparently meaningful topics. His mind moved in and out of the conversation as he continued to contemplate what had taken place less than an hour before. Chase enjoyed reconnecting, but the event and the impending visit with his mother weighed heavily on him.

When Frank marched through the front door toward the kitchen, Chase had just finished his second cup. "Well good morning, Chase. You're up early! Didn't expect that."

"Yeah I know. Had this crazy dream or somethin' I'll have to tell you about later after we see Mom."

"Sure. Well, since you're up, I've got some fresh bread and a few pastries, so why don't we eat, catch up, and then go to the hospital?"

"You guys go ahead. I need to take a quick shower. I'll be down right after that." As much as he desired to converse with them, Chase determined that his mission was to visit his mother, stay as long as needed, and return to Linda and the kids sooner rather than later. He understood that it must be special for Frank to have his kid brother around after all this time, but it wasn't as if they never talked. Or maybe he simply felt uncomfortable back in his old neighborhood, a place with too many bad memories.

CHAPTER 12

On the way to the hospital, Chase tried to sound interested in the conversation, nodding and agreeing, sharing a little about Amy and Ryan, listening to more stories of how the town had changed over the years, who still lived there, and who had moved. Frank and Allie asked him a couple of times if he felt all right; he said yes, that he was just tired, which at the moment seemed mostly true.

He didn't care for hospitals. Too many sick people, obviously, but the problem didn't stop there. A certain odor prevailed, a mixture of dirty socks and disinfectant that filled his nose and hurried his pace. Several years had passed since his last visit to one of these places. He stayed in touch with Aunt Betty, periodically calling her to check in and usually eluding the subject of religion. One day she phoned with news of a sudden fall and a broken hip. Chase jumped in his car for the hour drive to Riverside. His visit encouraged her, though it forced him to tolerate more declarations of Jesus' love for him. Later rescued from the repellant odor, Aunt Betty made a full recovery at home.

"She's in here," Frank announced, walking first into room 302. "Morning, Mom. Guess who's here?"

"Frank? Is that you?"

Chase peeked around his brother's larger frame and saw a shell of what used to be his mother. He held back a gasp. Wrinkled and frail, she was nearly unrecognizable, certainly not the strong woman he so fondly remembered. Frank had warned him, saying that the rare disease she had contracted, Avian something, continued to take a toll on her body, rapidly aging her. Still, Chase was unprepared for what he saw; his mother had become a mere semblance of the person he once knew. Did he dare express concern? Could he touch her? Would she even remember him?

"Chase?" She peered at him. "Chase! It's you! Come over here!" She weakly held out her bony arms as he bent over the bed and gingerly met her hands with his. "Oh son, it's so good to see you. It's been way too long."

"I know, Mom. I'm glad I'm here. How are you?"

She winked. "They tell me there's nothing they can do to fix me, so I guess I'm not too good!"

"Well at least you've still got your sense of humor!" Chase relaxed with the knowledge that her faculties were intact. Looking into her cloudy eyes, nearly closed over by sagging skin, he searched longingly to see the mother of his youth.

"Sit down, Chase. … No, closer to me. … There you go. Where are Linda and the children? Are they with you?"

"No, they couldn't come right away, but I can send for them if, um, if you—"

"If I'm gonna die right away?" she interrupted with a chuckle, coughing with difficulty as she smiled at the three of them.

Chase squirmed. "Well I didn't mean that, but, well, I don't know. Let's just play it by ear."

Allie saved him. "Hey Mom, why don't you tell Chase what you told Frank and me yesterday?"

"What, that I'd break his neck if he didn't come to see me?"

"Of course not! You know what I'm talking about."

"I found out your father died two weeks ago," she said dryly, staring at the TV on the wall.

Chase stiffened, startled by her words, though somehow not saddened. "Really?" he managed. "How'd it happen?"

"Heart attack. Probably never did give up drinking."

He looked over at Frank and Allie. "Why didn't you guys tell me?"

"You were already on the plane out here," Frank said. "Thought it best if Mom told you."

"Was there a funeral?"

"Lane was the first to get a call. His number was evidently the only one in Dad's wallet. All we know is that Dad lived in Jersey for who knows how long, died of a heart attack, and was buried a couple of weeks ago."

"Wow," Chase quietly responded, shaking his head.

They spent another ten minutes or so reminiscing, avoiding any events that revolved around their father, and sharing jokes and lighthearted stories. Chase remained dazed by the news as they talked on and on. Why should he be surprised that his dad had died suddenly and apparently alone? Why should he care? He had no good reason to feel sympathy or grief or even regret that he didn't get a chance to see him after all these years.

But perhaps he felt regret after all, having been robbed of the chance to know his father in adulthood. His dad never did meet his wife and his children and never had the opportunity to see his youngest son as a successful man. And what about his recent incredible experiences? Wouldn't it have been great to share with his father the internal and external changes beginning to manifest themselves as well as the lifelong lies suddenly exposed? Wouldn't it have been something to see his father's reaction when they reunited after so much time apart?

No, probably not. His dad clearly chose to walk out on everyone, obviously deciding never to see his family again. So why think about him now as if somehow things could have been different? As if somehow his own long-overdue appearance would have transformed his father's life? Still, it would have been nice to see him one more time, at least to say good-bye. But maybe he should … no, but then again …

Chase pulled himself from his thoughts. "Frank, Allie, do you guys mind if I spend a few minutes alone with Mom?"

"Not at all," said Allie. "We'll wait for you in the lobby. Good-bye, Mom." She bent over to kiss her on the cheek. "See you soon."

"You better!" the sickly woman exclaimed, receiving a peck from Frank on her wrinkled forehead.

Chase shifted awkwardly on the bed, waiting for the large hospital room door to close. "Mom," he began, inching closer to her, "I'd like to share something quite amazing that happened to me a few days ago."

"Sure, honey. Go ahead."

He related every detail of the spider story, looking for any sort of affirmation. Chase watched her eyes, once or twice thinking he noticed a certain twinkle. When he finished, his mother reached for his hand. "This makes a lot of sense to me."

"Really?" he asked incredulously.

"Yes … um, can you help me with this, Chase?" she asked, attempting to reposition the pillows behind her. "Thank you." She cleared her throat several times, and Chase noticed that it caused her pain to do so. "I'm not sure how much you're aware of my upbringing, how the kids in school used to tease me because I was so shy. Of course that only added to my fears and my feelings of rejection. For most of my life, I was terrified about what people thought of me." She coughed and then continued. "When I finally stood up to your father, it was the first time I could remember fighting for myself and my rights."

"I had no idea."

"Yes, and for many years not much changed, but after you suddenly left, I began to see myself differently. I made new relationships at church and enjoyed life like never before."

"How come you never told me all this?"

"Oh, I don't know. I didn't think you'd find it very interesting."

"Well you're probably right," Chase agreed, "but now I see why my story rings true with you. Sounds like we have both made a few good changes."

"Chase, just hold on to what you know to be true. Don't listen to the lies any longer. They'll try to return, so you have to be strong and resist them. After a while, you'll be able to tell the true you from your lied-to self more and more quickly."

"Wow! That's amazing, Mom! I can't believe you have such insight in this area. I didn't think anybody had gone through what I just experienced."

"I did. Just in a different way."

"Well I can't wait to hear more. I'll be back every day to see you."

"We shall see how long that lasts."

"You mean how long you're, um, going to—"

"Live?"

"Well … yeah. Can you tell?"

"I will never die!" she exclaimed with a hoarse chuckle. "At least in your memories."

Chase hugged his mother and gave her a kiss on the cheek. "Okay, see you soon."

As he entered the lobby, Allie questioned him. "You okay? You seem kind of out of it."

"Yeah, I'm fine. I think I need a nap."

Chase saw that he had missed a call from Linda since he had silenced his cell phone in the hospital. Back upstairs in his room, he returned the call.

"Hi, hon'!" she answered with notable enthusiasm. "How are you over there?"

"I'm okay. I'll tell you in a bit. How are the kids?"

"Everything's normal. They miss you already."

"I miss them too. Anything new?"

"No. I'm just trying to stay busy. Have you seen your mom yet?"

"Just got back. She's pretty chipper despite her condition, but nobody knows how much longer she has. What's really weird is that I just found out my dad died a couple of weeks ago."

"Oh Chase, I'm so sorry. That's awful."

"Well you know me and my dad. But it's crazy that I never saw him again. I've been thinking that I might drive down to Jersey and visit his gravesite."

"Oh?"

"Yeah, just something I'm considering. Hey, did you get my email?"

"I read it a while ago. That's why I called. Quite fascinating, to say the least."

"I'll say. What do you think?"

"I copied this thing from the Internet after doing some research. What happened to you last night, or I guess this morning, could be something others have experienced."

"What do you mean?"

"Well at first I thought it was just a vivid dream, but then I considered your spider-web incident and wondered if something bigger is going on. That led me to discover an explanation called *doppelganger*."

"Dopple what?"

"*Doppelganger*. It says here that it's someone seeing his or her double, a lookalike. 'It's also used,' and I'm quoting, 'to describe the sensation of having glimpsed oneself in peripheral vision in a position where there is no chance that it could have been a reflection ... In some traditions, a doppelganger of a person's friends or relatives portends illness or danger, while seeing one's own doppelganger is an omen of death,' although we don't have to believe all that," she added.

"Thanks a lot," Chase said with playful sarcasm. "You've made my day."

"I'm just saying that this is astounding, something quite significant. We don't have to buy all the omens and the warnings of death, but maybe we should at least—"

Chase jumped in. "Hey, maybe it's about my dad dying."

"Okay," Linda answered hesitantly, "but I think it's how you already explained it, a death of your old self, some sort of a contrast between the old you and the new, real you."

"Yeah, maybe you're right. And as you said, maybe there's a connection between this vision and the spider-web one, like the doppelganger thing is actually the result of this process of finding freedom from lies. Hey, could you email that to me?"

"Sure."

"Anything else going on?"

Linda knew the reason behind his question but kept to herself. "No, just the same old things."

"All right. I'll call you and the kids later. I miss you a lot, wish you were here. Mom says hi, by the way."

"Give her hugs and kisses. Talk to you soon."

Chase sat back on his bed, reflecting on their conversation. He checked and saw Linda's email—no message, just the links she had found. He read the first one intently, learning about famous people with similar experiences. "Abraham Lincoln?" he whispered. "Never heard of such a thing." Scrolling back to the top of the page, he stopped at a definition of doppelganger: "Having glimpsed oneself in peripheral vision in a position where there is no chance that it could have been a reflection."

Well it definitely was not a reflection, he thought. *I indeed saw myself, the man I used to be, the one who looked so similar to the victim in the spider web.* Closing his laptop, Chase speculated apprehensively about the death omen. Could that imply some supernatural premonition of his own death? No, that didn't make sense. So it must mean what he and Linda agreed that it meant, seeing his old self now dead, or sort of dead. But he could also be right in thinking it concerned his dad, though he doubted that because he didn't see him in the vision or the dream or whatever it was. His growling stomach told Chase he needed food; a cigar might be nice as well.

"Thought you were taking a nap," Frank said from behind the newspaper as Chase lumbered downstairs.

"Couldn't sleep after all. I talked with Linda for a while, and I think I'll go for a walk and grab a bite to eat."

"I'll be making lunch for us pretty soon!" Allie called out from the kitchen.

"Listen, Frank. I'm not trying to be rude or anything. I really appreciate staying here, and I do want to connect with you guys. It's just that a lot of crazy things have recently happened to me, not just with Mom and now Dad, but personal stuff, and I need time to collect my thoughts. I'm sorry, but I need a little space."

Frank shrugged. "Hey, no problem with me. We just want to see you."

"I know. Me too. I'll be back."

"All right. See you later."

CHAPTER 13

C hase knew the area well and headed up the street toward the corner market five blocks over. The Macklin boys grew up only about a half-mile away in the other direction. He and Frank would often ride their bikes over to Ted's Market on Baker Street to check out the new Topps baseball cards, eagerly ripping open a pack and scouring it for a famous ballplayer or a rookie card. They had talked about their hobby several years ago, Frank proudly stating that most of his cards were safely tucked away in the attic. Chase never knew what happened to his small collection and recalled with regret some of the '70s cards he once had: Tom Seaver, Rod Carew, Bob Gibson. He wondered about their value three decades later.

Nearing the market, Chase noticed the old neon sign remained, though Ted had to be long gone since he must have been at least sixty when they were children. Nothing else had changed much: same cracked sidewalk, same creaky swing door, same glass countertop, scratches and all.

"So you're still making sandwiches, huh?" he playfully asked the young girl behind the counter. She couldn't have been much more than eighteen, her blond hair pulled back in a bun, revealing larger-than-normal ears contrasted by narrow eyes and a button nose. She looked bored.

"Yeah. What can I get you?"

"I used to come in here way before you were born, back when Ted used to work here."

"The old owner?" she asked with indifference.

"That's the one. How long have you been working here?"

"Five months or so."

"You guys sell any cigars?"

"A few over there," she answered, nodding toward a small humidor by the register.

"Great. Can I have a ham-and-swiss on rye with everything on it? Oh, and a water. I'll take a look at what you've got."

Strolling to the park across the street, lunch in one hand, freshly cut Punch cigar in the other, Chase felt quite pleased that he hadn't been overwhelmed by recent events. He remembered when he and Frank used to play at this park. Unfortunately, when he was a young man the park and the woods were frequent spots for his drug deals. He wouldn't think about that. Sliding onto one of the old benches, he began nibbling on his ham-and-swiss. As he took a swig from his bottled water, an old white Cadillac pulling up to park in front of him caught his attention.

"Is that you, Chase?" he heard a voice call out through a partially opened window.

Standing up to get a better look, he covered his eyes with his hand and took a few steps forward. The voice spoke again. "Looks like it's you. Been waitin' here in the area, hopin' ya might come around."

He recognized the gruff voice. Still squinting from the sun, Chase drew closer. "Murphy?"

"Hey, nice to see ya, Mack. Thought I'd find ya 'round here. Heard about your mother, ya know."

"What do you want?"

"Come on, kid. It's been all these years and you're not glad ta see me?"

"It's not like we left on the best of terms."

Murphy let out a loud, raspy laugh, a bit of saliva forming at the crease of his mouth, yellowed teeth peeking through. He seemed pleased with

Chase's obvious discomfort. "Oh yeah, that's right!" Placing his head near the window, he lowered his voice. "Come closer so I can see ya better."

Chase didn't move.

"Listen, kid. Things've changed. Got some money for ya. Hop in the back."

"No, that's okay. I'm a little busy right now."

"Looks like it," said Murphy with raised brows as he noticed the unwrapped cigar in Chase's hand. "As I said, things've changed. Ya don't know it, but that story ya gave all those years ago I found out ta be true. A couple of my connections were able—aw, it don't matter. Just get in the car so I can make it right."

"No offense, but I'm a bit uncomfortable doing that."

Murphy laughed again and rolled his eyes. "Suit yourself, but really, hey, I'm not kiddin' here. I got a lot a money for ya, kinda my way of makin' up for what I did. What about we meet somewhere else? Maybe, uh … oh, I know. Let's meet over at O'Malley's. You know the place."

"Course I do."

"Seven o'clock then. I'll just be there with him," Murphy said, nodding toward his driver, "so bring people with ya if that makes ya more comfortable.

"Let me think about it. I just arrived and a lot of things are going on."

"Just trust me one more time, Mack. See ya at seven." He quickly turned his head to the left. "Let's go, John."

Chase stumbled dazed back to his bench and considered the extreme oddity of recent events. The last person on earth he thought he would ever see again had somehow found him at the park on his first day back. He had come to visit his ailing mother, only to discover his dad died two weeks before. And all of this happened after the discovery that his wife was seeing another man, at least in some fashion. Then there was the professional counseling, something he swore he'd never do, the vision of a mammoth spider, and now the doppelganger thing just this morning.

What could be happening in his life? Were these mere coincidences, or would there be a climax revealing some sort of connection between everything? And what should he do with regard to Murphy? He didn't have to show up, but what about this money he mentioned? Could he trust Murphy after all these years? Could it possibly be worth the risk? Maybe Frank would come with him. No, he wouldn't do that, especially if he thought it dangerous. So why even go himself?

Chase tossed the rest of his sandwhich in a nearby trash can, pocketed his unlit cigar, and ambled back to Frank's. He was suddenly tired, and his head found the pillow as soon as he entered his room and lay on the bed.

"Chase? It's time for dinner!" He awoke to Allie's vocal alarm. "Chase? Are you up?" she asked, rapping on the door. "Time for dinner! Hope you're hungry."

He glanced at the clock. Six-thirty. "Yeah, I'm up. Be right down." He lay there a few minutes more, mulling over his options before he finally rose, grabbed his jacket, and made his way downstairs. The first bites of the meal tasted great, and he thanked Allie.

"You're welcome! Frank and I are just so happy you're here! I wish the circumstances were better, but at least we're together. Lane and Kathy will be here after dinner. They can't wait to see you!"

"You know what? I'm going to have to see them tomorrow. I hate to do this to you, but something's come up. Remember Murphy?"

Frank stiffened. "Of course we do. Why do you ask?"

"I just saw him a few hours ago, and he wants to meet with me over at O'Malley's."

"What, are you crazy?"

"Frank, I've been thinking about it, and it's been what, thirteen years now? He's just too old for me to be concerned. Said that he made a mistake with me and that he's got some money to give me."

"Some money?" Frank asked with a snigger. "Sure he does. Come on, Chase, this guy has never been someone you can trust, to say the least. And it doesn't matter how long it's been or even if he's eighty! The guy's a crook. Always has been. Why would you even consider such a thing?"

"I don't know. Maybe I'm just curious. We used to be fairly close, and I was simply thinking that if—"

"You were a kid!" Frank cut in, his voice growing louder. "He was taking advantage of you! Man, you're stubborn." Seeing his brother's resolute eyes, Frank relented. "Okay, if you're going, then I'm coming with you."

Allie burst in. "Oh no you're not! You can't set foot into this situation. Last time you did that—"

"She's right, Frank. You don't have to do this."

"Well neither do you!"

A knock interrupted their argument, and Chase's other brother and his wife charged through the front door. Lane, three years older than Frank, had moved out of the house before their dad deserted them. Chase always admired him, not merely for being the older, wiser brother but because only he dared to stand up to their father. A long scar was still visible on his forearm from a fight in which Dad had cut him open with a broken bottle. Chase viewed him as sort of a hero, battle wound and all, unafraid of the man who tormented his family. Lane didn't seem as tall as Chase remembered him, but he looked quite handsome for forty-one and still in great shape. Kathy was quieter, an obvious opposite of Lane.

"Hey, everyone!" he called out. Chase left the kitchen first. "Well look at you, little brother!" Lane hollered. "How in the world are you?"

"Fine," Chase managed in response after his brother's bear hug. "Great to see you."

"You too! How long has it been?" Lane asked, releasing his grip and looking into his eyes.

"Too long. That's for sure."

"I'll say. Phone calls and emails sure aren't the same."

"True."

"Well it looks like we're just in time for dessert!"

Allie rushed over to embrace Kathy. "Actually, just in time to settle an argument!"

Chase shook his head. "No, we don't need Lane to get involved in all of this."

"All of what? What's going on?" Lane asked, looking from person to person.

"Chase wants to go and see Murphy," Allie said.

"The old drug dude?"

"Yes. You remember him."

"I remember." He turned toward Chase, who slumped on the sofa while the others remained standing. "Why would you do that?"

"Lane, I don't want to explain myself again. I just saw him and he wants to meet me, like right now, and give me some money."

"For no apparent reason," added Allie.

Lane looked around the room. "Anyone think of the possible danger here?"

"Exactly!" Allie exclaimed. "Murphy's not one to take lightly."

"I'm not," Chase objected. "Like I told Frank and Allie, he said he'd made a mistake with me all those years ago and wants to make it right. Come on, Allie, you don't have to be so concerned. I've considered the risk, and I really don't think there's a reason to be afraid."

"Well you're not going there alone!" Lane declared. "I'll go with you."

"Oh great," Chase moaned. "First Frank and now you. I can handle this on my own, guys."

Frank reached down and tugged on his arm. "Right, just like you handled him before. Now come on. We got you covered."

Allie shook her head and then shrugged at Kathy.

The three jumped into Lane's car and drove the few miles to O'Malley's, Chase sitting in silence. It felt good to know they had his back, sort of like being a young boy in trouble who had his two older brothers going with him to make it right. He didn't consider this necessary, but then again, Murphy had proven to be quite unpredictable in the past. Better to have them at his side just in case something went awry. Lane broke the silence.

"Chase, you go in first since I've never even seen the guy. Frank and I will keep a sharp eye out for anything unusual. Now this probably won't be a big deal since it's at a public place, but you never know. If anything happens, grab a bar stool, a beer bottle, anything you can use as a weapon, and don't think twice. Just react quickly."

It struck him as funny to hear his brother give lessons on barroom brawling. Chase recalled his very first fight, which took place in the same bar. Seventeen and just starting to sell for Murphy, he followed orders to meet a new contact at O'Malley's, some guy Murphy told him about who knew somebody else with money. Murphy didn't trust the situation, so he sent the new kid over to check it out.

Chase remembered the evening well. He sat in a booth, waiting for a nondescript person. The typical late-night crowd, not more than five or six older men, huddled near the chain-smoking bartender. When a lanky, shovel-faced youth stepped through the darkened doorway and looked back and forth, Chase waved him over to his table and then held out his hand. Ignored, he placed both hands in his lap, his left lightly clutching a dinner knife, not very sharp but pointed on the end with serrated edges. Effective if necessary.

The kid plopped himself down across from Chase with a smirk on his sallow face. "You got stuff to sell?" he asked with an upward motion of his head.

"I wouldn't be here if I didn't."

"Don't get smart with me, punk. If you got the blow, we got the money. How much can ya get us?"

Chase didn't like his mannerisms. "Slow down, butch. I don't make decisions like that."

"You called me butch?"

"Just an expression," Chase answered, hands beginning to sweat as he gripped the knife more tightly.

"You guys got a bad reputation, ya know. Your boss is a cheat. But hey, if you got blow, we got buyers."

"We don't need buyers." Chase slid out from the booth and started to walk away.

"Hey, punk, what's that in your hand?" As soon as the rogue reached for his arm, Chase turned on him in one quick motion, stabbing his bicep and then smacking him in the face with the back side of his right hand. Hesitating for just a moment when blood began to rush from the kid's nose, Chase dropped the knife, hit him full force in the face again, and took off into the street.

He told Murphy about it the next day. Murphy laughed hysterically. The whole thing smelled fishy from the beginning, he informed his newest employee. Impressed that Chase sensed the same thing and acted instinctively, Murphy decided to take him under his wing. He handed him a pistol, telling him it would work better than a table knife if he ever ran across scum like that again. Although never forced to use the gun, Chase found many more occasions for fights.

The three entered the smoke-filled bar, carefully surveying their cramped surroundings while attempting not to bump into people. The place was obviously much more popular than in the old days.

"There he is," Chase said, nodding toward Murphy, "and just that one guy with him."

They walked toward the back, Lane and Frank keeping alert for anything suspicious. Chase trained his eyes squarely on his old boss, who had a cigarette dangling from his lips.

"Mack, I see ya brought reinforcements with ya."

"No, these are my brothers. This is Lane and that's Frank."

Murphy stared at Chase. "Okay, whatever. Sit down."

"So what's up?" Chase asked, as each of them grabbed a wooden chair at the round table.

"Are ya hungry?"

"No, just ate."

Murphy lit another cigarette. "How 'bout a few beers?"

"Sure."

"John, go get us some beer and me another drink." Looking straight at Chase, he unpocketed an envelope and shoved it across the table. "I said I had money for ya, but this here's even better, keys to my old house."

Chase's brow wrinkled. Murphy continued as if not noticing his bewilderment. "Listen, Mack. Remember how I once told ya that if ya ever had kids, I wanted to be their godfather and that I promised to take care of 'em?"

"Sure."

"Ya got any by now?"

"Children?"

"Yeah."

"We have two."

"That's good. Well I don't go back on my word, but ya took off forever and I had no idea where ya went. When I heard about your mom, I figured you'd be around, so I been keepin' my eyes open. Couldn't believe I was lucky enough to see ya today. Coincidence, I guess. Anyway, I'm movin' permanently to my place in Florida. Everything's in storage, waitin' to be moved. This here's my gift." He nodded at the envelope.

Chase opened it and saw a couple of keys along with a title deed. "You're giving me your house? Why?"

"I already told ya. Makin' good on my promise. Just my way of cleanin' the slate. Guess I'm gettin' soft in my old age." He laughed alone.

John placed the drinks on the table and sat down. Perplexed, Chase continued to stare at the keys and the document. "So what am I supposed to do with these?"

Murphy took a sip of his whiskey. "Whatever ya want. It's all yours, Mack."

Lane shifted in his chair. "This is really amazing, quite generous. What's the catch?"

Murphy shot him a scathing glance, his yellowed teeth menacing. "I'm gonna pretend I didn't hear that." As suddenly as he had attacked Lane, his demeanor softened when he turned back toward Chase. "Listen to me, Mack. I'm only gonna say it once. Everything's clear between us now. I've lived up to what I said, and you do whatever ya hafta do. The house is paid for, so sell it if ya hafta. I don't really care at this point. Just do me one favor."

Chase knew there had to be something. Lane leaned back incredulously, arms falling to his side. Frank frowned.

"What kind of favor?" Chase asked.

Murphy slowly stubbed out his cigarette in the ashtray with emphasis. "Remember me at Mass."

Chase smiled with relief. "Well I don't do that anymore, but I will remember you and tell my kids what you've done."

"That'll work. Now finish those beers 'cause John and me are hungry."

Chase started to rise but for some reason felt compelled to offer his old boss something in return. He leaned over the table. "Say, Murphy, one day I'd like to share with you some of the things I've experienced since I last saw you."

"Why should I care?"

"I thought … well, I thought that—"

"We're suddenly best buddies?" he exclaimed with a chortle. Murphy shook his head, seeing Chase's look of dejection. "Get a grip, Mack. Take this gift a mine for what it is and get outta here!"

"C'mon, Chase. Let's go." Lane stood, grabbing his brother's arm. Chase didn't move, paralyzed by Murphy's insolence. "C'mon," Lane repeated with another jerk of his hand. "Let's leave."

Chase slowly rose, keeping his eyes on Murphy, hoping that perhaps he would say something positive or at least less combative. *No*, he thought with disappointment. *He'll never change. Far too arrogant.*

Chase held on to the envelope as if somehow afraid of it while Lane guided him away from the table. No one in the bar took notice of them.

Once outside, Frank took Chase by both shoulders. "Listen, I don't trust that old man. Why should we believe he's changed? The whole thing is a bit too ideal."

"I don't know, Frank," Lane said with a furrowed brow. "You may be right, but my gut tells me this is legit, though it is pretty unbelievable."

"Well you can't be too safe with a person like that."

Chase moved toward the car in a stupor, barely listening, fingering the envelope. Maybe Frank was right. But then again, he agreed with Lane. How could he be certain? "Let's drive over and check it out," he said without emotion, not caring what anyone thought.

"Sure," agreed Lane. "What do we have to lose?"

"Who knows?" mumbled Frank.

CHAPTER 14

The house appeared unchanged, four maples out front, neatly placed brick guarding the driveway, overgrown ivy still protecting each window. The larger key easily unlocked the front door. "This is unreal," Chase said, thinking about his last visit to this place when he had stumbled in, shot and bloodied.

Stepping into the small living room with acacia flooring, now stripped bare of all furnishings, Chase noticed discolored outlines where paintings and pictures had hung. Shuttered windows begged for attention, paint chips falling from the trim to reveal the wood beneath. He remembered each piece of furniture as it once stood, the grandfather clock that chimed annoyingly at the top of every hour, the deep-brown leather sofa and matching love seat that Murphy made certain were always polished, the locked antique desk holding important papers and who knows what else.

The memories belied the room's present condition. Chase walked over to the metal grate for the floor heater and rocked back and forth on it, shifting his weight, pretending to inspect its sturdiness and safety. He rolled his eyes at his own ridiculous behavior.

The three upstairs rooms appeared to be in fair condition, all rather undersized and nondescript but quaint nevertheless. Chase noticed a rank, musty odor, particularly as they entered what he assumed to be the master bedroom. Not exactly pungent, it was still strong enough to compel a person to scrub the walls and the ceiling. The reek might simply be due to the age of the home, but more likely it was a combination of mildew and cigarettes. Linda would never move in with this smell, regardless of the source. He'd need to do something about it as soon as possible. But when would that be? And who was he kidding? Linda would never live here.

"Well, I guess this place is mine," he said with an apathetic shrug as the brothers made their way down the mahogany stairs.

"Not too bad a deal," Lane offered, wondering why Chase seemed so glum. "Doesn't make any sense coming from a guy like him, but what are you going to do, turn it down?"

"Maybe," Frank said. "We should probably consider all the possibilities."

"I agree," muttered Chase. "Just can't figure the whole thing out, whether I should be excited or cautious."

"Perhaps both," Frank said. "Anyway, let's get back to the girls. I'm sure they're wondering what's taking us so long."

"You're probably right," Lane agreed with a nod. "Let's go."

Chase slowly followed, locked the door behind them, and then hesitated. "Hey guys, can we talk some more about this first? Frank, why don't you call Allie and let her know we'll be home shortly?"

"What's up, little brother?" Lane wanted to know.

"There are a couple of benches in the backyard. Why don't we sit for a few minutes and think this through?" Chase led the way around the side of the house to an unlocked gate while Frank assured Allie they wouldn't be much longer.

The yard used to be wonderfully kept, its centerpiece a huge rock fountain surrounded by rose bushes and three stone benches. The grass, now overgrown, shared space with weeds springing up all over the lawn and around each tree. Neglected shrubs pressed against the fence and over the edge guard of the lawn. The rose bushes still stood but without a bloom and barely clinging to life.

Chase recalled how meticulously maintained the area was all those years ago. He and Murphy would occasionally sit by the fountain and have a few drinks, rarely discussing anything intimate—merely business, money, and the next job. Chase grew somewhat fond of the boss everyone else held in contempt, but he had enough wisdom never to ask any personal questions. The arrangement seemed to work well for both of them.

Though the landscape, lonely and bleak, cried out for attention, Chase felt strangely refreshed as he lowered himself onto one of the benches. "Well," he began, running his hand through his hair, "I just wanted to hear your opinion about my situation, meaning what I should do with this place." He hesitated. "I mean, wouldn't you agree it's a bit strange that Linda and I suddenly own a home here in New York?"

Lane still stood while Frank sat next to Chase. "Listen, little bro," Lane counseled with his typical bluntness, "I admit it's the most unusual thing I've ever heard of, but I can't imagine what Murphy could do to you if he does have an underlying motive. He's not going to turn around and sue you or burn the house down while you're in it! He said he made a promise that he planned to keep, so maybe he's actually telling the truth. What do you think, Frank?"

His brother cleared his throat for effect. "Well, it could be possible that Murphy's in trouble with somebody he's wronged. If we look at the worst possible scenario, what if he's unloading the house to escape the area? If that's what's going on, then whoever lives here may end up becoming a target of mistaken identity, you know, like somebody setting off a bomb, thinking Murphy still lives here."

"Really, Frank?" Lane asked with a roll of his eyes. "You actually think he's that diabolical?"

"I'm just pointing out different ways of looking at this. Can't be too careful."

"And I appreciate that," said Chase, "but I honestly don't think there's anything more to this than an old man moving on. My thought is to simply fix it up and sell it."

Frank placed his hand on Chase's shoulder. "Well if you're really not worried, then why don't you just move in yourself, you and your family?"

"I can't move back here."

"Why not? It's been years, Chase. You're not hot anymore. Nobody's after you."

"I know that. I mean, I guess we could move here. I just don't know what we'd do as far as work goes."

Lane leaned over. "You're in sales, bro! You can get a job anywhere. Besides, the house is paid for. I'm not saying this is what you should do, but it'd be great having the family back together again," he added with a wink.

"Sure it would," Chase agreed, smiling. "That could be a good thing, but hey, I doubt Linda could survive the winters here!"

"Sounds like you've got a lot of excuses," Frank said. "What's really bothering you?"

Chase thought for a moment. "I'm not quite sure. Maybe I'm just trying to talk myself out of it since it feels so much like a dream. Or perhaps I don't want to get too excited about the possibilities only to have Linda squelch it all. I don't really know. Listen, I guess all I can do is speak with her and we'll figure things out together." Chase forced a smirk. "I just wanted the input of my two big and wise brothers."

"Yeah, sure!" said Lane, grinning. "Now is that it? Are we done?"

"For now, yeah."

"Well good 'cause I need some dessert! Maybe two pieces of that cake I smelled at the house!"

Frank shook his head and turned toward Chase. "It's unbelievable. He still has the metabolism of a teenager."

Lane raised his hands high in the air and loudly proclaimed, "I am a gift from heaven, my brothers! A gift from heaven!"

**

They buried their mother four days later. It was a Thursday afternoon and around fifty degrees, typical for that time of year. Chase had visited her every day, encouraged by her wit and wisdom but frustrated by her steady physical decline. On each occasion, they shared their similar experience of discovering a life free from personal lies. Chase cherished these rich moments, hoping his days with his mother would stretch into weeks. He wept at her bedside the morning she took her last breath.

The cemetery rested just outside of town. The garden-like three acres of manicured lawn was adorned with an even mixture of maple, ash, and London plane trees. The clouds began to wrap around the sun, sending a slight chill over the small group huddled near the freshly dug grave. Family and several close friends sat on white plastic chairs atop a piece of green outdoor carpet.

Chase had encouraged Linda to stay home to avoid an unnecessary expense. She said that the kids could get out of school for a few days and that her boss would completely understand, but Chase won in the end. The family, chiefly Allie, also argued with him, insisting that he view this as a chance for everyone to meet his wife and his children. He promised to bring them out over the summer, quieting his critics.

Lane and Kathy's two boys could not attend since both were away at school. Frank and Allie remained childless. Pregnant before Chase fled to California, Allie experienced complications and lost the baby. She never could conceive again. Aunt Betty responded to Chase's email, lamenting that travel had become nearly impossible but saying she'd pray for them.

The smartly robed priest stood directly in front of the coffin and pictures of their mother, which were surrounded by a colorful flower arrangement. After a solemn greeting and a short opening prayer, the priest announced that he would read from the book of Wisdom, chapter 3. Rather good-looking with dark skin, high cheek bones, and a straight nose, he spoke in a soft but commanding voice, never hesitating. His head remained focused on his notes the entire time, the only variation coming when he frequently reached up to adjust his dark-framed glasses.

> The souls of the just are in the hand of God, and no torment shall touch them. They seemed, in the view of the foolish, to be dead; and their passing away was thought an affliction and their going forth from us, utter destruction. But they are in peace. For if before men, indeed, they be punished, yet is their hope full of immortality; chastised a little, they shall

be greatly blessed, because God tried them and found them
worthy of himself.

As gold in the furnace, he proved them, and as sacrificial
offerings he took them to himself. In the time of their visitation
they shall shine, and shall dart about as sparks through stubble;
they shall judge nations and rule over peoples, and the Lord
shall be their King forever.

Those who trust in him shall understand truth, and the
faithful shall abide with him in love: Because grace and mercy
are with his holy ones, and his care is with the elect. Wisdom
3:1-9

The priest then gave his homily, though Chase caught very little of it
after hearing the words *faithful* and *holy ones*. He thought, *Was my mother
a holy one? Surely a good Catholic woman, and if anyone deserves heaven, she
certainly does. But what makes a person holy? I guess she lived a rather saintly
life if she tolerated Dad all those years, but holy? How does this priest know?
Who is he to talk about someone he met maybe half a dozen times?* Chase felt
strangely comforted by the words but didn't understand any of it.

As the priest droned on, Chase stared at the coffin. *She had proved to
be a good mother*, he thought, *particularly with the challenges she had faced.*
A tear formed in the corner of his eye as he reflected upon his visit to the
hospital and how stunned he was to discover that she had understood the
power of her own personal lies and had conquered them but had kept this
to herself for no apparent reason. He loved her dearly and wished he could
have had more time with her.

After the Lord's Prayer, then another prayer and a short blessing, Lane
stood, embracing each family member. There were many tears. They
flowed easily from Kathy and Allie and a few family friends, and even
Frank had a couple stuck in his eyes, Chase noticed. The priest pocketed
his glasses, offered his condolences, said some nice things about their
mother, and then slowly walked away. The family drove silently to Frank
and Allie's for dinner.

The aroma from a simmering pot of stew greeted them as they hung their jackets by the door and began to set the table. "Smells fabulous, Allie!" Lane shouted, sticking his nose in the pot.

"Well your wife helped too!" she replied.

"Oh yeah. Good job, honey!"

"Chase, you've been awfully quiet most of the day," Allie said. "You okay?"

He sat by himself at the kitchen table, staring straight ahead, motionless. "Chase?"

"Oh, sorry, Allie. I'm fine, just thinking about Mom and everything. I guess you feel a little older around death."

Lane reached out to touch his shoulder. "I'm over forty, man! You're still just a kid!"

Allie drew closer. "Chase, I know what you mean. Death makes us all think more about our own lives, what old age will bring, how long we're going to live, all that type of stuff. I remember when my own mother died. It was really hard, a reality check, I guess. Makes you wonder about a lot of things."

Still staring blankly, Chase said to no one in particular, "I think I'm going to Jersey tomorrow."

Frank objected. "Chase, you don't need to do that to yourself. Why would you want to go see Dad's grave? You don't even know where to go! The only information we have is that he lived in Trenton."

Lane sided with Frank. "Listen, little bro, you can do what you think you have to do, but I can't see that it's going to help. Dad left us a long time ago. He didn't want to see us when he was alive, so I'm sure it doesn't matter now."

"I understand what you're saying. Believe me I do. It's just … just something I need to do. I haven't told you guys what happened to me a few days before coming here, but maybe it's time."

Everyone took a seat and began passing the plates of food. "Go ahead!" Allie said eagerly, reminding everyone of her gregarious personality. "We'd love to hear what's going on, and try not to leave out any details!"

Chase told the story of the spider web and the lies but omitted Linda's relationship and their counseling sessions. The longer he spoke, the more the events solidified in his mind. He discovered new words and new concepts, and he could describe the events more clearly than before. When he recalled the spider web and how a giant hand had freed him, he said that meant he had been rescued from himself. As soon as the words left his mouth, Chase realized their significance. He hadn't merely been rescued from the lies but had been delivered from the one who had believed them and had lived under their spell. He been unable even to recognize his condition, let alone live free of lies.

The lies took on new meaning as Chase perceived that he had empowered them by accepting them as true. They were no longer merely concepts, such as abandonment, fear of trust, or lack of vulnerability; they became alive as he identified himself in their midst. He was in some way personified in them, so attached to the lies that they became his identity, who he truly believed he was. But his recent journey, just a week old, left him determined to become so attached to the truth about himself that truth would dictate who he was from this time forward.

The entire time Chase spoke, the others stared at him, spellbound. When he mentioned the doppelganger, Allie wanted to know more. "Wait a minute. You mean to say you saw yourself?"

"Yes."

"Like a vision or something?"

"Well, I've described it as such, but I'm not sure if that's the right word. It appeared as real as all of us sitting here when I walked up behind myself and spoke to Linda. After the new me saw the old me, I made a vow that I'd never again go back into that old body."

"Weird," Lane commented.

"Weird but real," Chase said. "It must be part of this new journey to rediscover myself. I mean, I know there will always be areas that'll require work and attention, areas in which I'll need prodding and reminders because I've lived most of my life under the power of these lies. I have definitely experienced some immediate relief, but I'm certain that much of this will be progressive. You guys have nothing you can use to compare my habits and my lifestyle since we haven't seen each other for so long, but Linda does. That's why I can't wait to get home. So much has happened in such a short time that I've become fairly distracted from that initial experience in the web. And I guess that's why I feel the need to go to Dad's gravesite. I don't know exactly why, just a sense that it's important."

"So when are you going to leave?" asked Allie.

"Early tomorrow morning. It's a long drive."

Allie's face saddened, her lips pursed. "So this is it? I mean, it's been great having you here, but it looks like we'll have to say our good-byes tonight."

"Guess so. But listen, as I said before, I'll make plans for the family to come out in the summer. We'll have to do something with that house, of course, but it'll be great to vacation out here with everyone."

"Have you spoken to Linda about it?" Allie anxiously asked.

"About what?"

"Your new house!"

"Just briefly after convincing her to stay home during the funeral."

"What did she say? Tell us!"

"Oh, she was, well, a bit taken aback by the whole story. I mean—"

"Was she excited?" Allie interrupted.

"I wouldn't consider it excitement exactly," Chase said with a grin. "More like bewilderment over what we're going to do with it."

"You can move here!"

"Yeah, I did mention that option to her," he said, shrugging. "We'll see."

They continued to talk through dessert, peppering Chase with questions about the spider, the hand, and doppelganger. Attempting to lighten the moment, the brothers took a few playful jabs at Chase. He was far too young to be found talking to himself! A man-size spider? Sounded like a scene in *The Lord of the Rings*! Could he be certain he'd seen himself? Maybe it was a mummy after all!

Chase tolerated the jesting, but his mind drifted in and out of the conversation as he attempted to focus on the trip ahead of him, energized to see what tomorrow would bring and eager to get back to Linda and the children.

When he felt comfortable enough to excuse himself without showing rudeness, he said his good-byes and then took double steps up to his room to see about changing his ticket out of Kennedy. He found a flight the next afternoon at three-fifty, arriving at LAX at seven-forty, perfect considering L.A. traffic.

Then he searched the Internet for cemeteries in Trenton and discovered that they kept records online. After checking five or six of them for Robert Macklin with no success, he realized his best option would be to call the coroner's office on the way down. He got the number and calculated that he needed to leave Trenton between twelve-thirty and one to be at Kennedy by two. Chase set the alarm for four in the morning in case he needed several hours to locate the gravesite.

He didn't sleep much, periodically turning over to check the time in case he overslept. When the alarm finally sounded, he jumped out of bed, took a quick shower, packed his bags, threw on a jacket, and headed out to his car. Still yawning, he prepared himself for the five-hour drive.

CHAPTER 15

About halfway to Trenton, Chase knew he needed something to keep him awake. Pulling off at an exit in Binghamton, he noticed a coffee shop with a drive-thru close to the freeway. "I'll have a large latte. Oh, and do you have muffins?"

"Yeah."

"Okay, I'll take a blueberry one."

Chase paid the sleepy-eyed teenager at the window, yawned, took a few sips of java, and headed back onto the highway. In an effort to stay alert, he began to hunt for other lies he had possibly believed about himself, lies not previously exposed. He became deeply reflective.

At age fourteen, Chase had determined that he needed to take care of himself since no one else would and that he didn't need anyone since he could manage on his own. Both could be viewed as understandable decisions based upon his circumstances, but he suddenly found himself calling them lies. After all, he had a fairly nurturing mother and two older brothers he could have asked for help and advice but never did.

And how could a young teenager do everything alone? And what type of attitude would such a mind-set create? He thought of the word *independence*, something on which Chase had always prided himself, but now he considered the probability that such an independent mentality might not be healthy. It might be productive, but in his case it was surely based upon the belief that only his dad could take care of him, and since his dad had walked out on the family, no one else could replace him.

All of this must now mean that he needed to work at becoming more mindful of others, allowing people to assist him when necessary. But how would he begin? Would this mean behaving in ways completely foreign to him? Would he have to do the most unnatural things until they eventually became natural? He wasn't sure.

Chase contemplated these questions until another lie popped into his head: since he hadn't received love from his parents, he couldn't extend love to others. Perhaps this was why he'd had difficulty telling anyone but his children that he loved them or why he found it so hard to be affectionate with others, a handicap tied directly to the layers of lies about touch.

His parents did not speak words of endearment or encouragement to each other and rarely to their boys, and so the verbal expression of love, and its physical expression through touch, were not modeled. The challenge for Chase was recognizing the lie hidden beneath these truths: that the love denied him was an excuse not to express love for others. How could he not have seen this before? What happened in that hideous spider web that opened his eyes to a new understanding of himself? And what was the significance of the hand that pulled him out of the web, or did it have any significance? He nibbled on his muffin.

Chase continued to reflect for another hour, his mind bombarded with even more lies he had accepted about himself. He had feared that if he became too honest with people, they might use the information against him. He had been stung too many times in relationships to risk hurt or rejection again, so he had made a choice not to trust. As other lies crossed his mind, Chase realized how utterly trapped he must have been because, in believing them, the lies had indeed become him. *Profound*, he thought.

He then pondered the concept of truth, typically the opposite of what he had long accepted, and what the truth would sound like if given a chance to prevail. People might or might not use information against him if he opened up, but he had to begin to be more honest and vulnerable for his own sake and for his sanity. The only way he could have healthy and vibrant relationships was to trust, to risk being hurt and rejected again.

But what about that other guy? Chase had continually attempted to suppress his fears during this time apart from Linda. He had to be away, but what bad timing with his mother on her deathbed right after he had learned his wife was in some sort of a relationship. Sure, he and Linda called or emailed every day, not merely because Doctor Rhinegold encouraged communication but because they were connecting for the first time in months, not just intellectually through discussions of work but with a fresh emotional bond.

However, what if she'd continued that relationship in some way? What if Linda was living a lie herself or masking her pain by reaching out elsewhere? Chase knew she loved him. She told him repeatedly that she missed him and couldn't wait to see him and hold him and sit down to talk with him. But what if there was something else going on?

**

Linda was thrilled when Chase called her during his drive, informing her of his decision to fly home that afternoon and asking her to bring the kids when she picked him up at the airport.

She had busied herself at work to help the days pass more quickly. After she had cut off any continued contact with Stan, Linda forced herself not to think about him but rather to divert all of her attention to Chase and the children. She must have written five or more emails the first few days, phoning her husband every night just to talk and to keep her mind alert and focused. Such steady contact comforted her a bit when Stan's intrusive call came on Thursday.

The familiar number displayed itself on her cell. Linda let the phone ring and go to voicemail. A few moments later the same number appeared again. She drew a deep breath, exhaled, and opened her phone. "Stan?"

"Hi, Linda."

"What do you think you're doing?" she asked with a calmness that belied her emotions. "I told you it's over. I said never to call me again. Do I have to change my number to show that I don't want to hear from you anymore?" Though she wanted to send a stern warning, she sounded as if she were making a plea.

"Linda, listen. I'm not a mean person. You know that. I'm just missing what we both enjoyed so much and wanted to see how you're doing."

"I'm doing great," she said irritably. "Is that good enough for you?"

"No, it's not. I don't think this is really you. You've never acted this way before."

"Stan, as I said the last time, you don't know me, so don't give me any more lines. Maybe you're not mean, but you're going to find me very unpleasant if you continue this illusion."

"An illusion? Come on, Linda. You're saying that we never had anything between us?"

"I never said that, but I definitely don't feel anything for you now!"

"But you know that feelings are fickle. I believe we enjoyed something far deeper than feelings."

"Stop the manipulation. Just leave me and my family alone."

"I'm not trying to manipulate anything at all. It's just that—"

"I'm going to say it one more time, Stan. It's over. Whatever you think we had, go on and think it, but we're done. Do you understand?"

"Okay, okay. I'll let it go. I won't call you again. But you can't call me either. If I'm going to bury everything, you can't dig it back up."

Linda sighed, sensing it was finally over between them. "Oh believe me, I won't. I love Chase and I'm committed to him and our marriage."

"And what if things change?"

"They won't."

"But Linda, this is not—"

Cold and detached, she closed her phone without responding. Stan got one thing right: she was not normally like this. But life had changed in a pleasantly surprising way, leading her to focus on the survival and the future happiness of her marriage and her family. If that required grim firmness, then so be it. And if Stan ever did call again, and it meant finally being honest with Chase, she would do that as well. Linda vowed to remain resolute in her decision.

When Chase had called her on his way to Jersey, Linda heard in his voice an anxiousness to come home, which created her own sense of urgency to see him until he asked again, as he did nearly every day, if everything was all right. She understood the implication but feigned ignorance and assured him nothing new had occurred on the home front. Though distraught at keeping the phone call secret, she convinced herself the truth would only damage their relationship. No need to fuel his suspicions. Anyway, the relationship had ended, so why bring up issues that would simply hurt someone else? And this hadn't been a real relationship, just something that had veered way out of control. Sure it felt pleasurable for a time, but it was nothing serious, at least from her perspective.

**

Chase exited the highway in Trenton, stopped at a gas station, and checked the time. A little after nine. Pulling out the number from his pocket, he called the coroner's office. Surprisingly efficient, the person on the other end returned after a few minutes with his father's location, Riverview Cemetery.

The attendant at the station gave him directions, and Chase drove away with renewed focus. After weaving through morning traffic for twenty minutes, he finally pulled up to the cemetery, got out of the car, and wearily stretched.

Nestled near the Delaware River, Riverview carried a fresh, springlike fragrance. As he walked through the trees, Chase wondered why people were born in ugly, sterile places and buried in such lovely, serene settings. A bit ironic, he thought.

Chase was still not certain why he felt compelled to see his father's grave, but he had been pulled toward this destination for some reason. Would he feel the need to talk to his dad as if he were alive? Would he ask him questions, knowing he couldn't answer? Could he gain some sort of personal satisfaction or even healing for his soul simply by coming? He had no idea.

Since it was only half past nine, Chase had plenty of time to make a random search. He read many of the century-old tombstones, some plain and simple, others ornate and almost beautiful. Chase and his friends used to play at the local cemetery near the woods, and he had always been fascinated by these places. But now how sad it was to see markers for infants and teenagers; how bizarre to notice couples buried next to each other, some having died the same year, sometimes within months. Several people had the strangest names, and he found the inscriptions for the deceased quite interesting.

As Chase continued his search, his stomach announced its need for food. He was exhausted and thought he should have asked for help finding the gravesite. Perhaps he wouldn't have enough time after all. Just when he had decided to turn around and look for the cemetery office, he stopped. Chase nearly walked past a nondescript marker while arguing with himself, but he caught the name Macklin out of the corner of his eye. He turned to make certain. "Robert Macklin, died April 1, 2000." Very plain and simple.

"So this is where everything ended, Dad," he found himself saying, surprised that he so quickly started a one-way conversation. He stared at the modest marker and thought about the wasted life buried beneath it.

"Was it worth it?" he asked aloud. "Was it worth leaving your family, dying alone, no one at your side? You probably didn't care, or maybe you did but drank away your guilt. I don't even know why I'm talking to you. You never listened before."

Chase stood there for several more minutes, torn between his anger and an urge to cry. He began to understand his issue of abandonment. After his father's sudden disappearance, Chase had for years placed the responsibility for this desertion upon himself and then turned to drugs to alleviate the guilt. *But why am I guilty?* he thought. *I didn't do anything that caused Dad to behave as he did.*

"That's it!" he cried out. For some reason he had taken responsibility for his father's actions, believing he was somehow to blame for his dad leaving the family. *Doesn't make sense,* he thought, *but maybe at fourteen a person doesn't know any better.* Looking at the simple headstone, Chase loudly addressed his dad again. "It was you! You, not me! I'm not going to believe any longer that I had anything at all to do with you abandoning me."

The word *abandonment* continued to reverberate in his mind. He wondered if his way of relating to others was directly connected to this experience, if somehow he had emotionally abandoned loved ones and friends out of fear that they would abandon him, a type of self-protection. He had never considered this possibility before; it seemed strange that a person would abandon someone else and would in return receive the very treatment he feared. He would have to ask Doctor Rhinegold about this.

Then Chase suddenly recalled that this was one of the lies coming out of the web, the one he hadn't given much attention. So maybe that was why he had felt driven to come here, to discover the source of this issue.

He deliberated for a moment upon the other words that had rushed at him in his vision, words still etched in his memory: *vulnerability, touch, pride,* and *anger.* Probably anger at his dad and at himself, he concluded. But what was the deal about pride? Where did that come into play?

Chase pondered the pride his dad displayed. It was ironic but true. He would tell his sons never to forget who they were. "You're a Macklin!" he often declared. "Don't ever let anyone look down on you. You're better than everybody else."

Dad was so arrogant, Chase thought, reflecting on how he had accepted this lie as truth and how it must have been interwoven with the other lie about not needing anybody. He had held some obvious fear-based lies all along, but he speculated that there must be a few pride-based lies as well. Determined to put an end to all of them, he took a step back and spoke one more time to the headstone.

"This is it. Thanks for nothing, Dad. All these years of lies. Well, rest in peace wherever you are."

Chase knew he shouldn't blame his father for his own personal lies, but his farewell felt right since he didn't think his dad deserved anything better. Without turning to look back, Chase headed for his rental car to find something to ease his growling stomach.

On the way to the airport, he rang Linda again. She answered cheerfully. "Hi, Chase! What's up?"

"Just left my dad's gravesite a bit earlier, and now I'm on my way to Kennedy."

"How'd it go?"

"Quite a relief actually. I'll tell you all about it when I get home."

"Okay. The kids and I will see you when you get here!"

"Sounds good. I love you, Linda."

"Love you too, hon'."

CHAPTER 16

Any thoughts of catching up on sleep during the flight quickly faded when Chase found himself crunched in the middle seat, sandwiched between a man working on his laptop and a woman accidentally brushing his elbow a bit too frequently. Far too tired physically and mentally to entertain further thoughts, Chase regularly stretched his legs as far as the seat in front of him allowed, moving them back and forth. He awkwardly excused himself a couple of times and stood at the back of the plane, performing a few exercises against the wall until the flight attendant would send him back to his prison.

After Chase had arrived and recovered his bag, he shook off his weariness and responded enthusiastically when Amy and Ryan came running up to greet him.

"Hi, Daddy!" they gleefully exclaimed, falling into his outstretched arms. He embraced them tightly, showing how much he had missed them. Linda's beauty left him breathless as she gave him the warmest kiss he could remember. Her dancing green eyes appeared to glow in the evening lights.

They didn't arrive home until nearly eight-thirty. Linda prepared a late dinner while Chase played with the children. The laughter and the giggling kept Linda smiling, thinking she finally had her family back. Chase eagerly told them about his brothers and their wives and how much they wanted to see everyone. He spoke tenderly of his mother and her wit.

"Daddy, did your mother want to see us too?" Amy asked.

"Oh yes, she did. I think she was very proud of you and Ryan."

"What about your father?"

"Well … um, he's not alive either, Amy."

"What happened?"

"I don't really know. Never had a chance to see him. But hey, wouldn't it be great to see your aunts and uncles soon?"

"Yes! Can we?"

"Sure! Why not? As soon as we're able to."

Chase and Linda put the children to bed after baths and walked hand in hand to the bedroom. An intensely amorous night followed; it was nearly overwhelming considering his fatigue. Falling immediately asleep, Chase awoke the next morning with a dream still fresh in his memory. He jumped into the shower, hurriedly dressed, and found Linda in the living room, caressing a cup of coffee.

"Well good morning!" she exclaimed cheerfully. "You slept forever!"

"Yeah, it was a long day," Chase answered with a wink and a smile. Making his way to the kitchen, he poured himself some coffee and returned to sit beside her. "I had a crazy dream last night."

Linda snuggled closer. "Wow! You're becoming quite the dreamer! Tell me about it."

"I was in our home, not this one, but I knew it to be ours. My dad appeared, looking very old and wrinkled, simply standing there in our living room. I walked right up to him and punched him in the face! He just took it and stared at me. I punched him over and over, screaming something at him, but I don't remember the words. When I stopped, he was still expressionless, bleeding from the nose and the mouth. Then he finally spoke. He said, "Son, will you forgive me?" I yelled something again and hit him until he vanished into thin air. Then I woke up. That was it. What do you suppose it's all about?"

Linda shook her head. "Do you think your father felt badly about himself and what he did to you and your family?"

"You mean this was a dream about what he somehow hoped could have been?"

"I don't know, something like that."

Chase peered out the window. "But look at what I did to him! I pummeled him to death!"

"Hon', it was just a dream."

"Oh, I know, but I'm trying to pay attention to all this stuff, especially when it has to do with my dad and me. I've been thinking that it's not so much about him as about my anger issues."

"Well that could be."

"Thanks a lot," Chase said with a forced grin. "I mean, we both know I show anger at times, but I don't yell and hit. Even with my dad I wouldn't have done that. I would have been too afraid. Babe, all I can think of is that there must be some pent-up junk still inside of me. Do you remember anger being one of the words in the spider web?"

"I forgot about that."

"Maybe this is one more step toward my freedom. I guess it's another thing to discuss with the doctor."

"Are you still planning to meet with him again?"

"Yes. I need to. We both do."

Chase didn't notice her discomfort. Linda tried to hide it with a quick "okay" and by getting up for more coffee. Calling out from the kitchen, she said, "Hey hon', you haven't told me about your visit to your father's gravesite. How'd that go?"

"Pretty amazing, I guess." He waited for her to return before continuing. "I spoke to him as if he could hear me. It felt good—you know, processing some of the stuff I'm going through."

"Anything specific?"

"Yeah. For one thing, I'm no longer going to take responsibility for his actions."

"You've done that?"

"Always have, I guess. Anyway, the visit must have been worth it because of this dream."

"Sounds like it, hon'. And I'm happy to see you're still working through things from your past."

"Well, I think we all need to be responsible for just our own actions." Chase didn't mean for this to be a jab at his wife, but her curt response showed that the line hit home.

"Thanks for sharing with me."

The next several days went quite well. They spoke about their new house in New York, Chase hinting that it might be nice to move there. Linda laughed at the suggestion, which made him think a move would never happen. He joined in her laughter to make certain she didn't take him seriously, though part of him considered this a real possibility.

Linda continued to notice positive changes in her husband. He would do little things like open the car door for her, sit next to her on the sofa, and tell her he loved her. And then came the more incredible moments of sharing his feelings, demonstrating vulnerability in areas long locked up. He called her his best friend or at least said that's what he wanted her to be. This was something Linda had always dreamed of but had considered impossible a few months ago. He even mentioned God for the first time she could recollect.

"I've been thinking," he said one day, "how God must have made a man and a woman to come together to have the most intimate of relationships. And then I thought about best friends, how that's really the most intimate of all relationships. This led me to conclude that God couldn't possibly have intended us to have anyone other than our partner as our best friend. I mean, I know some husbands say their wives are their best friends, and I used to think that was nice for them, but I decided that it was unrealistic to believe that everyone could enjoy such a relationship.

"I know I'm getting deep. But here's the deal. If I'm not my wife's best friend and she's not mine, where will we go to fulfill that need? I simply chose not to have that need fulfilled since I never recognized it as a need in the first place. Maybe that saved me from an illicit relationship with someone else, but I think it resulted in a lie that kept me away from what I now see: that you and I are meant for each other, that we complete each other. I think it's a lie to believe that someone else could fulfill that need and maybe a lie to think that someone else should. Don't you think it's possible that the whole scenario is a lie? I mean, if I choose someone other than my wife as my best friend, offering that person the most intimate of all relationships, is that okay?"

Linda hesitated for a moment, making certain he had finished. "Wow! This really is deep. And I have to confess that I haven't done very well with my own issues in this area. I've held back from you, maybe not intentionally, but I guess just to protect myself from being hurt. Can we work on this together, hon'?"

"Of course we can," Chase said with a slight smile.

Linda fingered her hair. "Now I have a question about part of this— not that I'm disagreeing."

"Sure, go ahead."

"What about guys having friendships with other guys? Or what about my girlfriends? It just seems that some things are much easier to share with those of the same gender."

"Well I don't fully understand all of the dynamics, but you do hear people say that since they can't tell everything to their spouse, they need to have a best friend to confide in. I'm sure there's an element of truth there, but I want you as my best friend, and I hope that in time I will earn your trust."

Linda melted. She tucked her arms underneath his and gave him a kiss, whispering in his ear, "Chase, that is the most special, most intimate thing I've ever heard. I want you, too, as my best friend."

Chase had scheduled an appointment with Rhinegold for the following Monday. Linda suggested going out shopping on Saturday since she needed new clothes for work. In the past he would have balked or least complained about being too tired, but he recently considered how he could be more involved with his wife and try to enjoy the things in which she took pleasure.

The closest outdoor mall presented many opportunities for someone eager to indulge. Linda needed a couple of new outfits and of course all the accessories. Strolling out of a store, purchases in hand, they heard a voice calling out from behind them.

"Linda?"

She turned and nearly dropped her bags. "What on earth are you doing here?" she snapped.

"Shopping," Stan said with a smirk.

Chase glanced back and forth. "What's going on, Linda? Who is this?"

"Oh, hi," Stan said, walking toward them. "You must be Chase. I'm Stan, an old friend of Linda's."

Linda grabbed Chase's hand. He could feel her grip tighten when she asked, "What do you need, Stan?"

"Oh nothing. Just saw you walk by. Coincidence, I guess. How is everything?"

Linda couldn't take it any longer. "Chase, this is the guy," she whispered.

Chase swung around. "What? What guy? You mean this is the—"

"Yes."

Chase looked straight at the intruder. "What do you want?" he asked, his voice acrid.

"Hey, man, I don't want anything. Just being nice."

"Get out of here!" Chase demanded gruffly.

Stan came closer. "Not so fast. You have no idea what's going on with Linda and me. It's like you're blind. She has needs that you just—"

Before he could think, Chase reached back and punched him in the face. Stan crumpled over. Chase took advantage and hammered him in the stomach. He then waited until his enemy stood erect, holding his side and feeling his jaw. "Listen, man, this is my wife you're flirting with! If I ever see or hear of you again, I'll find you, and I won't be as nice. Understand?"

"Coming from you? No."

"You want me to finish it all right now?" Chase asked with a threatening glare, hoping he'd agree.

Stan shuffled away without answering.

Embarrassed that everything had come so dramatically to light, Linda took Chase's hand and meekly apologized, tears beginning to stream down her cheeks.

"It's okay, Linda. You don't have to worry any longer. Does this jerk live around here?"

"No," she responded through her tears. "Can we sit down?"

"Sure."

They settled on a wooden bench next to a large planter, one of many that decorated the wide walkway between the shops. "I'm so sorry, Chase. I've kept this whole thing a secret for too long."

He felt his heart drop, anticipating the worst. "Okay," was all he could say.

"I was honest in saying that we made contact for a few weeks, and when I found out you were suspicious, I cut it off. What I didn't tell you is that he sent an email one day after you went to New York, prompting me to call him and break it off again."

Chase gulped. "So you called him."

"Yes," Linda said through her sobs. "I knew that I needed to make it clear that the whole thing was just in his head, nothing real. I told him never to contact me again. I didn't tell you because I didn't think you'd understand or that you'd worry too much and leave New York early to be with your family."

"So tell me the truth. Were there more calls?"

"Not from me! I wanted this whole thing over with. I mean, it wasn't even a 'thing' to me. I got pulled into something I never really wanted. I opened up to someone I considered an old friend, someone I knew long before I met you. I had no idea he was looking for anything more than that."

Chase's stomach churned, his mind reeling. "What exactly was he looking for?"

"Hon', nothing of substance ever existed. I told the truth last week when I said I never saw him. There were only emails and a few phone calls. He tricked me into believing that my needs weren't being met, obviously implying that he was available to meet them."

"How did that make you feel?"

"Chase, I can't go there. You don't need to know the things we talked about. It wasn't real."

"Well it's real to me!" he said, his stomach feeling as if it were in his throat.

"I'm sorry, hon'. That's all I can say. He deserved what he got today. I'm glad you were here." Linda reached to take his hand again, but Chase wasn't satisfied.

"But what if I hadn't been here?"

"I don't know. I'm sure I would have told him the same thing I've been saying, to leave me alone."

"Did you fall in love with this guy?"

"Please, honey, don't do this. It's over now."

Linda's response caused Chase's internal knot to increase. He shook his head.

"Can you forgive me?" she asked.

Immediately he remembered his dream, with his dad asking the same question. He knew he wouldn't lash out at his wife, but what about his rights? Could he forgive her when he felt betrayed? "I don't know. I need to process it all."

Linda carefully brushed her checks with her fingers and slowly dabbed underneath her eyes. She felt overwhelmingly fragile. "Well, can we at least talk to Doctor Rhinegold about it? Maybe he can help us."

"Sure."

Their shopping excursion over, they drove home in silence. Chase was uncertain of his emotions. He looked at Linda out of the corner of his eye a few times, noticing the tears but unwilling to comfort her. He allowed her to feel remorseful.

When they reached the house, Chase handed Linda the car keys and told her to pick up the kids at the sitter's. He walked slowly to his bedroom, opened his humidor, and grabbed a cigar. Alone in the backyard, he was tormented by his thoughts.

How in the world had this happened? Sure, he had been distant. Sure, he had pushed them apart and kept to himself. But what did he do to deserve this? Or maybe he did deserve it. After all, Linda's needs weren't being met, so she obviously reached out to someone who would listen to her. But then again, no one deserved this type of treatment.

So what now? Everything had been progressing so beautifully. He had undergone changes, she had responded to him, and their love life was better than ever. They were having fun again, communicating, and getting to know each other with renewed respect. He had just begun to discover his true identity outside of destructive lies that had dictated a false identity over the years. But now what? How would he deal with such a troubling situation, a wife who kept secrets, who lied and didn't want to talk about it once exposed? How could they continue toward restoration and reconciliation on a path paved with deception? Could everything he held true be suddenly unraveling?

On the other hand, could Linda's behavior result from a repressive, self-protective nature similar to his own? Did he think himself better than his wife? Could she too have been unknowingly trapped with no way of escape? The possibility brought Chase a bit of relief. He felt that they indeed would be able to work through everything together.

Chase lit his cigar, took a few puffs, and considered another potential issue. If Linda held back the truth to protect him, what made him think that she had revealed the entire truth and that nothing serious had taken place between her and that guy? Did they perhaps meet someplace? What if they had fallen in love and she didn't know what to do about it? What if they …

"I can't think about that," Chase said aloud. Until today, he had thought that he had to earn back her trust, but now the opposite seemed truer. Chase had no idea how to treat Linda when she returned with the children. He had to act normal, but he didn't feel normal at the moment.

The family watched a movie together that night, Chase attempting to ignore his emotions and to banter playfully with Amy and Ryan. He watched Linda from his chair, but after thirty minutes or so of observing her distress, he got up and sat next to her. Linda buried her face in his chest. Chase held her tightly, caressing her hair, wanting to believe her, and hoping for another breakthrough. He replayed his encounter with Stan, attempting to think the best of his wife without being naïve.

Linda didn't move from the safety of his arms. He felt the beating of her heart, smelled the fragrance of her perfume, and was content merely to remain present for her.

Linda's breathing calmed. This felt right. She was comforted by her husband, who, though understandably distraught, demonstrated his love and tenderness. "I need you, Chase."

He didn't respond but held her more tightly.

Linda finally rose to put a sleepy Ryan in his bed, while Chase sat on Amy's comforter. "You know I love you, Amy."

"I know, Daddy."

"I mean I really love you," he said with emphasis.

"I know!" she said, giggling.

Chase gave her a hug and a kiss, stroking her hair until she fell asleep. He gave her another kiss on the cheek before entering Ryan's room.

"Hey, buddy. You awake?"

"Kinda."

"Well I love you a lot, Ryan." He continued, not expecting his son to respond. "It's going to be different around here. I want to do some fun things with the family, go camping, Disneyland, the movies—"

"Disneyland?" Ryan asked, his eyes widening.

"Sure. Why not? I don't expect you to understand, but your dad is going through some big changes, and I want to be around more. It'll be cool!"

"Okay, but I want to go to Disneyland!"

"We'll do it soon. Now go to sleep and I'll see you in the morning." He leaned over and kissed him on the forehead.

"Night, Daddy."

Chase carefully opened his bedroom door. The lights were out. Not wanting to disturb Linda, he stealthily slipped out of his clothes and crawled into bed.

Linda stirred. "You okay, hon'?"

"I don't know. Just tired."

"Me too. Please know that I love you. I am so sorry, but I'm willing to work through everything with you."

"I know," Chase responded wearily. "We'll go see the doctor and take one step at a time."

Linda put her hand on his shoulder. "I love you, Chase."

"Love you too."

CHAPTER 17

C hase had made a morning appointment with Rhinegold. After they dropped off the children at school, Chase put on the oldies station to avoid any uncomfortable conversation. *No reason to delve into deep matters on our own,* he thought. Linda stared straight ahead, wondering what had happened to the tender moments of the previous night. *Can't rush him in these things,* she concluded.

"Well hello, you two!" Rhinegold said cheerfully. "Come on in." As soon as they settled themselves, the doctor continued. "It's been nearly two weeks since I've seen you. Let's catch up. What's new?"

Chase recounted his doppelganger vision along with everything else he'd experienced since they'd last met. The doctor wanted to know more about each ordeal, visibly amazed that so much had occurred in such a short time. Chase didn't mind; however, he wanted to discuss what he considered the primary issue.

More than twenty minutes passed and Rhinegold backtracked to the doppelganger. "Now you said the person you saw in the hallway resembled the one entangled in the spider web?"

"Listen, Doc," said Chase impatiently, "I don't want to monopolize the whole time today. We need to discuss something that happened between the two of us."

"Certainly. What is it?" he asked, not appearing at all offended by Chase's abruptness.

"Well just yesterday we saw the guy Linda was having an affair with and—"

"It was not an affair," Linda cut in sternly.

"All right. I'm sorry," Chase said, looking at her. "The guy you had some sort of an emotional connection with. Anyway, Doctor Rhinegold, we were shopping yesterday and he appeared out of nowhere. I didn't like his attitude, so I punched him out."

"You hit the man?"

"Yeah, a few good ones. Told him to stay out of our lives."

"Had there been any contact with him prior to this?"

Linda squirmed. Chase answered. "That's part of the problem. Linda hid the fact that she called him at least once and he—"

"It was only once," she interjected firmly.

The doctor wanted to prevent an argument. "Linda, why don't you finish telling the story?"

She glanced at Chase and then back at the doctor. "Well, I know the things you told me to do and not to do, but, um, I just felt I had to call him one more time."

"Okay."

"So I did after Chase left for New York."

"Chase knew nothing of this contact then."

"No. I didn't want him to worry with everything going on out there. I just called the guy and told him that he apparently wanted something I didn't, that I was committed to my husband, and that he should no longer call me. I said that we never had anything between us."

"And then what happened?"

"I hung up and thought that was it."

"Until he interrupted your shopping."

Linda leaned forward and spoke with concern, almost in a whisper. "He doesn't even live around here, Doctor Rhinegold. I don't know how he could've possibly known where we'd be."

"Oh, I'm sure he didn't, but guys like this typically don't give up. He did know where you live, correct?"

"Yes."

Chase shook his head. The doctor noticed. "What's going on inside of you?"

"I keep finding out new things the more we talk! First I thought that not much occurred between them and that it was over. Then I find out there have been at least two conversations, and now she says the guy knows where we live. This feels a lot bigger than it did originally. Makes me wonder if there's even more."

Rhinegold noticed Linda looking away and taking a deep breath.

"Linda, can you understand how Chase is feeling?"

"Sure I do. I didn't want this sort of thing to happen in the first place, and I certainly didn't want it to hurt our relationship."

"So is there anything else you should be telling Chase?"

"There are no secrets if that's what you're asking. He keeps prodding me, trying to learn more about the specifics of what we did or how we communicated. When Stan showed up yesterday, that was the first time I had seen him in nearly twenty years." She looked over at her husband. "That's the truth, Chase. We never got together, no physical contact, just talking on the phone and a few emails."

"Chase, can you accept what Linda is saying?"

"I guess I have to. I can't keep torturing myself with all the what-ifs. It's just hard. That's all."

Clearing his throat, Rhinegold said, "Things like this are never easy. Trust has been broken, and that takes time and a lot of work to restore." He turned toward Linda, inching forward in his leather chair.

"Listen to me closely, Linda. You admittedly were lonely and felt ignored by Chase and unwittingly allowed yourself to be drawn into a dangerous game of cat and mouse, completely unaware that the cat was out to get you. Oh, you probably sensed that the situation was wrong, that continued conversations and flirtation were not a good idea, but this felt comforting and satisfying and gave you something to look forward to.

"In fact, even the secrecy of it all became stimulating. When secrets are kept, your adrenaline kicks in, telling you what you're doing is fun and exciting. You want more; you've got to get your fix. That is precisely why it's so difficult to stop. A relationship becomes an addiction. And though promises to quit are genuine, they are often empty due to the power of the addiction. So let me ask you, Linda, can you see this relationship as an addiction that will destroy your life if you continue?"

"Yes. I'm not going to continue it," she answered resolutely. "It's totally over."

"Good, but can you see that what you had was as powerful and deadly as heroin and that had you kept going, your addiction would have grown and your family would have been destroyed?"

"No, I never thought about it that way."

"Well thank goodness it lasted only a few weeks. Much less addiction. Easier to quit. So keep that picture in your mind. No matter what that guy may have told you, he is as deadly as heroin. You would have lost everything, okay?"

"Okay." Linda fingered her curls, embarrassed.

"And Chase, I urge you to slow down with your desire to uncover all the facts. It's best if you stop asking and prodding since it isn't going to help the situation. If you believe your wife, there is not much to discover anyway. I think it's time to set all this aside and to pursue the path you were on, the path to rediscovering yourself, which of course led to the rediscovery of your marriage. Don't allow this predicament to tear apart the beautiful thing that is being built."

He paused a moment, fingering his chin. "Now let me ask you something, Chase. If you continue to press for what you think is the whole truth in this crisis, and if you continue to punish your wife by not relenting in your quest to uncover all the details, but learn that such behavior might destroy your marriage, will you keep it up?"

"Of course not."

Rhinegold nodded. "There is your answer. And one more thing. Chase, do you find any connection between your behavior and Linda's?"

"I did think about that."

"And what did you conclude?"

"That I'm not the innocent one here. I've got my own issues, probably ones that created this whole mess in the first place."

"Could that awareness provide you with a bit more compassion for Linda?"

"Yeah, I think it can." Chase reached for Linda's hand, meekly smiling.

"Well good," the doctor said with his own smile. "I truly appreciate the way you both are willing to take responsibility."

"Thanks," Chase said. "But before we're done, can I ask you a question?"

"Sure. Go ahead."

Chase rubbed his forehead. "I've been considering my abandonment issue and wondering if a thought I had is normal: the idea that I have emotionally abandoned other people due to my fear of them abandoning me. Maybe it's what I did to Linda, you know, leaving her emotionally empty based upon my own insecurity. It sounds crazy to do to someone else the very thing I fear, which of course leads to my own abandonment in the end."

"No, Chase, that's not crazy. It's not healthy, but when a person experiences abandonment, he often will vow never to be abandoned or rejected again. So to guarantee that won't occur, the person will push people away to protect himself."

"That makes no sense whatsoever," Chase said, rolling his eyes. "It's so naïve. And actually kind of stupid!"

"But Chase, you've said yourself that this was a lie you've held on to. Since when are lies wise?"

"That's a good point."

"Initially lies may sound prudent, but once you see them for what they are, it's not at all unusual to feel stupid for believing them."

"Well the abandonment one still sounds crazy to me."

"It's definitely dysfunctional, but I am so pleased to hear how much you're learning about yourself. You must be aware that many people, perhaps even most, never find freedom from their misguided self-belief systems."

"Never thought about it."

"Let's go ahead and set up another appointment in a couple of weeks."

"Can we check our schedules and get back to you?"

"Sure."

CHAPTER 18

They never met with the doctor again. The two of them quickly resolved issues that Chase once would have ignored, tried to bury, or approached with short-lived attempts to change his behavior. When he needed assurance that Linda's recent emails did not include her former friend, she patiently showed him Stan's email address and how she had blocked it. When Linda desired relief from her troubled mind, Chase held her close and spoke words of endearment. Their romance was reignited with intimate date nights, cuddling, and small but meaningful gifts shared with each other.

After a few weeks of this renewal, Chase no longer felt the need to revisit Linda's recent past, nor did she mention how his previous behavior had driven them apart. They did speak once about being rescued, Linda from a perilous game that would have destroyed her own life and the lives of those she loved, and Chase from a web of lies about himself that resulted in unintentional isolation from treasured people.

Chase realized that he had forced his wife into her own separate world, transforming them into uncongenial roommates futilely attempting to survive segregated lives. As he continued to process the lies, Chase took increasing responsibility for all that had happened over the last several months. He did this not to relieve Linda of her responsibility but because he understood that marital bliss was unattainable if they clung to the independent lifestyles to which they had grown accustomed.

They spoke at length about the possibility of relocating their family to New York, taking advantage of a home without a mortgage, and living near the children's aunts and uncles. A move would involve securing new employment, but Chase's positive attitude was persuasive. "And perhaps if everything works out well, you can stay at home and take care of the children since our expenses won't be nearly as high," he said one day.

Linda agreed to take an exploratory vacation during summer break to acquaint herself with the area and to follow up on the résumés they had already begun emailing. In the meantime, Chase arranged the promised trip to Disneyland, after which he wanted them all to visit Aunt Betty, knowing of her physical ailments and her continued loneliness with the unexpected loss of her husband a few years back. The Macklin family had first met his aunt at Ron's memorial service, and Chase wanted to stay in contact. He did warn Linda, however, about Betty's religious inclinations.

The weeks crawled by, at least for Ryan, who nearly every day asked when they were going to Disneyland. The plan included a fun-filled weekend in Anaheim, a drive over to Riverside for the night, and then a flight from L.A. to New York the following day.

When June finally arrived, they packed their bags for a two-week vacation and headed down to Orange County, Amy and Ryan playing and giggling most of the way. Disneyland proved to be everything they had dreamed about and more, but trying to get the children into the car after two days of kid heaven proved quite a challenge. They didn't want to leave. They didn't want to go to Aunt Betty's. They wanted to go home! Chase bribed them with soft-serve ice cream, keeping their complaints to a minimum.

Betty had moved into an apartment after Ron passed away. She proudly showed them an extra room with a double bed and a large foam mat pulled out for the little ones. "Will this be okay for everyone?" she wanted to know as the four of them peered into the bedroom.

"Perfect," Chase replied. "I think the kids will have fun with us sleeping in the same room together." He told his aunt the children were exhausted and promised she could spend time with them in the morning.

Once they had them situated and kissed them good-night, Chase and Linda found Betty waiting in a cushioned rocking chair. Now in her mid-seventies, her light skin deeply wrinkled and pulling away from her bones, she appeared frail but retained her mental sharpness.

"Well have a seat! Chase, it's so good to see you again. And Linda, it's been far too long."

Linda smiled. "I agree. But Chase always speaks so fondly of you to everyone."

"Even though he never listens to me about Jesus?"

Chase shook his head. *She didn't waste any time*, he thought, trying to remind himself of why they came, wondering if the visit would be worth the mental torment. "Aunt Betty, it's not that I don't listen to you. It's just that I'm not interested in religion."

"It's not religion. I keep telling you that."

"I know you do, but it's all the same to me."

"Linda, what do you think?" Betty asked, moving her head slightly and squinting.

"About what?"

"Jesus!"

"Oh, I believe in him. I was raised in church."

"But do you have a personal relationship with him?"

"Not really, I guess. I'm not sure."

"Well maybe we can talk about that."

Chase had already had enough. Knowing the inevitable direction in which his aunt would lead them, he leaned over and whispered to Linda that he had warned her. Then he asked with suppressed enthusiasm, "Aunt Betty? Would you like to hear a crazy thing that happened to me a few months ago?"

She sat as erect as her body allowed. "Of course! What is it?"

Chase related his entire experience with the web of lies, pleased that he had found a distraction from her Jesus talk but increasingly uneasy when he observed her smiling and nodding. When he finished, Betty gleefully clapped, not quite the response Chase anticipated.

"Do you know whose hand pulled you out?"

Here she goes again, he lamented to himself, annoyed that his diversion didn't work. "Come on, Aunt Betty. Can't I just tell a story without you trying to interpret it?"

"But it's easy!"

"Maybe for you, but my life is not like yours."

"That doesn't matter. It was obviously the mighty hand of God reaching out to rescue you. Who else's could it have been? And whose voice do you think said, 'Watch me'?"

Chase shook his head. He should have known better than to open up to his aunt. Realizing the downward spiral would continue regardless of his answer, he quietly said, "My own."

"Your own?" Betty said in disbelief, looking over at Linda for confirmation. With a squint lasting longer than normal, she leaned forward and asked her nephew in a petulant tone that was completely out of character, "Do you think you can save yourself from yourself?"

"What do you mean by that?" Chase snapped, not really wanting to know her thoughts.

"Well," Betty said, as if she alone held the answer, "we don't have the capacity to save ourselves. That is why Jesus died on the cross. Oh, sure, it happened over two thousand years ago, but he is still the only one who can rescue us from our sins."

Chase turned to Linda and whispered, "Would you mind if I went outside for a while? I hate to leave you alone with her, but I simply can't take this any longer."

Linda glanced over at Aunt Betty and whispered back, "Okay, if you have to. But she's just an old woman telling us what she believes."

"Thank you, babe. Have fun!" He kissed her on the cheek, stood up, and declared to his aunt, "I'm sorry. I need to take a walk and get some exercise. We have a long day tomorrow."

"Can't stand the heat?" Betty asked with a wink.

"Just need some fresh air. I'll be back."

Chase stepped out onto the front porch and sighed wearily. He was happy with his choice to dismiss himself but hoped Linda wouldn't be mad at him later. *She'll be okay*, he thought with a huge exhale. *She's a strong gal.*

Producing a small cigar from his shirt pocket, he lit it and felt better as he strolled through the well-lit neighborhood. He realized again the stubborn tenacity of his aunt, how she used any angle she could find to opine about God and religion. How could that hand have been God's since he wasn't even thinking about God? And the voice? It was certainly his own, but what difference would it make if somehow God spoke through him that day? Everything would have played out the same.

Chase wiped his brow, cleaning his hand on his shorts. He had never considered himself impious in a disrespectful way. He had always believed in God and had felt that sufficient. God certainly couldn't expect anything more from a person. But could he be pertinacious or even ignorant in not considering a deeper reality? He didn't know. He preferred ignoring the discussion altogether.

His thoughts turned to the next day—driving to LAX, flying out to see his brothers, and showing the family a potential new home. Though it had been only a short time since his last visit, he found himself missing his roots—Frank and Allie, Lane and Kathy, and even Murphy in an odd sort of way. He reminded Chase of the old days, which certainly weren't his best years. *But it's funny*, he thought, *how memories play upon the emotions, how we can miss even depressing or difficult times after a long separation, almost like an old friend. A person may not want to return to that season of his life but apparently can have a certain fondness for the past.*

His mini-cigar nearly finished, Chase checked his watch. He'd been gone twenty minutes. Probably time to get back. He meandered to the house, continuing to reflect upon upstate New York and the memories, wiping perspiration off of his face at nearly every step.

"Hey, ladies," he said cheerfully as he reentered the living room. "Man, it's hot out there! Are you all done catching up?" Without waiting for an answer, he continued. "Hey, it's getting pretty late. Linda? You want to get some sleep?"

"Sure. I need it."

Chase bent over to kiss his aunt. "We'll see you in the morning. By the way, do you have any coffee?"

"I keep a little bit of instant just in case."

"Okay, thanks." Chase hated instant coffee.

As they were preparing for bed in the bathroom together, Chase smirked. "Well, tell me, did she convert you?"

"Hon', she's so nice. I think she simply needs people to talk with. I listened to her life story for a while and how she met Ron and then—"

"But what about the Jesus stuff?"

"Oh yeah, that too. It wasn't a big deal. You know what, though? She did make me think about how we're raising Amy and Ryan."

Chase drew back defensively. "What'd she say?"

"Just that we should seriously consider taking them to church, that there are good morals they can learn, other children to connect with and so on."

"You know what? I'm not sure why I came to see my aunt. Maybe because she was there when I needed help all those years ago or maybe since she's the last connection to my mom and dad. Anyway, I guess I deserve it since I'm the one who brought up my story."

"But hon', I love hearing you share it! Don't worry so much about what she thinks."

"Yeah, you're right."

CHAPTER 19

O nce they secured their luggage at the Syracuse airport, Chase led the way to Hertz and rented an SUV for the drive to Frank and Allie's. This visit was greatly anticipated by everyone since, despite repeated attempts and promises to come to see them in California, Frank and Allie had flown out only once, right after Amy's birth.

Chase called his brother about ten minutes before arriving and then pointed out a few memorable sights to his family as they entered his old neighborhood. "That over there is the high school we all attended, and just behind it ... can you see that old abandoned warehouse back aways? Yeah, when I was little, a few of us neighborhood kids hung out there a lot. Called ourselves a gang," he added with a chuckle.

"You were in a gang?" Ryan asked.

"No," he said with another laugh. "We just called it that. Even had a name—the Black Widows." The words jolted him, Linda too. "That's pretty weird, don't you think, babe?"

"Definitely. That was really the name of your club?"

"Yeah ... Hey, and look! That blue house is where I kissed my first girlfriend!"

"Chase," Linda scolded him.

"I'm only joking, kids."

Linda shook her head.

When they finally pulled up to Frank and Allie's, the family saw the two of them standing in the driveway, waiting. Allie ran over and pressed her face against the window. "Oh my!" she shouted. "Look at these children! They're beautiful!"

"Well let us get out the car, Allie!" Chase said with a grin.

Amy and Ryan tolerated her enthusiasm as she hugged and kissed them. "I'm your Aunt Allie!" she proudly declared. "They look like Macklins all right ... And Linda!" she exclaimed, pulling her close. "It's so nice to see you again! You're prettier than ever!"

The brothers shook hands and then gave each other a shoulder embrace. Frank patted the children on their heads and shared a quick hug with Linda while Allie gleefully continued her compliments. "Well come on inside!" she eventually said.

As they gathered in the living room, Allie beamed with excitement. "So how is everyone doing? How was your flight? Tell me about it."

"The children had a good time," Linda responded with a smile. "Very first flight for them."

"First flight? Well, children, that must have been fun!"

They both nodded, uncomfortable in their new surroundings. Linda noticed. "Why don't you two run upstairs with your suitcases while we talk for a bit? Which room is theirs?" she asked, looking at Allie.

"Second on the right. Frank, would you mind showing them the way?"

"Sure. Come on, kids. Follow me. Here, Amy, let me help you with your bag."

"Lane and Kathy are coming over for dinner," Allie said. They could smell a wonderful aroma wafting from the kitchen. Allie leaned forward. "But before they get here, I just have to tell you who I ran into just yesterday. You're not going to believe this." She paused to build drama.

Chase bit. "Okay, Allie, tell us."

"Sadie."

"Sadie? You saw Sadie?"

"Yes! I went shopping and nearly ran into her in the store! She was looking at this scarlet dress, holding it up and—oh, I guess that doesn't matter. Anyway, I recognized her immediately, though it took her a moment to place me. She lives only about five minutes from here, married for a long time with three kids! Can you imagine that?"

Chase shrugged nonchalantly. "It is pretty strange to think about it."

Linda interrupted with a wry smile. "Anyone want to tell me who Sadie is?"

"Oh, I'm sorry, babe. You know the story of my last night here. Remember the girlfriend I had at the time?"

"I guess so."

"That's Sadie."

Allie jumped in. "So we're talking for a bit and I ask her if she ever gave up drugs. Well she said—"

"You actually asked her that?" Chase interjected.

"Yes, of course I did. She wasn't embarrassed at all. She said she kicked them when she got pregnant."

"Good."

Allie sat back triumphantly, invigorated by the way she had steered the conversation. "But Chase, you're not going to believe this. Guess who she once saw?"

Completely unable to keep up with her energy, he answered listlessly, "I don't have a clue."

"Your dad!"

"What?"

"The kids are unpacking," Frank announced as he came down the stairs. "I told them dinner would be ready pretty soon."

"Frank, I'm talking about Sadie and your dad," Allie said, pretending to be annoyed at the interruption. Looking back at Chase, she continued. "So Sadie tells me she saw your dad a few months after you left."

"She never met him," Chase objected. "How did she know it was him?"

"Be patient. I'm getting there." Allie paused again for effect. "Anyway, Sadie told me that one night she went to one of the local bars with her boyfriend and overheard a couple of men talking. One of them said he was a Macklin and proud of it."

"Doesn't that sound like Dad?" Frank offered.

"Frank, let me finish. So Sadie just walks up and asks him if he said his name was Macklin. Well, he was slurring all over the place but said yes. She then asked if he had a son named Chase. He said yes again!"

"Amazing," Chase observed, shaking his head. "I can't believe this."

"Yeah, but I'm not done yet! So they talk for a while about you and then—"

"Great," Chase mumbled.

"And then your dad tells Sadie that if she ever saw you again, would she tell you that he was sorry for the way things turned out, that he really did love his kids but that he thought it best to stay away. He asked her to say that if his boys could ever find a way to forgive him, that would be nice."

"Nice?" Chase said sarcastically.

"Don't hold me to the exact word, just something like that."

"But you're sure he said he was sorry and hoped for some sort of forgiveness?"

"That's what Sadie told me."

"And he actually mentioned that he loved us?"

"I guess so."

Frank studied his brother's reactions. "I can see what you're thinking, Chase. I felt the same way. Dad saying he loved us? I don't know about that. Wait a minute. I just heard Lane and Kathy's car in the driveway. Why don't you guys surprise them at the door?"

"I'm not finished!" cried Allie.

Lane barreled into the house without knocking, Kathy right behind him, nearly bowling over Chase and Linda as they were about to open the door. "Hey, what's going on, bro? Almost killed you guys!" he shouted, offering a warm embrace. "This must be Linda! Great to meet you after, what, ten years or something? Linda, this is Kathy. Hey Allie, time to eat?"

"Lane, I'm in the middle of the story about your dad and Sadie!"

"Finish it later! I'm hungry!"

157

"Oh, all right," she agreed, not too happily. "I'll go upstairs and get Amy and Ryan. Hey, Kathy," she said with a complete change of attitude, "you won't believe how much they look like Macklins!"

Linda had heard similar comments, or perhaps compliments, throughout the years. She knew her children strongly resembled Chase, but this made her feel insecure, even more so when Allie kept mentioning the Macklin name. Linda couldn't present anyone other than herself to support the resemblance to her own family. She had nothing but pictures to demonstrate the similarities and certainly no one with her to brag about those likenesses. She knew this to be petty, but she couldn't help her feelings.

"Look at them, Kathy!" Allie said proudly, pointing as the children made their way downstairs. "Don't you think they look just like Macklins?"

"I don't know, Allie," Lane said with a shrug. "I see a strong likeness between Linda and the kids, especially with little Amy. Look at her mouth and her eyes."

His words stunned Linda. Could he have read her mind? Could Lane really be that sensitive, or perhaps just extremely kind, or both? She grabbed Chase's hand and whispered in his ear, "That was nice of him to say."

"Well, he's a nice guy," he replied, but not too softly.

"What'd you say there, little bro? That I'm nice? I don't know about that!" Lane began strutting around the room, flexing his muscles, the children giggling at his jocular antics. "I'm a pretty mean fella. Look at me!"

"Okay, okay," Allie said, joining in the laughter. "I think it's time to eat."

The dinner conversation centered upon Linda, Amy, and Ryan. The aunts and uncles wanted to hear about work, school, teachers, and their trip to Disneyland. They listened to Linda tell the story of how she and Chase met, what her job entailed, and how she managed to put up with Chase for so long. Allie then changed the subject, becoming the first to ask about the house.

"So tell us, what do you think of your new home? You're not going to sell it, are you?"

Chase loved her directness. "We don't know yet. As I told you awhile back, we just want to take a look at it, walk the neighborhood, check out the school, and follow up on some possibilities of working in the area."

"So then you're definitely moving here!" Allie responded excitedly.

"We're considering it. No need to rush such a big thing."

"Hey, why don't we all go over there together tomorrow after work?" Lane suggested.

Chase hesitated. He expected their visit to be more of an adventure and hoped his family could see the place without the influence of others. On the other hand, one of the reasons for a possible move included living near these four. He looked over at Linda. "What do you think, babe?"

"Sure. That'd be great."

Lane quickly responded. "Well there you go! We'll come over around five or so and carpool over."

Later that night Chase told Linda that he guessed it might be a good idea to get this part over with so they could enjoy their vacation as a family. He had the details mapped out: a road trip through Vermont and New Hampshire, over to the coast of Maine, and on to New York City and the Empire State Building. From there they would head to Philadelphia for a couple of days before finishing their excursion in Washington, D.C. Chase had never been to any of these places except for New York City, so his eagerness for adventure matched his family's.

The following day after lunch, the four walked to a few of the areas Chase once frequented. He bought Amy and Ryan candy and sodas at Ted's Market, took them to the park, showed them his elementary school, and pointed out the places he and Frank used to ride their bikes. Linda observed how quiet and peaceful the town appeared and concluded that it must be a safe. The afternoon passed quickly, and they found their way back to Frank and Allie's, with Lane and Kathy just arriving as well.

"Everyone ready?" Lane asked enthusiastically. He didn't wait for a response. "Frank and Allie, you come with us. Chase, I'll follow you."

They all agreed and hopped into their cars for the ten- minute drive. Chase, pleased that everyone would share this newly discovered treasure together, described the house to his family with as much detail as he could remember. He warned Linda about the rank odor in their bedroom and promised to rectify the situation immediately.

Coming up to Washington Street, Chase hesitated at the yellow light and then sped through it, realizing he would have to pull over and wait for his brother. He slammed on his brakes when he saw an old pickup ram Lane's car, spinning it around and sending it fifty feet or so past the other side of the intersection.

"What's the matter?" Linda screamed.

"It's Lane!" Chase shouted, parking by the sidewalk and jumping out of the car. "Keep the kids here!"

As he raced to the scene, Chase's fears intensified when he noticed the front end was nearly separated from the rest of the vehicle, everything a tangled mess. He glanced at the pickup, sprawled on its side. Thinking the worst, his heart pounding, Chase called out, "Lane! Frank! Are you all right?" He came closer to peer inside the dark vehicle and saw his worst nightmare. No one stirred. A small crowd gathered as tears poured down his face. He looked for Lane and Kathy but couldn't see much through the wreckage. Frantically he turned toward the back seat. "Frank? Allie?"

"I think we're okay," he heard Frank say in a shaky voice. "What happened?"

"An accident." His eyes searched toward the front. "Frank, I don't think they made it!" Wiping away the tears so he could see, Chase reached out to touch Lane's body. "Frank, they're not responding!"

"Kathy!" Allie screamed as she reached forward in vain. "Kathy! Say something!"

By that time, Linda had begged someone nearby to watch the children for a moment. Anxiously she pressed through the crowd. Chase saw her, pulled her to himself, and wept in her arms. "I think they're dead, Linda. I think Lane and Kathy are dead."

Within minutes, the police responded to a cell phone call, EMTs right behind them. Chase and Linda watched helplessly as the experts administered first aid. Chase noticed one of them shake his head while examining the bodies. A policeman patiently spoke to the bewildered pickup driver as the ambulance sped away with Frank and Allie. In a daze,

Chase asked another policeman if anything more could be done. Left with no answers and realizing the futility of staying, he and Linda slowly walked arm in arm back to their rental car. Linda insisted on driving.

"I can't believe I ran that yellow light!" Chase loudly moaned, pounding his hand on the dashboard as they sped toward the hospital. "I should've stopped!" He hit the dashboard again.

Linda reached over to touch his shoulder. "Honey, please don't blame yourself. It wasn't your fault. The other driver must have timed his approach just when the light changed, probably going way too fast."

"You kids all right?" he asked through his tears.

"Yes, Daddy," they responded, fearful of saying anything more and not used to seeing their father cry.

Chase stared blankly ahead. Everything felt surreal. In one moment they'd gone from a joyful family excited about the possibilities of the future to one struck by tragedy. Why didn't he stop instead of trying to beat the light? They didn't have any time limit. What was his hurry? *How do you deal with death thrown at you so unexpectedly?* he wondered. *Where do you place it in your plans for tomorrow, or the next day, or even the following year? And what about the uncanny number of deaths in the last few months—Mom, Dad, and now Lane and Kathy? Is it all merely bad luck, coincidence, the hand of God, or fate? Or does any of that matter?*

Chase knew he had to be strong for Linda and the children and maybe for Frank and Allie, who might not be fully aware of what happened. But how could he show strength when he felt responsible for the calamity?

"It's not my fault," Chase whispered to himself, repeating Linda's words. "Of course it's not. I know she's right, but man, I'm not sure I can handle this. I should've stopped," he said aloud to no one in particular.

"Chase, don't do this to yourself," Linda said. "It could've happened to anyone."

"Yeah, but it happened to me, to us, to the whole family."

"I know," she answered tearfully. "We'll get through it somehow. Please don't torture yourself like this."

"I'll try not to."

They parked near the hospital entrance. Chase told Amy and Ryan that he and their mother needed to see their Uncle Frank and Aunt Allie and that they would have to stay in the waiting room. After a few questions at the emergency check-in, Chase and Linda entered a room with four or five curtained partitions. They peeked through each of them, and the last one revealed Frank standing at Allie's bedside.

Chase moved toward them, Linda's arm tucked in his. "Frank! How are you and Allie?"

"Hey, Chase, Linda," he answered, visibly in pain. "I'll be okay. They're running some tests on Allie. What about Lane and Kathy?"

Chase slowly shook his head. Allie burst out sobbing; Linda stepped over to comfort her, stroking her hair, softly crying with her. The brothers embraced, weeping in each other's arms. Minutes passed. Frank spoke first, wiping his nose and holding Chase by the shoulders.

"How, Chase? How can they be dead and we're alive? I don't get it."

"I don't either," he said, running his sleeve underneath his nose. "I guess … I suppose the way the car split in half … I don't know, Frank."

"Well what happened? Felt like a train hit us."

"Lane caught the tail end of the yellow light, and an old truck slammed into you full force."

"A drunk?"

Chase shook his head. "I have no idea. Hey, Allie," he said, stepping closer to the bed, "everything's going to be all right. We're here for you, whatever you need."

Allie held on tightly to Linda's hand without a word, gazing across the room through misty eyes.

After a few more minutes of silence, Chase whispered to his brother that they should take the children home but that if he and Allie were released, they should call him, no matter what the time, and he would pick them up. They embraced again, Frank allowing more tears to flow. Not knowing what else to say, Chase gently patted his back. Linda squeezed Allie's hand and then before leaving reached over to gently touch her foot underneath the blanket. "See you soon, Allie. It'll be okay. We love you."

CHAPTER 20

For the next hour, during the drive home and while putting them to bed, Chase and Linda attempted to detraumatize their children, helping their young minds process the tragedy. Amy and Ryan asked about Uncle Frank and Aunt Allie. Chase and Linda said they would be fine and would probably be home tomorrow.

Ryan wanted to hear stories about Uncle Lane; he thought he was funny. Chase complied, recalling the time he was in the shower at age nine and his brother somehow managed to unlock the bathroom door, remove all of his clothes and the towels, and quietly exit. The next sound Lane heard came from his brother screaming at the top of his lungs for help. The children giggled.

Then one day, Lane convinced Frank that the two of them should take Chase to the woods and desert him. Lane thought this was hysterical, though he never heard the end of it from their mother.

"Tell us more, Daddy!" Ryan cried. After a few more stories, Chase and Linda tucked the children in, leaving the bedroom door open. Chase called the hospital to check on Frank and Allie. They would be staying the night. The doctor would see them in the morning.

He and Linda appreciated the comfort of the sheets and blankets as they crawled into bed. Chase lay quietly for a while, agonizing over the sudden and painful losses, uncertain of their implications. Could there be some malevolent entity in space that held a grudge against him and his family? Was there an infernal plot to destroy those closest to him? Or could there be an inexorable purpose that had evaded his awareness and understanding? He peeked over at Linda, already drifting off, and whispered. "Linda, you still awake?"

"Sort of," she answered groggily.

"I'm sorry, but I've been thinking about how eerie these past few months have been. I just don't get it. Is there a deeper message out there we're supposed to figure out? Could someone—not God of course—could someone or something be against us? Or is it just one of those things?"

"I have no idea. I guess it's just one of those things, tragic as it all is."

"Yeah, that's what I thought." Chase's eyes welled up, and his tears fell onto his pillow. "I can't believe this happened. There was no couple on earth like Lane and Kathy. Outside of you and the kids and Frank and Allie, they were the only family I have. How do you process moments like this?"

Linda turned to see his tears freely flowing. "Hon', I'm sorry." She gently wiped his cheeks. "I just don't know the answers. Horrible events are sometimes impossible to understand."

"So what are we going to do?"

"As far as what?"

"As far as looking at the house and traveling around the East Coast. I can't see us continuing our plans after tonight."

"I agree. I'm actually thinking we need to move here."

"What?" He raised himself on his elbow, brushing away the tears from his eyes. "Really?"

"Frank and Allie are going to need us. They have no one, Chase. I can't imagine going on with our lives and leaving them here alone."

"Well, maybe you're right. I'm not certain what to do at this point."

"Why don't we go see the house and call it our own? Perhaps that'll distract the children enough. Maybe us as well."

"I doubt that, but let's talk about it in the morning. I'm drained." He rolled over to kiss her. "Thanks for being here for me. I need you, Linda."

"That is so good to hear you say, hon'. You really have changed."

"I don't feel all that changed anymore."

"It'll all come back. I understand how you feel, though."

He wondered if she did.

Released the next morning, neither Frank nor Allie suffered injuries of major concern, Frank a few bruises and neck strains, Allie some back pains that would require several months of physical therapy. The family buried Lane and Kathy a few days later in two plots next to Chase's mom, same priest, same message. Lane and Kathy's two boys flew out, but what could anyone say in a situation like this? Chase had no idea. He left it to Allie to find the right words.

Chase showed his family the house. With just a little more than a week left before the return flight, Linda quickly tackled the organizational challenges, deciding where each piece of furniture would go and what they might need to purchase. Amy and Ryan agreed on their rooms. They were a bit smaller than what the children had now, but Linda's creativity allowed them to keep their beds and dressers and all their belongings without having to jettison anything. The elementary school was within walking distance, and the four strolled over one day to speak to an administrator about the school year that would begin in September. Extremely friendly, he welcomed the children to their new school and promised to introduce them to their teachers.

The rest of the details appeared relatively easy: fly home, place their house on the market, sell one of their cars and some unnecessary furnishings, say good-bye to a few friends and coworkers, and pack up their remaining belongings into a large moving truck. Chase would drive the truck back with Linda and the kids following in the BMW.

Chase wanted to explore the possibility of working in New York for the chemical company, an idea he needed to discuss with the owners. He calculated that the family's monthly expenses without a mortgage payment might allow Linda the luxury of not having to work. And should his plans fail to materialize, the equity on their home in Glendora had grown to the point that they would have enough money to live for quite some time.

On the day before their departure to California, Chase told Linda he needed to take a walk. A warm morning sun greeted him as he stepped into the street. He heard the chirping of birds competing for positions on the telephone wire above. Wispy clouds adorned the sky, floating by in the gentle breeze. Kicking a rock to the other side of the street, Chase forced himself to focus on what he had been processing for the last several days.

Perhaps everything was a nightmarish illusion, he thought; perhaps each vision merely his mind's way of coping with stress and anxiety. After all, extreme marital issues precipitated the initial vision, and he couldn't be positive it took place the way he had related it. In fact, the web itself was quite possibly a lie. Though it appeared real, what he saw may have hidden an emotional breakdown of some sort. That must have led to the other experiences, which could certainly be attributed to the identical mental and emotional trouble of his—

Chase stopped himself. What was he thinking? He could not honestly deny the changes taking place in his life. Even others had noticed. His thoughts turn toward Lane. Was that it? Had Lane's tragic death left him conflicted, torn between anger and peace, resentment and satisfaction, confusion and resolution? He didn't know. The event certainly brought nothing new to the table. Or perhaps it did. Could it be that the finality of death exposed a skewed perception of his visions, that it awakened him from an unreal dream and stopped him from chasing after an unattainable mirage? And if so, how could he pretend to move forward based on what might indeed be illusions or, even worse, fraudulent experiences?

On the other hand, maybe his situation mirrored the encouragement he provided to salespeople throughout the country. Surely if he had the ability to shore them up whenever they struggled, he should be able to find a way to fight through his own difficulties.

Chase found himself at the park where two older men sat with a checkerboard between them. He had never played and thought it may be a nice way to distract himself from his thoughts. "You gentlemen mind if I watch awhile?" he asked, approaching.

"Not at all," said the one wearing an old navy hat and a brightly colored jacket. "You play?"

"No. Just curious."

"Well it's easy. Two sides, simple moves, short games."

"No, Harry, it's not that easy," insisted the balding man with glasses sitting across from him. "There happen to be a lot of strategies involved. Why don't you let me teach you, son?"

"No way, Carl. It's better if I teach him. I can make it much more understandable."

"Who wins most of our matches?"

Harry rolled his eyes.

"Listen," Chase interjected, "why don't you just go ahead with your game, and I'll watch. You can both tell me the rules and the strategy as it progresses."

"Sure, okay," Carl said with a condescending look at Harry. "What's your name, son?"

"Chase. Chase Macklin."

The two turned in unison, Carl wearing a deeply furrowed brow. "Macklin, you say? Not Bobby Macklin's son."

"Well, yeah. I'm the youngest. You knew him?"

"Knew him! I'll say we did. Went drinkin' with him in the old days. Never could keep up with him, though. Boy, that guy could drink!"

"I know," Chase responded dryly.

"Whatever happened to your dad?"

"He died a short time ago."

"Oh, that's a shame."

"I'm sorry," Harry added.

"No, that's okay," Chase said, almost cheerfully. "He left his family years ago and we never saw him after that."

"Yeah, we know," Carl said, looking absentmindedly at the board. "He was a nice guy, though, always telling jokes, making everybody laugh."

"He talked a lot about his sons, three if I remember," Harry said to no one in particular, looking up at the sky.

"Yeah, there were three of us." Chase's use of the past tense startled him. "I'm sorry but I need to go," he announced impetuously, starting to walk away.

Carl, face painted with disappointment, pleadingly called out to him, "You don't want to learn the game?"

"Maybe later," he hollered back. "Nice to meet you."

"Well it's been a pleasure meeting a Macklin boy! Hang in there! Your move, Harry."

Chase hurried back to Frank's house, frustrated with his inability to dismiss the anger he felt toward his father and baffled by the enigma of Lane's death. He decided to set aside his feelings and his mental torment for the time being.

CHAPTER 21

I f only he had stopped at the light! Everything would have been different with Lane still alive. No wavering. No doubts regarding his personal resurrection. No taunting thoughts of throwing it all way.

After being home for a few days, Chase sat outside on the patio swing on a warm summer evening, cigar in one hand, beer in the other. Looking up at a full moon, along with a lone star announcing the approach of darkness, he ruminated upon all the events since April and wondered if he were the only one who wrestled with mental conflicts. He felt compelled to return to the night it all began with his vision of the spider web and those first lies exposed. Chase knew that he must deal with his questions about reality, so he started with the lies since they seemed more tangible.

Prior to Lane's death, Chase had understood their progressive nature, how a person like himself, so emotionally vulnerable since childhood, came into agreement with mostly untrue ideas about himself, subtle notions, easy to accept. Once he agreed with those personal assessments, other lies followed, building layer upon layer of self-deception. The behavior this encouraged confirmed what he believed about himself.

Once he came into full agreement with the many layers of lies, he unknowingly entered into a dysfunctional attachment to their power. The lies actually became him. Completely unable to separate himself from them, and lacking the ability to pull his true self away from the lies, Chase was fully enmeshed in a sticky web. Truth, declaring itself in various ways over the years, would simply cause him to tell himself, *Well that may be true, but it's not me.*

Chase now realized that as long as one is trapped in a vicious web of personal lies, truth struggles to unravel them since one's attachment to the lies become so strong. Truth, in fact, becomes foreign to the ears, unable to break through what is familiar and has dominated one's thought life.

Relighting his cigar and sitting back with a few reflective puffs, Chase felt better for acquiring a more realistic view of his recent experiences. He concluded that these events must involve a wickedly intense battle for his soul.

Chase looked out upon the unkempt yard and again thought of Lane. Suddenly deep sobs exploded from within him. Unable to control them, he held his face, tears streaming through his fingers. Tossing his cigar onto the concrete, he allowed himself, perhaps for the first time, to feel the anguish of loss.

"I'm so sorry, Lane," he said half aloud. "I'm so sorry, Kathy. It'll be so good see you again in heaven."

Though uncertain of that reality, he felt right about expressing his desire. Removing his hands from his face, Chase let the tears remain. For some reason he had a sense of serenity for the first time in weeks.

Chase's thoughts returned to his lies when he envisioned an old European castle. *Could it be,* he wondered, *that when you come into agreement with lies, they're like an impregnable fortress over your mind, your emotions, your actions, and your lifestyle? And if that's so, then for truth to enter and to take residence, the fortress must be destroyed.*

"Wow!" he said aloud. Chase reasoned that truth must certainly possess the ability to defeat lies, but he guessed it depended upon what one did with truth, how one received it. Since truth is so often rejected because it is unfamiliar to a lie-filled mind, change apparently must come either from more exposure to the truth or a radical deliverance from the lies, which is what happened to him that night a few months ago on this patio.

These reflections helped Chase understand his continual battle with mental and behavioral patterns of the past and why he sometimes regressed to that old man he swore never again to resemble. He realized that discovering his lies and obtaining initial liberty from them weren't enough; more important he had to continue to reflect the truth about himself in everyday life, overcoming his previous habitual behavior.

This would indeed be a battle, perhaps a lifelong war, and Chase knew he had to fight it not merely in times of relative bliss, such as when he and Linda enjoyed an awakening in their marriage, but through dark and challenging times—marital difficulties, bitterness and unforgiveness, tragedy, and even death.

Mentally exhausted, Chase slowly rose, left his cigar on the ground, and made his way to the bathroom before crawling into bed. He looked over at Linda with a weak smile, knowing that his conclusions allowed him to overcome the daunting temptation to reject his freedom, at least this time.

It took several more weeks to organize everything for the move. They found a buyer for their home. Escrow would close around the middle of August, giving them just enough time to settle in and to prepare the children for the new school year. They considered seeing Doctor Rhinegold once more but decided their marriage and family life were better than ever. Linda felt securer due to Chase's transformation, and Chase no longer viewed Linda's previous relationship as an issue. Their excitement about the move, along with the many preparations, kept them fully occupied.

When the day finally arrived, they asked neighbors to help load the truck. Linda bought a few pizzas and drinks, which they all shared afterward. Chase climbed into the Ryder, while Linda situated the children in the car behind. Hoping they could relax and enjoy the trip, Chase had scheduled a full week of hotel stops and sightseeing along the way.

Frank had to tolerate Allie's impatience for the entire seven days. She wanted to make certain that he hired a landscaper to tidy up Chase and Linda's yard, that he called the children's school to verify their enrollment, that he finished a few of projects in their home, and that he phoned Chase from time to time regarding the family's trip to the East Coast.

Frank complied with all her requests, handing his wife the phone when she wanted to hear more about the details of the Macklins' adventure. Allie shouted with glee when Linda told her about the Grand Canyon, the Rocky Mountains, the Children's Museum in Chicago, and even about Amy and Ryan playing in the pool at each of the hotels.

The Ryder eventually appeared. Chase stepped out both weary and ebullient, Linda and the kids right behind. Not a moment passed before Allie called out, "Hey everyone! Welcome to New York! I picked up some sandwiches at the deli. Are you hungry?"

Chase smiled at her energy and efficiency. "Great to see you too! Let's get this thing unloaded first." They all exchanged hugs and then dove in for the next couple of hours. Several of Frank and Allie's friends were there to assist them, the men happily doing all the heavy work while the ladies unpacked boxes in the kitchen.

"Linda, this is going to be so much fun having you two around!" Allie exclaimed. "I'm so happy we're going to be neighbors! Isn't it all just so amazing how things worked out?"

"Yes, it is! Thanks so much for helping us."

After the truck was emptied and the sandwiches were consumed, Chase and Frank returned the Ryder and then came back to assemble the beds and to arrange the living room furniture under Linda's careful watch.

The Macklins loved settling into their new home and neighborhood during the next few weeks. Even the formerly reclusive Ryan quickly made friends down the street in both directions. Chase wanted to try his hand at rewiring the ancient electrical work and at fixing some of the plumbing, but his ever-cautious brother convinced him otherwise.

Allie had mostly recovered from her injuries. She and Frank shared dinner with Chase and Linda at least two times a week, stories of Lane and Kathy dominating most of their conversations. Though it was soothing to share these tales and to laugh together, they were haunted by memories of the tragedy. It seemed like yesterday; perhaps it always would.

Chase often allowed his tears to flow unreservedly, no longer punishing himself by taking responsibility for the deaths but unable to find freedom from the utter despair of loss. However, he did not desire to be free of grief so soon; Chase somehow felt he would dishonor their memories by turning the page at this point.

On a couple of occasions, Linda explained to Frank and Allie how different Chase had become, pointing to his attitude, to the way he communicated with and treated others, and to his tenderness. One night the conversation grew more intense. The four of them were at Chase and Linda's, and the children had gone to bed at eight. It happened to be Chase's birthday.

"So tell us, Chase," Frank said with a grin, "what does it feel like to finally come into manhood?"

"Oh, thanks a lot!"

They all laughed and raised their glasses for a toast. "Seriously, Chase," Frank continued, attempting not to smile, "have you considered installing an elevator in your house since the stairs may be problem at your age?"

Allie joined in. "Are you going to need any help showering or getting dressed? We could always chip in for a live-in maid!"

"You guys are horribly cruel, especially since you're older than me! I'm only thirty-five. Just wait till you're forty, Frank."

Linda cleared her throat. "So honey, what would you like to accomplish in your next thirty-five years?"

The others chuckled but then realized the serious tone in her voice.

Chase stared at the ceiling as he considered the question. "I think that I simply want to enjoy the moment, and by that I mean allowing myself to live within time rather than becoming a mere observer of it."

"You're getting deep," Frank said, looking at the others for support.

"Maybe so, but I've had a lot of time to think about things these past few months."

"When?" Linda asked with a mischievous grin.

Chase rolled his eyes. "Well, despite the fact that we've been incredibly busy since the move, everything feels new, more peaceable, and time seems much more manageable, maybe not because of the area but more due to the things I've undergone this year. You guys know what's happened to me. If I do live for another thirty-five years, I want to be able to look back and to know that I overcame what previously kept me from who I was meant to be, rejecting the lies I had so long believed, and that I lived my remaining years according to the truth of who I am."

The others sat in silence for a moment, so he asked them, "Does this make any sense to you guys?"

Allie spoke up. "Sure it does! We all could use some positive change, but not everyone will experience what you did."

"I've thought about that too. And though I agree with you, I'm convinced everyone lives with lies that need to be exposed and destroyed. They may or may not be similar to my own, but they nevertheless exist."

"What would you say is your biggest?" Allie wanted to know. "That is, if you don't mind telling us."

"Not at all. My abandonment issue is near the top since I think it opened the door for other lies to enter. I was certainly plagued with them prior to Dad leaving, but I'm sure that event solidified what already existed."

"What do you think is one of mine?" Frank asked meekly.

Chase thought for a second. "Probably that you're smarter than me!" he answered with a loud laugh. "Got you back!"

"Okay, okay, but seriously now."

"Seriously?" Chase fidgeted. "I don't know, maybe fear of rejection."

"Why would you say that?" Frank asked with a puzzled frown.

"Just a hunch. Lane and I—" Chase suddenly stopped, chest heaving in and out. Taking a deep breath, he continued. "Sorry about that. Guess I still have a hard time mentioning his name."

"We totally understand," Allie said with a sniffle.

"Anyway, Frank, the two of us got most of the attention, he the jovial one, me always in trouble. Could it be that you felt left out and a bit rejected, which in turn maybe led you to believe a lie that you're not very, um, valued or accepted?"

"Never thought about it."

"Well I don't want this to turn into some sort of a therapy session, but I do believe it's healthy to consider the possibilities. We shouldn't ignore what may help free people from false perceptions of themselves, thoughts that more than likely affect their behavior."

"Okay, doc, we got it!" Frank said, hoping he spoke for the rest. "Everyone want a refill?"

"I want to hear more!" Allie said eagerly, holding up her glass.

Chase shrugged. "I don't know what else to say. Thanks, Frank."

Allie sat forward. "Well what about abandonment? You're saying that came from your dad's choice to disappear?"

"Absolutely," said Chase without hesitation.

Allie dropped her head. "I think my problem is feeling rejected by God."

Chase shifted uncomfortably on the sofa. "What do you mean?"

"I've never been able to have children. Even talking about it after all these years is difficult. It's just that … well everyone else I know has children, so why not me? What did I do to deserve this? It seems like punishment or something."

"By God?"

"Yes."

"I wouldn't have a clue. What do you think, Linda?"

"Oh, thanks," she said, rolling her eyes at Chase and twirling her curls. "Well, Allie, if God is who I think he is, he wouldn't sit up there in heaven and choose this person to have children and that person not to have them. So I guess what Chase is suggesting is that maybe you've bought into some sort of lie, not just about God but about your own feelings of unworthiness."

Tears suddenly streamed down Allie's face. Frank set his glass down and put his arm around her, wiping a few from her chin. "Don't cry, Allie.

You're not unworthy. You didn't do anything to deserve this." He looked toward this brother for help.

Chase cleared his throat. "Listen, Allie. This may be the beginning of something good for you. For me, revealing a lie became the starting place toward becoming free of it. Now I'm not an expert by any means, but perhaps you can explore feelings of unworthiness and shame, and if you discover these are the lies afflicting you, see if you can embrace the truth about yourself. It will typically be the opposite of what you've believed. This may not be easy, but I know it'll be worth it."

"Thank you," Allie managed to say in between sobs. She then held out her glass with a forced smile. "Happy birthday."

CHAPTER 22

C hase found work after a couple of months. The owners of the chemical company finally decided to employ him at a distance to supervise their national sales force. Even better, a manufacturing company out of Syracuse, expanding throughout the country, needed someone to coordinate marketing and sales nationwide. He would need to commute to the corporate office every Monday but could work the rest of the week out of his home via the Internet and telephone, ideal in that Linda would be able to assist him. Juggling two similar positions proved challenging, but he loved it.

On one of those Mondays, around six at night before Chase came home, Linda prepared for Tuesday's workload. An email with an unfamiliar address caught her attention. Out of curiosity she opened it, gasping when she realized its source. Her heart raced as she read it.

Dear Linda,

It's been about six months since you put an end to our beautiful relationship. I know you asked me not to contact you again, but I became concerned when I drove out to Glendora this morning, found your home, and discovered that your family wasn't living there any longer. The neighbors told me you moved to upstate New York. What was that all about? I don't want to have to track you down, so just let me know that you're okay. You can use my new email address.

Your good friend,
Stan

P.S. Just to let you know, I still have my same cell phone number.

Linda closed the email, trembling and confused. She reopened it, fingering her curls, staring blankly at its words. How would she deal with this? Should she respond? Dare she inform Chase? What about a phone call to Doctor Rhinegold? She took a deep, slow breath, feeling alone, isolated, and helpless. Her tears fell softly onto her hands, frozen on the keyboard. It wasn't her fault, she assured herself. But then why the shame? Why continued secrecy? Why—?

"Hey Linda, I'm home!" Chase called out, bursting through the front door. Linda quickly hit the delete button, emptied her email trash, used a nearby Kleenex to fix her mascara, and stepped out of their home office.

"Hi, honey," she managed to say as cheerfully as possible. "How was your day?"

"Well I'm going to need some help since corporate wants to open up a distributorship in California. Great news but a lot of work. Hey, what's wrong?"

"What do you mean?

"You've been crying."

Linda bit her lip. "Well … yeah. I just received an email from you know who."

"What? No way."

"I'm sorry. I thought this thing was totally over. There's been no contact all these months, but I guess he changed his email and sneaked one through on me."

"Can I see it?"

"I already deleted it. I wasn't even sure about telling you."

Chase reached out to embrace her, caressing her back with both hands. "I'm glad you did, really glad you did. Listen, you don't have to respond to this Stan guy." He said his name with disgust. "Just ignore the jerk. He's not worth it."

"Thank you, hon'," Linda said with a huge sigh, giving him a kiss. "Thank you so much for understanding."

Chase didn't feel all that understanding. He knew that this was not a game, that a predator, a tormenter, a destroyer still lurked and that there was only one way to deal with such a person. Without emotion, resolute in his decision, Chase said, "Give him a call and hand me the phone."

"What?"

"I'm going to talk to him."

"Chase, don't do this to yourself; it's over."

"That's what you keep telling me, but obviously it's not. Let's put an end to it once and for all."

"Really? You really want to talk to him? What will you say?"

"I don't know. Just get him on the phone."

Linda slowly punched in the numbers and handed Chase the phone with incredulity.

"Linda? Is that you?"

"No, it's her husband."

"Oh. Where's Linda?"

"That doesn't matter. Listen, dude, you've been stalking my wife for months. This is it. You're done. No more contact. Understand?"

"Coming from you? No. I'd like to hear it from her own lips."

"You already have, moron! Your charade is over! I'm telling you right now—"

"I love her."

The words struck Chase full force in the abdomen. Struggling to maintain his composure, he held the phone away from his ear, trying to formulate a response. Instead, he hit "End" and threw the phone on the sofa.

"What an idiot! That guy's a complete jerk. And by the way," Chase added angrily, "change your cell number. I've told you that before."

"I will," Linda answered meekly. "And Chase, thank you."

"You're welcome."

He stormed up the stairs, still shaking from the confrontation. She stared at her phone, stupefied, and shook her head, wondering.

CHAPTER 23

Linda thoroughly enjoyed working at home with Chase, sharing her experience in marketing and completing most of the necessary organizational tasks that Chase would have neglected. However, the next few days proved rather tense, Chase avoiding eye contact and Linda feeling insecure and needing comfort. He even returned to an old habit of staying up late to watch a Lakers game so that she would be fast asleep before he retired upstairs.

"Are we ever going to resolve this issue?" she wearily asked one night after dinner.

"It's up to you."

"Chase, I don't want to fight any longer. It doesn't even feel like a fight. You did the right thing in calling him, and now it's over. Why can't we simply move past it all?

"I already have."

"So why are you punishing me with your silence?"

"I don't know. I'm not certain what to believe any longer."

"You don't trust me?"

He wanted to. He knew he needed to, particularly since his inability to trust had been identified as one of his lifelong lies. "I trust you, Linda, just not him. Can you give me more time to process it all?"

"Why don't we process it together?" she pleaded. "After all, I am involved in the situation."

"I'm aware of that. Listen, why don't we simply forget the whole thing until … unless he contacts you again. I can bury the issue. Let's move on from here and consider it resolved."

"That's fine with me," she agreed with a sigh. "That's all I can ask for." At least she felt that way at the moment.

"Okay then." Chase pecked her on the cheek and helped her with the dishes.

**

Amy and Ryan loved the arrival of winter, which gave them their first experience with snowballs, their father becoming the victim of his own instructions of how to make and throw them. One Saturday afternoon in December, Frank came over shivering from the cold with an invitation in hand.

"Hey Chase, you remember Danny Eister?"

"Sure."

"Well he's getting married next month and sent out an invite. Thought you and Linda might want to come. I'll give him a call if you do."

"Is this his first marriage after all these years?"

"No, actually it's his third!"

"Wow! That's crazy. When is it?"

"January 20. You guys wanna go?"

"Sure. That'd be great. Hey, why don't you join me for a cigar? I was just about to head outside."

"Come on, Chase, you know I don't smoke anymore. Haven't for years."

"Oh, it's no big deal, just a cigar. I've got the perfect one for a beginner." Without waiting for a response, Chase hurried to his office and pulled out a couple of Dominicans, Frank following reluctantly behind. "Here you go," he said with a grin, handing his brother one with a lighter wrapper than the Maduros he preferred. "Let's go out back and talk. I'll grab a jacket first. You want a beer?"

"Wait, Chase," Frank said as he stared at the foreign object in his hand. "I don't need to do this. Really."

"Just try it. You want a beer or not?"

"Sure. Fine."

Chase cleared snow from one of the old benches and wiped his hand clean on his pants before they sat down. Clouds shadowed the fountain behind them, the sun peeking through just enough to create an illusion of large white spots on the otherwise gray work of art. Chase cut both cigars, handing one to his brother and instructing him how to keep it lit. After taking a few puffs and watching coils of gray smoke rising against the stark white background, Frank said he liked it—a little.

"So what do think about Bush being our new president?" Chase asked nonchalantly, pulling the collar of his jacket more tightly around his neck.

Frank frowned. "You want to talk politics?"

"Well, not really. Just wondered what you thought."

"I voted for Gore, so I don't know. Hopefully he'll be good. What about you?"

"I've never voted in my life, but I think Bush may be all right."

They sat in silence for a few minutes, watching the smoke billow away in the chilly breeze. This was the first time the brothers had shared a cigar together, and Chase enjoyed the experience immensely. He hoped Allie wouldn't be too terribly mad at him. "How are you and Allie doing," he finally asked, "I mean, as far as considering the possibility of your own lies?"

"You mean the ones we talked about at your birthday?"

"Yeah."

"Oh, I don't know. Allie still has a hard time understanding why she's unable to have children. We don't talk about it much. Thought about adoption years ago, but she never wanted to do that."

"What about you?"

"Oh, I thought adopting a child might help, but—"

"No, I mean about the rejection issue."

"I don't know, Chase. I really don't think it's all that big of a deal. That was a long time ago. I'd rather not even go there."

"No, I understand. I'm not trying to dig up past hurts. It's just that I've discovered the freedom that's possible after dealing with issues that've been covered up by lies about ourselves. But hey, if you feel you're okay, that's great."

"Well wait a minute." Frank hesitated and took another puff. "It's not that I feel okay and everything's fine. I mean, you're probably right about me feeling rejected by Dad, but I think it goes deeper than that. I totally resent him for what he did to all of us, particularly to Mom. I can't just forgive and forget."

"Hey, I know, and believe me, I can relate. But what good has it done us to leave it at that? Mom and Dad are gone but we live on. It's not as if we can punish Dad with our anger and resentment. I'm realizing that we're punishing ourselves if we continue down that road."

"Like it's doing something to us instead of him. Sounds pretty obvious," Frank said, "especially now that he's dead."

"Right. And it not only affects us but those around us. If I remain resentful toward Dad, that decision, along with the rejection and abandonment issues I held on to, will continue to influence my behavior toward others. At least that's what I think."

"Well it definitely sounds like you're on to something here."

"How's your cigar, by the way?"

"Fine. I don't think I can handle much more, though."

"You don't have to. No problem." Chase tapped off about a half-inch of his own ash and continued. "So anyway, you and I were teenagers when everything happened, and now we're adults. This issue with Dad is just one of the many lies that've trapped us for far too long. I don't know about you, but I'd like to become free of every lie if that's possible. I know it'll allow my perception of others to change, which will then cause me to treat them in a healthier fashion, I mean as far as expectations and such. Do you see where I'm going with this?"

"Sure, but what exactly do you think the lie is?"

"Good question. I would think that it started with the belief that Dad should have not done what he did."

"He shouldn't have!" Frank insisted.

"I agree, but that's the tricky thing about lies. Sure he shouldn't have left us, but we're not responsible for his actions, just for our own. I'm thinking that as long as we hold on to something like injustice, it only increases the power of the web around ourselves. It has no effect on the other person."

"I can see that, but I don't understand how my reaction to Dad's behavior is some sort of a lie that I believed."

"Well how about this? You may believe the lie that you could've done something about Dad's departure, or that you were somehow responsible, or that your anger and resentment are justified punishment for him. I'm suggesting that becoming free of the lie is a much better way to go."

Frank wore an enigmatic expression. "So you're saying I need to forgive him?"

"I wouldn't know. I'm not a therapist. I'm just saying, based on my recent experiences, that the way we live our lives and treat others is directly related to the lies we've accepted as truth. And in this case, the truth is that Dad chose his own path. There's nothing we could've done to change that, so we simply have to let it go and live our lives. You want to keep Dad bound in chains, but they have instead bound you."

Frank thought for a moment. "Okay, Chase, maybe you're right, but it's a bit too much to process right now."

"You'd rather talk politics?"

"Not really!"

Several days later, Chase crafted a letter to Amy and Ryan on a single sheet of paper. He then scribbled on the outside of an envelope a message saying they should read it after his death. He and Linda had already set up an official trust, but he felt it necessary, even if he lived for another fifty years, to have something in writing that explained his recent experiences, personal reflections from a loving father.

Dear Amy and Ryan,

At I write these words, you are much too young to grasp what I want to tell you, but by the time you read this, you will be mature enough to understand. I lived a good life, loved your mother with all my heart, and treasured both of you beyond words. You will have certainly heard me relate the story about the spider web of lies I was freed from and how my life was never again the same. I will have told you about the hand I saw and the voice I heard, which some have concluded were the hand and the voice of God. I am not certain of this, nor perhaps are they.

Since this will be my final communication with you, though written when you were young, please consider my advice very seriously. Without a doubt, you too have lies that have bound you, keeping you from becoming who you should be. Most often these lies are based on fear, but they can also be based on such things as pride, insecurity, and anger. If it was really God who rescued me from myself, then seek him out so you can live free of self-deception. If I was simply getting in tune with what already resided within me, then seek what is within you.

As you can see, I don't know for sure how things happened to me, but I do know, as clearly as I know anything, what it was that occurred. The *what* will be one the greatest things you will ever find, because your lies will have been exposed and you will discover liberty from harmful attitudes and destructive behavior. If you learn the *how*, meaning that the source of your rescue is something within you or God himself, and you conclude this is important to the process, then you will have come even further than I did.

My greatest hope is that you will find freedom from lies about yourself that you've accepted, became attached to, and then have allowed to dictate your behavior. I remember hearing once that the truth will set you free. Well it did for me, and that is my deepest longing for you.

I love you both dearly,
Dad

Chase read the letter carefully once more before folding it, placing it in the envelope, glancing at his instructions on the envelope, and sealing it. Walking across the bedroom, he pulled out of his desk a small box of important documents and placed the envelope inside.

CHAPTER 24

"Chase, you look so nice!" Linda marveled.

"Well it is a wedding we're going to. And look at you! You're beautiful!"

"All I really care about is staying warm."

"Good luck!"

"Thanks a lot."

Danny Eister scheduled his wedding for four o'clock. Known as the Protestant kid down the block from the Macklins, he was two years older than Chase and just a year younger than Frank. They played together growing up but lost contact after high school when Frank entered college and Chase immersed himself in life under Murphy. Frank reconnected several years later, he and Allie attending both of Danny's previous weddings. He assured everyone that this one would be his last.

On the way, Chase peeked at Linda. "You know what, babe? I just realized I've never been to a wedding like this before, just Catholic ones. I hope nothing's weird."

"At a wedding?" she said with a giggle. "What do you think they might do there?"

"Well you don't have to laugh at me! I don't know. It won't be the same, no priest or anything.

"As if you really care about that type of thing. Come on. Let's just have a good time."

When they entered the church parking lot, Chase noticed how small and nondescript the building appeared; it was nothing like the ornate Catholic churches. He couldn't figure out why someone would choose such a place for a wedding. Nothing much to it. Finding a space close to where Frank parked, he went around to open Linda's door.

"Chase, it's freezing!" She huddled next to him, teeth chattering. "I just, just can't get used to this weather."

He laughed loudly. "I agree, but that's life on the East Coast! It's not all that bad, but hey, you should be quite warm underneath all those layers!"

"Yeah, sure."

The church's interior surprised him: dark wooden pews with the sun peeking through stained-glass windows on the left side of the building. The carefully maintained wood floors were accented with rich, golden-brown carpet. At the altar, set off with an ornate, stained-wood railing, the carpet climbed up a step onto the stage before disappearing behind a pure white curtain with a golden sash. *This place was probably built in the 1940s,* Chase mused. Though much different from the church his family rarely attended, it felt comfortable in a way.

A man in a tuxedo escorted Chase and Linda to the third row on the right, and Frank motioned for them to sit next to him and Allie. The two were no sooner seated when Danny and the minister headed down the aisle toward the front. Frank leaned over Allie and whispered. "Chase, you're late! You almost missed it!"

"Yeah, I know," he whispered back. "Linda and I were—oh man, don't look behind you. On the other—Frank, don't look! Murphy is on the other side of the aisle. I can't believe it."

Frank's brow furrowed. "Murphy? What in world is he doing here? Are you sure?" Frank sat back and slowly turned to look out of the corner of his eye. He saw enough to verify that Chase was right.

Pleased that the wedding lasted only about twenty minutes, Chase took Linda's hand after the ceremony and followed the group out of the church. Murphy limped beyond the five or six people in front of them. Walking down the steps to the parking lot, Chase called out, "Hey! Murphy!"

"Hey what?" Murphy spun around as he spoke. "Oh, Mack, it's you. Saw ya inside. Figured I'd see ya at the reception. How ya doin', kid?"

"Fine. This is my wife, Linda."

"Nice to meet ya."

"Well it's nice to meet you," she said, holding out her gloved hand. "Chase has told me so much about you."

Murphy let out a guffaw. "That can't be good!"

"No, it is! Especially your generosity with the house."

"Naw, that was no big deal. Didn't like it no more. Too cold in there. My old bones prefer the Florida heat—speakin' of which, I need to get outta here. See ya at the reception." He turned and stepped into his car without another word.

Most of the guests were already seated at the veterans hall when Chase and Linda arrived. They found Frank and Allie at a table by themselves. Linda joined them while Chase headed over to the drink table where Murphy stood by himself.

"So what brings you here, Murphy?"

"Oh, I'm an old friend of the bride's parents. Nice folks. Wouldn't miss it for the world."

"How've you been?"

"Not too good, Mack. Gettin' old, ya know."

"I noticed something's wrong with your leg. What happened?"

"What happened? Nothin'! Just gettin' old," he repeated.

"Well I'm glad you're here. I've wanted to talk with you about all the things I've been through over the years, particularly this year, but I didn't think it'd ever happen. Would you like to grab a table?"

"Sure. Lemme get another drink first."

Chase spied a place where they could be alone. He began his story back in 1987, recounting how he flew out to California to start a new life. He told Murphy about finding work, about slipping up the day he smoked pot, about his first marriage, and about meeting and marrying Linda. Murphy seemed genuinely interested, peppering him with questions. Chase felt he might be ready to hear about the spider web. He observed Murphy's intensity increase as he shared the story.

"A huge web, ya say?"

"Yeah, with me in it."

"Interesting."

Chase told of hearing his own voice speaking to him and asked Murphy what he thought about that.

Murphy took a long swig from his glass, shaking his head. "Don't have a clue, Mack. Sounds a bit crazy to me."

"Me too, but my life has never been the same since that day."

"Good for you," Murphy responded with sudden indifference.

Chase pretended he didn't notice and pressed forward, recounting the exposure of the lies about himself and how he visited his father's grave.

"Ya never did like your dad."

"Oh, I know. But everything's different now."

"Okay, fine. So why ya tellin' me all a this?"

"Well, it's just that I think that, um, we all struggle with lies about ourselves and others. But the thing is, I've found out that a person doesn't have to continue down that road. There's real freedom to be discovered, freedom from yourself and from who you've always thought you were."

"So you're sayin' I got some lies!" Murphy snapped. "You're tryin' to change an old man? Is that what you're doin'?"

Chase pulled back defensively. He envisioned Aunt Betty talking to him about God. Had he come full circle and begun pushing his own route to deliverance upon others?

"No, not at all, Murphy. I'm sorry if I came across that way. I just wanted you to hear what I've been through. You can take it or leave it. No big deal."

"Well it's obviously a big deal ta you! Anyhow, thanks a lot for tellin' me. How are your kids?"

"Great! They love it here, especially the snow."

"They like the house?"

"Yeah, they really do."

"Good. Well I'm gonna get another drink. Ya better get back to your wife."

"Okay, Murphy. Take care of yourself."

"Always do."

"How did that go?" Linda asked as Chase slumped down by the three of them.

"Okay, I guess. I just shared with him what's happened with me over the years."

"That's it?"

"Pretty much."

"You seem a bit, I don't know, unsettled."

"Well, he is a rather exhausting man to communicate with."

"How's that?"

"I'm too tired to tell you!" Chase answered with a smirk.

Chase had a little too much to drink at the reception, and after putting the children to bed that night, he immediately fell asleep. He dreamed he was strolling down a sidewalk with some old friends, guys he recognized from his past, laughing at a few crude jokes. A man wearing a red bandana walked up to them, his tattered clothes and foul odor indicating a life on the streets. He struck up a conversation, most of it senseless chatter. Suddenly the man pulled out a knife. Chase's friends quickly deserted him. The man then lunged at Chase, stabbing him in the side. Blood spurted out, and the man attacked him again. Chase swung back, fists desperately pounding the air. He hurried to a nearby car, the man in pursuit. Chase climbed inside, bloodying the steering wheel as he sped away.

Chase found himself on futuristic-looking roads, similar to those in a video game, lights and colors streaming all around him as he pushed harder on the accelerator. When he saw police cars in pursuit with sirens blaring, Chase made a sharp turn into a tunnel. It was barricaded. He slammed on the breaks, jumped out, and spied a door in the tunnel that led to a stairway. Chase stopped cold when he saw the cops climbing the stairs toward him. Their faces were disfigured, and they had the bulbous eyes of aliens. Another door appeared in the stairwell. He opened it and entered but didn't close it. One of the aliens looked in and gave him an impish grin before shutting the door. Chase heard it lock.

He stood outside on a balcony, alone and with no way of escape. Chase became aware he was having a nightmare from which he needed to awake. Figuring a dangerous jump would surely rouse him, he climbed upon the balcony railing but hesitated for a moment, seeing absolutely nothing through the darkness. With no further thought, he jumped backward. The fall and his accompanying screams startled him. He awoke and found himself in a bed, familiar yet unfamiliar.

Chase rubbed his eyes and exited the room, recognizing that he was merely in another dream. He stood in the middle of a cocktail party in someone's living room. Everyone there was extremely friendly and talkative. A woman walked over and offered to show him around. He asked her how he could get back home. Chase abruptly awoke, this time in his own bed next to his wife. He lay there for a moment, forehead perspiring, and then checked to see if his screaming had disturbed Linda. Her heavy breathing provided the answer.

The following morning, he related his dream over coffee while the children watched cartoons.

Linda fingered her curls, frowning. "So you had a dream within a dream?"

"Yeah. Ever heard of such a thing?"

"No, never. I wonder what it means."

"All I can think of is that the dream represents the decision I made when I first left New York, at least the first part when my friends deserted me and I was stabbed and then chased. Maybe jumping into another dream has to do with going west in my attempt to discover a new direction."

"Well that makes sense, a dream about your life."

"Yeah, that's kind of what I'm thinking."

"But you did say you asked the woman how to get home."

"Right, and perhaps that home represents finding the real me."

"That's nice," Linda said with a smile. "Welcome home then!"

"Yeah, good thought."

CHAPTER 25

As the months went by, Chase planned his family's delayed summer vacation. Amy, just finishing the third grade, showed incredible eagerness to see more of the country after learning the basics of American history and memorizing all fifty states and their capitals. She wanted to see Augusta, Providence, and Columbia. Chase said that South Carolina was a bit too far at this point but that they'd see as many cities as possible.

One night, several days before setting out for Maine to start their trip, Chase dreamed again. For whatever reason, he and Linda were supposed to sleep in a room without a bed, merely a mattress on the floor. Entering the room, Chase found just enough space to squeeze in between Linda and an old man who apparently came in before he did. After a few minutes, the old man jabbed him in the back, yelling at him to move over. Chase turned in anger, stood up, and told him to get out. He then calmed himself, patiently took the man by the hand, and led him out of the room, assuring him there would be another place to sleep. He found one, pulled out a sleeping bag, and left the room.

Chase awoke with the dream still fresh on his mind. He visited the bathroom, returned to bed, and had still another dream. Driving his car around an unfamiliar neighborhood, he saw Ryan as a teenager pulling up beside him. He asked his son if he knew the way out. Ryan confidently replied that he did and told his father to follow. Chase's car stalled as Ryan raced away. He roamed the neighborhood in search of his son for what seemed like an eternity. Filled with frustration, he finally reached his destination. Ryan said he had been waiting there for thirty minutes and wanted to know what had taken him so long.

When Chase rose the next morning, he mentioned both dreams to Linda, who shook her head in wonderment. "I can't believe you have so many dreams and remember them all!"

"Yeah, it's weird. They've all come in such a short time, but they aren't just any old dreams. These seem to be begging for meaning. I'm sure the first has to do with our intimacy as a couple, that something or someone is trying to rob us of it. Do you know who the old man is?

"I've no idea."

"Babe, it's me! Remember the doppelganger vision?"

"Of course."

"Well don't you get it? The doppelganger guy is the old guy in this dream! That old man is my old self! You know, of course, that prior to my spider experience we weren't all that intimate, particularly in the areas of communication and vulnerability."

Linda nodded, hand to her hair.

"So I think the old me was trying to tell the new me to move over. After my initial anger, I escorted him out of the room, which may mirror the point in the doppelganger vision when I vowed never to be like that person again."

"Wow, Chase, that's amazing! I think you may be right."

"Well it certainly makes me realize even more how this whole thing is a battle."

"What do you mean?" Linda asked, taking his hand.

"The first recognition of lies led me down a path of liberty that you and I both know is real. But I still have to fight with myself whenever old tendencies and behavioral patterns raise their ugly heads. Most of the time it's easy to be the new me since it feels so right, like being more open and vulnerable, touching you more often, dealing with abandonment issues—all that stuff. Other times it's hard, and I have to force myself to do things against my will or to break with what was familiar. I don't know. Maybe it's normal."

"Well I'm with you, hon'. I've seen the real you, and I don't ever want you to go back to the old guy. He's definitely not as much fun!" she said with a wink. "Would you like another cup of coffee?"

"Sure. Thanks."

Linda went to the kitchen, returning with two full cups. "And what about the other dream?" she asked. "What do you think that one means?"

"It puzzles me. Any thoughts?"

"I'm not quite sure. Could you tell it to me again?"

Chase began with Ryan, probably sixteen or seventeen, pulling up beside him in a car.

"So it's in the future," Linda said.

"I guess so. I don't know! You're the interpreter of this one," he said with a smile.

"Okay, go on."

When Chase finished with Ryan saying he had been waiting for thirty minutes, Linda's eyebrows rose. "What about this? What if it has to do with Ryan being able to figure things out faster and better than you?"

Chase rolled his eyes. "Oh, great!"

"Well, honey, you do have a lot to teach him. If there is some sort of truth in all of this, maybe you're going to help him avoid some of the things you went through, and maybe he'll end up being a quick learner."

"That sounds better." Chase scratched his head. "But I'm not sure where we were going. Both of us apparently knew the destination, but I was uncertain how to get there."

"Well we have around ten years to find out!"

"Yeah, right."

Linda said almost in a whisper, "Hey, hon', maybe you should call Doctor Rhinegold to see if your dreams are all somehow connected."

"Why?" he asked with a wrinkled brow.

"Well, it's just that dreaming so much seems rather odd to me, and you and I don't know about these things. Maybe he does."

"I'll give it some thought."

Linda moved closer. "One more thing. What do you think about taking the children to church?"

"What are you talking about?" Chase asked in a caustic tone.

"Taking them to church. That's what I mean," she retorted just as firmly.

"What brought this on?"

"Ever since we saw your Aunt Betty I've been—"

"Great. She really did get to you."

"No, she didn't, just the part about raising our children with some help in the area of religion and morality, something like that."

"Catholic or Protestant?"

"You mean which kind of church?"

"Yeah."

"Whatever you want."

Chase walked toward the kitchen. "Hey, if you want to take our kids to church, knock yourself out, but you won't find me going with you. And besides," he called out, "what makes you think they'd even want to go?"

"I think they'll have a good time getting to know other children!" she shouted back. "Chase, I don't understand why you're so stubborn in this one area. Maybe it's another lie."

Chase felt his anger rising, and he strode back into the living room. "No, don't go there, Linda! Don't start lecturing me about lies! It's not like everything is a lie!"

"I'm sorry. I shouldn't have said that. I just can't comprehend what you've got against taking our children to church. It's not going to hurt them, you know."

"Yeah, but if it means me going, then I'm not interested. You go ahead. See what it's like."

"Okay, fine."

"Good."

CHAPTER 26

Murphy died on August 31. Chase had a peculiar habit of reading obituaries in the local paper. He felt a bit more educated learning about those in town with rich life experiences. And, he had recently thought with a chuckle, this tied in rather nicely with his attraction to cemeteries. On Sunday, September 2, he abruptly stopped, mouth agape, placed his coffee cup on the table, and stared at the headline: "William R. Murphy, 1932–2001." Though no picture accompanied the obituary, Chase knew it to be his old boss. Born in Brooklyn. Moved to town in 1960. Business owner. No surviving relatives. To be cremated in Fort Lauderdale, Florida. No services planned.

"Linda!" he shouted from the living room toward the kitchen. "Linda, come here a second!"

"Sure. What is it?" she asked, concerned at the tone of his voice.

"Look here! Murphy died!"

She studied the obituary in silence and then noticed her husband's morose posture. "You okay?"

"Well, yeah, I guess so," he answered with a shrug. "It's just strange, don't you think?"

"What do you mean?"

"It seems like the end of a depressing chapter, the official end of an era in some way. Not that it hasn't been dead for years, but Murphy was the last connection to it."

"How does that make you feel?"

"It doesn't affect me one way or the other. Just kind of sad, I suppose."

"Hon', it says here that he had no surviving relatives. Did you know that?"

"Oh yeah, sure. That's the other unfortunate part."

"Well at least you were able to speak with him at the wedding."

"Yeah. That's a good thought."

Chase spent the next week buried in work, thinking often of Murphy and of the old days, noticing again how death seemed to magnify a person's accomplishments, though he knew full well that his old boss's wallet was fattened by other people's drug habits. He did own a couple of businesses in town; however, he told Chase long ago that they produced minimal returns. His was a lonely life with a lonely ending.

A few days later, Chase's world was rocked again. Frank called him about five minutes before nine in the morning.

"Chase! Do you have the TV on?"

"No. Why?"

"Turn it on! The World Trade Center just got hit by a plane!"

"What?"

"Turn on the news! I've gotta get back!"

Chase hurried to the television, shouting for Linda to come to the living room. They watched the World Trade Center in flames. Then, just a few minutes after nine, another plane crashed into the South Tower. Newsmen frantically attempted to make sense of how commercial planes could be used in a possible terrorist attack. Linda wept. Chase comforted her. He held her close and stroked her hair but couldn't think of any meaningful words to say. Mesmerized, they kept their eyes focused on the screen in horror and numbed shock, completely confused, seeking answers to their unspoken questions.

Frank called again. "Chase, are you watching all this?"

"Yeah. It's unbelievable! What do you think's going on?"

"I don't know. Some sort of an attack it looks like."

"Terrorists?"

"Sure seems that way. They're saying another plane is out there as well."

"Yeah, I know."

"Hey Chase, this is serious stuff. You guys want to come over? I'm going to take the day off to be with Allie."

"I need to check on Amy and Ryan first. I'll let you know."

He called the school, and the secretary told him all the children were in the cafeteria, waiting for their parents to pick them up. Chase and Linda jumped into the car and raced over.

Their kids had seen the news and wanted to learn more after climbing into the back seat. Chase said that they didn't know much at this point, that it was just some sort an attack in New York City. Amy began to cry when she noticed her father's panicked face. Ryan followed. Reaching back to comfort them, Linda said, "There's nothing to worry about. Everything will be all right." She hoped that was true.

Chase and the family burst into Frank's house without knocking and found him and Allie huddled on the sofa, staring at the television. They joined them, Linda holding Amy and Ryan tightly. With live coverage of the Pentagon in flames, Linda decided to take the children home to protect them from the horrific images.

"Okay," Chase agreed. "I'll stay here until we get a better idea of what's going on."

Fifteen minutes later, the South Tower collapsed, followed shortly by the crash of Flight 93 in Pennsylvania. The news anchorman spoke of possibly ten thousand dead in the attacks. Though the numbers decreased as reports came in, the three of them remained troubled and anxious.

"This is terrible," said Allie, staring straight ahead. "These are innocent people, going to work. How could anyone do such a thing?"

"Well I'm sure they're terrorists," Chase said, "and they hate us. Innocence means nothing to them. They'd love to take out as many of us as possible."

"But what did we do to deserve this?" she asked, shaking her head.

"Nothing. I've heard that they call us the Great Satan, which I guess means we all deserve to die, at least in their minds." Chase looked over at Frank. "What do you think we're going to do?"

"You mean the US?"

"Yeah."

"I've never been for war, but this time I hope we bomb 'em all."

"Where would we start?"

"Who knows?"

An hour later, Frank dropped Chase off at his house. Linda had the radio on to stay informed while distracting Amy and Ryan with on old Disney movie. She jumped up from the sofa when her husband came through the front door, immediately wrapping her arms around his waist. Chase quietly filled her in on what he had seen, and the two sat hand in hand, listening for new reports as they absentmindedly watched the movie.

Later that night, Chase retreated to the living room to reflect upon the day's significance. Could it be that the nation had believed a lie about itself? Maybe a lie about its invincibility? And if so, could the nation reject such a lie and change its way of doing things? He wasn't sure, maybe even about the lie. But he did know that this event underscored the need to remain vigilant, ever aware of the power of his own personal lies, perhaps exposed and broken, but still awaiting opportunities to reassert themselves if he assumed total freedom from them. Chase felt strong in the knowledge of his growing transformation but realized that he was not invincible himself and that relapses were possible, perhaps even probable.

The next Sunday, Linda helped the kids get ready for church. "How do you know what they're supposed to wear?" Chase asked cynically as he watched.

"Do you really care?" Linda replied.

"Guess not. Just wondering."

"Well could you at least lend a hand by fixing us breakfast?"

"Cereal?"

"Sure, that's fine."

Chase went off to the kitchen, pouring himself a cup of coffee and staring at five boxes of cereal in the pantry. He made his choice and placed the box and three bowls on the table with a gallon of milk. Linda had mentioned taking the children to church, and after the attacks she insisted the time had come. She couldn't understand his annoying stubbornness given all of his other changes over the years and found it particularly baffling at a moment such as this. Chase told her maybe another time, just not now. She had also suggested a closed-mindedness on his part, an unwillingness to learn anything new. He answered that religion offered nothing. Frustrated by her husband's intransigence, Linda gave up the verbal battle and chose to go alone with the children.

"So you're sure you won't come with us?" Linda pleaded once more as the three entered the kitchen.

"Yeah, come on, Daddy!" said Amy.

"Oh, your daddy's, uh, well, pretty busy this morning. You guys have a good time. I'll be here when you get back."

Linda raised her eyebrows and tightened her mouth. "What are you going to do?"

"I'll find something."

CHAPTER 27

Her research on the Internet the night before had revealed a Baptist church a few miles away, and since Linda had been raised in the denomination, she felt better about that choice than with the competing options.

The parking was lot full, so she found a place on the street, grabbed her children's hands, and wove her way through the cars. A woman in the entry area showed her the location of the Sunday school classes. Once she had them signed in, Linda seated herself near the back of the packed sanctuary, immediately noticing the cushioned chairs were much more comfortable than the old pews of her teenage years. As the piano played a nice tune, her eyes roamed the congregation, upwards of two hundred smartly dressed people in attendance that morning. A blue-robed choir prepared to sing a number while the minister and an apparent associate, both in suits, entered the stage from a side door and sat down in two reserved chairs.

After what Linda used to call the "warm-up," consisting of several rehearsed hymns, the associate stepped up and promoted a couple of social events. He then announced the offering baskets coming around and said a prayer. The choir sang another hymn while four men made certain the baskets reached everyone. Linda pulled out a twenty and dutifully made her donation. Then came a special song (though not too special in Linda's mind) by an older woman. The crowd graciously showed its pleasure.

Finally the minister stood and took a few slow, deliberate steps to the wooden lectern. He wore a dark brown suit with a pinstriped tie that didn't match all that well, his round face sitting on a short, thick neck that melted into his oversize frame. The Reverend Johnston adjusted his glasses and began reading from his notes, occasionally looking up for verbal support.

"Everyone knows that on Tuesday morning, September 11, four commercial airplanes were hijacked by terrorists and flown into New York City's World Trade Center and the Pentagon in Washington, D.C., killing everyone on board and thousands of innocent citizens on the ground. Our president has called this an act of war. Those who planned and organized this event have been labeled as cowards, as ruthless terrorists, and as enemies of the United States. Americans are stunned by these attacks and feel an overwhelming grief for the victims and their families. I have seen a mixture of anger and fear throughout our nation."

He raised his head and acknowledged a sprinkling of amens before continuing. "Those of you in attendance a few months ago know that we looked at the time when King David brought the ark of the covenant back to Jerusalem, and on the way, a man by the name of Uzzah was killed by God because he dishonored the Lord's presence. David became angry at the Lord and afraid of him at the same time. So David expressed the two emotions I'm seeing here in our country: anger and fear. I said, anger and fear!"

A few obedient amens took the minister back to his notes. "People are angry at those who have violated our land of freedom and have murdered the innocent. Yet at the same time, they are filled with the fear that terrorists will strike again—perhaps today, perhaps next week, and perhaps in ways that we've never imagined.

"People are also angry at those who have weakened international intelligence and national security, yet they are also afraid that no matter what we do, we may still be vulnerable. Anger and fear!" he shouted, pounding the lectern. "Neither emotion is a healthy place from which to respond. Both are likely to lead people to make choices they may later regret. And so even though anger and fear are normal human emotions, we should not allow them to influence the decisions we make!"

As the crowd clapped in approval, Linda noted how this sermon recalled what her husband had said about the personal lies that once ensnared him. Chase often pointed to his freedom from anger and fear. She continued to reflect as she listened to the minister.

"We as a nation have just experienced one of the most horrific events in our history, what President Bush has called the first war of the twenty-first century. But how should we respond? As Christians, we must look at our response in a twofold fashion. First, our nation must take strong action against its enemies to protect citizens and to ensure continued freedom. We should therefore do everything we can to support efforts to eliminate those who are terrorizing and killing innocent men, women, and children all over the world. Second, we must realize that these acts of war and terrorism are earthly expressions of a spiritual enemy. The obvious hatred toward America by those in terrorist organizations is merely a reflection of the hatred the devil has for mankind in general and for Christians specifically.

"And so our country is at war, and I believe we must support our country. Thousands of wonderful lives were stolen from us on Tuesday—sons and daughters, mothers and fathers, husbands and wives, friends and loved ones—most buried in the darkness of concrete and steel. As the mayor of New York so aptly said, 'We are all New Yorkers in this hour.' In addition, the body of Christ is at war. Our nation's future battles may be fought on foreign soil. However, our battle as Christians is not against flesh and blood but against the one who is behind the evil we see, the deceiver, the destroyer, the wicked one himself."

The Reverend Johnston spoke for another thirty minutes about the devil's tactics, about the need to stand together in prayer, and about how Christians must let their light shine into the darkness of the world. Linda's mind drifted in and out, her body restless during the long speech. She liked the first part, which seemed appropriately patriotic, but simply couldn't follow the spiritual dimension of the attacks. *Chase wouldn't like that*, she thought. *Better that he didn't come after all.*

**

After perfunctorily watching his family walk out the front door, Chase seized the time alone to process recent thoughts. He would have enjoyed a cigar but decided against it since Linda might think he chose that pleasure over going to church. Instead, he poured another hot cup of coffee and sauntered outside next to the fountain. A perfect fall morning greeted him, reds, oranges, and golds beginning to color the backyard trees. He loved Linda's enthusiasm when, just days earlier, she gleefully noticed the variety of colors in the neighborhood trees. Paying no attention to the stunning contrasts in his youth, Chase now shared his wife's appreciation of nature's cyclical beauty.

So why did he display stubbornness regarding God and religion and church? Chase reasoned that his attitude must have been born out of resentment for his father, but could there be a lie hiding beneath his cynicism? Perhaps the lie that no truth existed in religion since no truth resided in his dad? Or maybe the lie that God must not care about him? It seemed that way given his father's abandonment and his brother's death, events God evidently allowed. Had he become God's judge? Chase shivered at the notion. No, he didn't think he had fallen quite that far since he felt fine with God. His problem, therefore, must be more about the people who follow God. But why? Other than the obnoxious insistence that others accept their narrow point of view, Chase didn't have much of an answer, and he felt shallow citing the cliché of hypocrisy.

Ruminating without resolution frustrated him. Why could he figure out so many other areas of his life but not this one? Could it be that big of a deal to allow his children Christian influence? Or maybe his resistance was justified since the recent attacks appeared to be religiously motivated. But were Christians as dangerous as those other people? Or as brainwashed? He couldn't believe that. After all, his mom turned out okay with her Catholic faith. Lane and Kathy had continued to attend Mass on occasion. Maybe he simply rejected the concept of God being involved in a person's everyday life. Why would God care? Why would he want anything to do with a person like himself? And if he didn't, why should anyone want anything to do with God's religion?

"I think I may be getting somewhere," Chase said half aloud. He wasn't angry with God. He didn't consider himself recalcitrant or too proud, and he certainly wasn't impervious to reason. But since God apparently had no time for him, why would he want to give God any of his own time? Chase felt better, almost placid. He finished his coffee, strolled back inside, and found the Sunday newspaper waiting for him by his chair.

Before Linda and the children returned, Chase showered and began to work on a few neglected projects. In the middle of fixing one of the kitchen chairs, he heard the front door open.

"Hi, hon'. We're home!"

"Daddy, Daddy!"

"I'm in here," he called out while on the floor.

"Oh, there you are," Linda said with a smirk, "lying down on the job as usual!"

"Daddy, we went to Sunday school!" Amy said excitedly as she looked down at him.

"You liked it?"

"Oh yeah! It was fun!"

Ryan copied his sister. "Yeah, it was fun!"

"Cool. Now why don't you let Daddy finish working here, and maybe Mommy will fix us some lunch." He glanced up at Linda with a wink.

"Sure. I'm famished. Kids, why don't you go clean up and we'll eat in about twenty minutes."

Linda set her purse down, pulled out a couple of pans, and began preparations while Chase continued to work, searching for the question that would demonstrate interest without intrigue. "What about you, babe? How'd you like church?"

"It was good."

After a moment of silence, Chase craned his neck and looked up with a puzzled expression. "That's it?"

"You really care?"

"Sure I do. Tell me about it."

"All right," she said with a deep breath, thinking her husband might be at least somewhat interested. "Well, I sat in the very last row since the place overflowed with people. I've never seen anything like it. A buzz of anticipation seemed to fill the room, lots of people looking for answers after Tuesday—including myself."

"Did you discover any?"

Linda left the bacon and eggs cooking on the stove and peered under the table, speaking in a hushed voice as if she had discovered something worth sharing. "I think I did, Chase. After the songs and formalities, the minister spoke of the attacks. He was patriotic and very much to the point, but what caught my attention was when he dramatically emphasized two primary emotions our country demonstrated this week: anger and fear."

Chase cursed under his breath when the screwdriver slid off its target and landed on his other hand. "Okay," he said, wincing. "Makes sense so far."

"But Chase, don't you see the connection between that and the lies you were freed from?"

"Oh yeah," he answered with a shrug, rolling his eyes and licking his wound. "I actually did wonder whether our country's believed a lie about itself. But I don't see anything wrong with normal human responses during a time like this. Seems natural."

"I agree. The minister's point was basically about the danger of making critical decisions based upon the emotions of anger and fear."

"All right, I can buy that. Wow! You really liked this guy."

"For the most part. I just couldn't follow his examples from the Bible, though everybody else seemed to enjoy that part, you know, with all the clapping and the amens."

"Of course they did, babe. They're part of the group."

Linda ignored his sarcasm and returned to the stove. "And how was your morning?" she asked.

"Oh fine. Just taking care of a few things around the house." Chase didn't feel up to sharing his thoughts about God and religion.

"Well thank you. That was nice. And hon', the children sure loved their classes," she said with a smile.

"Yeah, I could tell. They want to go back?"

"Probably. I'm just not so sure I do."

Chase sat up on one knee and wiped his brow, attempting not to appear too interested. "Why's that?"

Linda stroked her curls. "I think this has to be a family affair. Chase, I can't see myself taking our children to church, or anywhere for that matter, apart from you. The last thing we need is to live separate lives again, as you once said, like two people living in their own individual worlds."

Annoyed, Chase straddled the chair to finish his job. "So what do you expect me to do, Linda, compromise myself by going somewhere that I simply cannot stomach?"

She wanted to cry out, "Yes! That is exactly what you should do," but she found herself saying, "No, that is not what I expect of you."

"Well good. On the other hand, if you do wish to return, I just may consider going with you one time. I guess it can't hurt that much," he added with a chuckle.

Linda placed the bacon and eggs on the table and then knelt down next to Chase. "Hon', thanks for at least being open."

"Sure, babe. After all, we are a family."

Monday arrived and Chase had to drive to Syracuse. He left early, having decided to phone Doctor Rhinegold to discuss the question of dreams. He left a message with his cell number and continued on. He got a return call from L.A. within minutes.

"Doctor Rhinegold?"

"Yes, Chase. How have you been?"

"Hang on a sec. Let me pull over."

He found a safe place to stop along the highway and placed his phone on speaker. "I'm glad you returned my call so quickly. Do you have a minute to answer one question?"

"Sure. Go ahead."

"I've been having an unusual number of dreams these past several months, and without going into the details, I simply wanted to know if a person can dream excessively. Is it normal?"

"So you've had quite a few."

"Yeah."

"Well, Chase, dreams are formed in the subconscious, and they often involve a processing of what your conscious mind has been dwelling upon or struggling with or the experiences that may be producing conflict or questions. Other times, dreams can simply confirm what you already know, a reminder in a sense that you're traveling down the right road. Still other times, it may just be the pizza you ate!"

Chase laughed. "Okay, I understand the possibilities, but is it normal for dreams to have recurring themes, to bring the same sort of message?"

"What type of message?"

"Well, as you said, confirming things that I already know or have recently experienced."

"Do your dreams seem accurate?"

"I guess if I'm interpreting them accurately."

"Well I am not an expert on dream interpretation, but I would suggest paying attention to them because your mind, and perhaps your emotions, may be reiterating a subconscious demand to consciously focus upon the significance of the message. Is that what you're doing?"

"Yes, I am. But let me ask you this. What about having a dream within a dream?"

"That occurred with you?"

"Yeah, recently."

"As I said, I'm not an expert and would find making a judgment difficult, especially without hearing about them, but perhaps consider the second dream more important, the first playing a set-up role for the next one."

"So this is normal."

"Chase, there have been many studies concluding that everyone dreams. Remembering dreams is another issue. Let's say, for example, that you've dreamed fifty or so times in the last couple of months, most nights multiple times, yet you have recalled only four or five dreams. What that tells me is that the ones you wake up remembering are indeed necessary foci for your life. Is that normal? In the realm of the subconscious, what would you say is normal, Chase?"

"I have no idea."

"Nor do I."

"So I guess I just need to go with the flow."

"Have they assisted you in processing your change?"

"I think so."

"Well there you have it. Listen, I need to catch my next appointment, but it's been great to speak with you again."

"Can you send me a bill?

"This one's on me. Say hello to Linda for me."

"Will do. Thanks so much."

"And one more thing, Chase."

"Okay."

"I'm proud of you."

"Oh … Thank you."

"I really am. Take care."

Chase stared at the phone in his hand. Had anyone ever said that to him before? Maybe Linda. He couldn't recall. But because they came from such a respected authority, he treasured the words. "I'm proud of you," the doctor said. The line echoed in his mind and stood in immediate contrast with all the other words spoken to him, words from his father, words from his friends, even words he had spoken to himself. "I'm proud of you." Although his family had pointed to the remarkable changes in his life since the spider-web event, this was by far the most powerful affirmation he had ever received.

CHAPTER 28

The years that followed proved unmemorable. Shortly after the attacks from the Middle East, widespread displays of patriotism waned. And though forever changed, within a decade the country seemed to return to a sense of invulnerability, audaciously borrowing and spending as if nothing could affect its prosperity. Chase flourished in his national sales positions. Linda continued to assist him from their home office but also took a part-time job as an administrative assistant at the local elementary school. The family never returned to church during those years. And Stan made no further attempts to contact Linda.

Amy graduated from high school in 2009, and having proved her academic excellence, prepared to go away to college in Providence at the beginning of September. Ryan turned sixteen and showed little interest in school, becoming increasingly distant from his parents and demonstrating early signs of rebellion, which greatly concerned Chase and Linda. They purchased a used 2005 Toyota pickup truck for his birthday, not as a reward but for practical reasons.

One Friday night, an hour past Ryan's eleven o'clock weekend curfew, Chase impatiently paced back and forth in the living room, fuming as he waited for him to return home.

The door finally opened, and Ryan meekly informed his father that two policemen were on the porch.

"What?!" Not waiting for an answer, Chase hurried toward the open door.

"Mr. Macklin?" one of them asked.

"Yes."

"We received a call tonight about some kids partying on a nearby street. When we arrived, your son was the only one we were able to detain. Even though the can of beer he held in his hand was unopened, he appears to have had one or two."

Chase glared back at Ryan.

"Listen," the officer continued, "it didn't seem significant enough to bring him in, but it'd be good if you set some guidelines. We did impound his truck just to get his attention."

"Okay. Is there anything else I need to know?"

"We already warned him that if it happens again, we won't be as easy on him."

"Thanks," was all that Chase could manage to say in return.

He closed the door, shook his head, and peered into his sons's eyes, his own narrowing. "Ryan, what do you think you're doing?"

"Nothin'."

"You think drinking in public is nothing?"

"I had one beer. That's all."

"No, you didn't. I know better than that."

"Whatever."

Chase shook his head again. "Listen, you got off easy with the cops, but you won't with me. You were out partying, and now you have to answer for it. How long have you been drinking?"

"I don't know. A while, I guess."

"Are you into any drugs?"

"No! I don't do that."

"All right, but this is bad enough. I went overnight from doing a few drugs to becoming a dealer. You don't want to go down that path."

"I'm not! Just havin' some fun."

"And you'll pay for that fun. Now go to bed and we'll talk in the morning."

"I've got plans tomorrow."

"Not anymore you don't! I'll talk to you later."

Chase crawled quietly into bed. Linda stirred and turned over. "Is Ryan home?"

"Yeah. He got into some trouble with the police but luckily nothing too serious."

Linda quickly sat up. "What? What kind of trouble?"

"Out drinking with some buddies. The cops caught him, impounded his truck, and fortunately just dropped him off."

"Really? Out drinking?"

"Yeah. I'll speak with him in the morning."

"I can't believe he's drinking! What are we going to do about it?"

Chase shrugged wearily. "All I can think of at the moment is to talk to him and to give him a warning. Let's just sleep on it, and hopefully I'll find out more tomorrow."

"Hey hon', you know what's weird?"

"No, what?"

"Just last night I was reading through my journal about the dream you had years ago with Ryan as a teenager. You know, the one about him reaching the destination before you? Pretty strange timing."

"Guess so."

"Well maybe this will somehow lead to the fulfillment of that dream."

"That'd be nice."

Chase attempted to sleep, but his restless mind mulled over the possibility that he had been shirking his parental responsibility. He wondered how much a parent should feel compelled to take in such a situation. How could he feel successful in rearing one child and fear that he had failed with the other? How could two children raised so similarly turn out so very differently? What did he and Linda do wrong regarding Ryan? Were there warning signs they somehow missed? Did he merely want to have fun without considering the potential consequences, or could the situation be much more serious? Of course underage drinking was serious regardless, but how long had Ryan behaved this way under the radar? He denied taking drugs, but could Chase believe his son at this point?

Finally he drifted off, waking from time to time with the same mental torments, unable to find answers. Chase groggily rose at seven o'clock and made coffee, still wrestling with his thoughts. He knew firmness would be necessary; however, he didn't want to push his son further away. What if this issue had arisen between him and his dad—that is, if his father had remained with the family when Chase turned sixteen? His dad would probably have beaten him, shouting and cursing that he better behave or move out. Chase told himself he would not be that type of father.

Linda came down in her pajamas and robe, joining him for coffee. Her face appeared worn and a bit gaunt, her hair sloppily pulled back around her ears. She greeted him with a forced smile. Chase returned the gesture with raised eyebrows. "Looks like you didn't sleep much either," he observed softly.

"No, I didn't. Couldn't help but wonder where we could have gone wrong, you know, as parents."

"Me too."

"How long are you going to let Ryan sleep?"

"Let's just eat breakfast, and I'll get him up after that."

"Okay, but what are you going to say?"

"I'll figure it out."

He roused Ryan at eight, ordering him to be outside by the fountain in twenty minutes. Chase waited impatiently, rehearsing questions and possible responses, his coffee cold by the time Ryan reluctantly sat near his father on one of the stone benches, head down. Chase demanded eye contact. "So what's going on with you?"

"What do you mean?" Ryan asked with a frown.

"I'm going to ask you again. How long have you been drinking?"

"Not too long."

"You said last night 'a while.' What does that mean—a month, six months?"

"Maybe a couple."

"Look at me again. Is it because all your friends are drinking?"

"I don't know," he answered sullenly, lowering his head.

"Are you okay with it? I mean, you don't see any problems with anything, even after what happened?"

"Like I said, we were just havin' some fun. Everybody does it."

"Son, do you think everything's about you having fun? Don't you realize that there are serious consequences when you break the law? You don't want to end up in juvenile hall or something worse, do you?"

"No."

"Then you have to start making better choices. You know that I was about the same age as you when I got caught up with the wrong people. I was extremely fortunate that I didn't end up in prison, but I told you how I got shot and had to flee the state. Because of all I've been through, it's important to me that you think through all the potential consequences of your behavior, but it has to be important to you as well. Listen, Ryan, you're a good boy. You don't have to bow to pressure from your peers and go down a road you'll later regret. Does this make sense to you?"

"Yeah."

"Ryan, look at me. Are you going to let me help you or not?"

"I don't have a choice, do I?"

"Well you're not going to have a lot of choices for a while since you haven't made good ones recently. You're going to be grounded for three months, and we'll continue to talk through all of this."

Ryan jumped up. "What do you mean grounded?" he demanded.

"Sit down, Ryan." He obeyed. "Grounded means you're not going to drive your truck or leave the house alone for three months, through the summer. Period."

"What, are you crazy? No way!"

"Ryan, stop it. Listen to me. This is the way it's going to be. You may not like it, but I never had a father who cared about me the way I care for you."

Ryan jumped up again and ran back into the house, the words "I hate you!" trailing behind him.

Chase followed him upstairs. He opened the slammed door and found his son crying on his bed. He stood for a moment, surveying the room for any signs of rebellion. Chase saw two posters of heavy metal rock bands. Next to them, in perspicuous contrast, hung an old picture of the family at Disneyland. On the other side of the room was a red-and-yellow sign he had never before noticed, the letters boldly and ironically announcing, "No Drinking Allowed!"

Chase rolled his eyes and sat down next to Ryan, attempting to comfort him. "Son, you're not going to understand this, but I love you with all my heart. I want the best for you, and where you're headed is not the best."

"You don't know where I'm headed," Ryan said, his face still in his pillow.

"Don't talk back to me like that. You've got a few months of restriction, and you need to focus on reimbursing us after we pick up your truck."

"How am I going to do that?" Ryan snapped.

"Whatever it takes. Paper route, mowing people's lawns, helping me around the house. You just need to make enough money to pay us back. And who knows, you may find something you really like."

"Are you done?"

"Yeah, sure. But, Ryan, take some time to think about this, and we'll talk some more." He touched his shoulder. "I really do love you, son."

Hearing no response, Chase furtively glanced once more around the room before heading downstairs.

"Sounded like that didn't go too well," Linda observed with a hint of frustration.

"No. I didn't expect it would. We talked about what he did, and then I grounded him for the summer."

"Three months? Really?"

"Yeah. It's just a number, but I'm not about to let him get away with this type of behavior. It'll all work out. He'll come around."

"I sure hope so."

Ryan's disposition radically changed after a weekend of sulking. On Monday morning he stepped into the kitchen with uncharacteristic alacrity. "Hi, Mom! Hi, Dad! What's for breakfast?"

"Well good morning, Ryan," Linda said with a surprised look at Chase. "You're in a good mood. Want some oatmeal?"

"Sure!" He plopped himself down at the table across from his father, who stared in bewilderment. "Hey Dad, do you have anything for me to do around the house today?"

"Uh, well, certainly. There's always something."

"Okay, just let me know. I'll obviously be here." He stole a glance at his mother, hoping for a smile.

She complied. "Ryan, what happened to you? Why the sudden change?"

"I don't know, Mom. I guess there's nothing I can do about anything at this point, so I just need to make the best of it."

Chase remained silent. Although it was nice to see his son's quick turnaround, he wasn't naïve enough to believe the conflict was over. Nevertheless, he thought, *What an amazingly positive start after such a miserable weekend!* He couldn't believe what finally came out of his mouth, however. "You know this could have turned out a lot worse."

"Yeah."

Linda couldn't believe her husband's insensitivity. Chase immediately tried to be more positive. "Well your mother and I are behind you."

"I know."

He kicked himself for changing his son's mood. Linda tried to pull Ryan out of it. Chase observed in silence.

After breakfast, he went upstairs, dug for the letter he had written to his children eight years earlier, and reread it. Quite pleased with his message, he found another envelope, copied his instructions on the front, placed the letter inside, and sealed the envelope.

CHAPTER 29

On the following Monday, his cell phone rang with Linda's number displayed. Working at his job in Syracuse, completely absorbed in a new marketing idea, the call surprised him.

"Hi, babe, what's up?"

"Ryan's gone!"

"What do you mean?"

"He's gone! I just went to his room to wake him and he wasn't there. I looked for his backpack and it's gone too. I think he's run away!"

Chase heard uncontrollable sobbing in between her words. "I'll come home immediately. Have you reported it to the police?"

"Not yet."

"Well do it and I'll be there as soon as I can."

"Okay. Hurry!"

Chase grabbed his laptop, shoved paperwork into his briefcase, informed the boss of his sudden emergency, and shot on to the highway.

No warning signs of such behavior, he thought. *Just the opposite, in fact.* Chase felt betrayed, not only by his son but by his own stupidity in believing change had occurred so suddenly and dramatically. "He's only a teenager!" he yelled, slamming his hand on the steering wheel. Chase wondered where Ryan would go, what friend might be sheltering him. Lost in thought and neglecting to signal a lane change, he nearly sideswiped a semi-truck. The driver pounded his horn in anger.

"Man! That was close!" Chase wiped his brow, checked the rearview mirror, and waved "sorry."

Forty-five minutes later he sprinted into the living room to find Linda weeping hysterically. "Chase! What are we going to do?"

Holding her close and brushing away the tears, he managed to say, "It'll be all right, Linda," not believing his own words. "Did you call the police?"

"Yes," she answered between sobs.

"What did they say?"

"They told me to come down and fill out a missing child report. Chase, I can't believe this is happening. Should we drive the neighborhood?"

"I'll call Teddy's parents. Maybe he went over there. If not, I'll try to get some of his friends' phone numbers. Babe, he's probably in the area. Don't cry. We'll find him."

"K."

Chase left her alone and hurried to the study. Teddy's mother had no idea where Ryan was but provided a few other possibilities. The first call proved valueless, and no one answered the second. He dialed the last number, perspiration mounting on his forehead and staining his armpits.

"Hello."

"Mrs. Thompson?"

"Yes."

"This is Chase Macklin. Listen, my son Ryan … Do you know him?"

"Of course! He's here with Zack."

Chase's chest rose and fell with relief. "Great. Well I need to come pick him up. What's your address? … Okay, thanks. I'll be right there."

He quickly hung up, informed Linda of Ryan's location on the other side of town, and rushed out of the house.

Feeling less anxious now that he knew Ryan was safe, Chase wondered if his own life could be a huge lie. He had, in fact, grown quite weary of the entire process of discovering lies and attempting to overcome them. Backing out of the driveway, he questioned himself. Could it be that every experience, including his initial vision, held some sort of demonic power over him? Chase pulled into the street and raced away. *Were demons even real?* he wondered. *And if so, did they control a person's mind? Or could each vision and dream, along with each conclusion and interpretation, be an illusion?*

Chase's life seemed to mimic a long movie with unbelievable tragedy and trauma, laced with hope but filled with disappointment. What if everything indeed proved to be simply a way of coping with reality? Could it all have begun with some sort of supernatural apparition that provided a sense of escape but that effectively led to personal imprisonment? And then, perhaps all by design, had a subtle trap been set by dark forces and eluded his cognitive awareness?

Chase knew he should be thinking of Ryan, but suddenly, out of nowhere, a phrase entered his confused mind. He had mentioned it to Linda and to Doctor Rhinegold but had somehow missed its significance. This time he heard it clearly, forcefully, from somewhere deep within himself and instantly understood that he dare not ignore it, that it somehow held the key to all of his mental and emotional struggles. Self-centeredness.

Of course! That was his primary problem, perhaps even the father of every lie he believed about himself. If he looked at his previous fear of vulnerability or of trust, Chase found self-centeredness demanding that he take care of himself at all costs. When he considered his past issues with touch, self-centeredness explained his jaded, scornful attitude toward others needing such comfort. If he were honest with himself, he had to admit that self-centeredness had given birth to his pride, which was possibly its first offspring.

But what about anger? That, too, Chase quickly resolved. Angry thoughts and actions proceed from a person's frustration that others don't understand him, don't consider his perceptions or ideas, don't allow him to remain in the center of his own created world.

The spider web appeared again, and Chase saw with his mind's eye the large, sticky strands accompanied by all of his old lies. Then, as if giving life to each of them, a carefully crafted mesh of web tauntingly displayed itself in the very middle—self-centeredness. There it hung, untouched. He shuddered.

Chase stopped at a signal. He realized his life could not go on as before since he had no idea how to defeat such an innate enemy. How does one stop an angry jaguar leaping through the air with its bared claws aimed at its victim's head? How does one fight off the razor-sharp teeth of an attacking barracuda or the powerful grip of a hungry crocodile? Self-centeredness, gloating at him from the web, implored him to try. He fought off the temptation.

Chase decided he was done with everything. How could he continue if no matter what he did, he'd be swallowed up by this vicious enemy? How could he go on if he faced the eventual defeat of all that he had lived for, all that he had ever known—the preservation of himself?

On the other hand, perhaps there indeed existed a way to defeat this enemy without destroying himself in the process. If self-centeredness was also a lie, maybe he could defy his own instinctual behavior by living with new purpose. Rather than conquering his dysfunctions and taking pride in those successes, a self-serving attitude, he could direct all of his attention to others and their needs. He would do this not to win another battle but to meet the spoken and unspoken cries for attention and love from those outside of his web. This would mean refocusing all of his energy and submitting his will completely to the task.

The light turned green. *But how can self-centeredness be a lie?* he wondered. *Isn't it true that people function with themselves in the very middle of their own worlds?* Chase recalled a line about loving your neighbor as yourself, though he couldn't remember the source. Didn't that imply self-centeredness since a person first had to love himself? He ran his fingers through his hair, resting his right hand on the back of his neck for several moments. *Perhaps,* he thought, *some lies are simply abused truth.* He didn't know.

Chase had only one desire at the moment, the only one worth fighting for, a deep yearning residing within him—to be a loving family. Nothing mattered more. Nothing else made sense. He would concentrate on Linda, Ryan, and Amy and forget about himself. "It's over," he said aloud resolutely. He would bury all thoughts about lies and move forward, focusing particularly on helping his son.

Ryan was more embarrassed than angry, though certainly far from apologetic, asking his father why he had created such a scene in front of Zack and his mother. He wanted to know the reason for his dad's panic. Of course he understood that he had broken the restriction. Of course he knew what he had done, though it consisted merely of spending one night away. No, they didn't drink. No, they didn't go out. And yes, he would never run away again.

"Are we finished, Dad?" he finally asked.

"Ryan, we're never going to be finished. We're family, and family stays together no matter what. Regardless of your disobedience, your mom and I love you and are here for you. You can always count on that."

"Okay," he responded sullenly with his head down.

Ryan loosely wrapped his arms around his mother's back, feeling her tight embrace but resisting her tear-filled pleas never to disappear like that again. After another minute or so of emotional appeals, Linda agreed to his request to go up to his room.

"Unbelievable," Chase muttered with a shake of his head.

"Are we losing him, hon'?"

"I think we may be. Come on, babe. Don't cry. I made a decision when I was driving to pick him up. I'm done with all the visions and the dreams and the attempt to convince myself that the world would be a better place if people experienced the same things I did. I can't take all the drama any longer. I think my own issues somehow created it all, you know, in a sort of dark way."

"What on earth on you talking about?"

"I'm tired. I'm tired of everything. The way I philosophize, the way I reason, my pride in coming further than most. I'm convinced that it's all an illusion."

"Chase, you're scaring me," Linda said, wiping away her tears. "I have no idea what's going on inside that brain of yours, but stop talking like this. We have to focus on Ryan."

"That's precisely the point. I've grown weary of being the center of my own world. I've realized that self-centeredness has driven my every thought and action. I'm done with that. I'm now fully committed to giving attention to you and the children. That's it."

"Well fine, but what are you saying about those personal changes that you know to be real?"

"Nothing's real. It's all an illusion."

"Look at me, Chase!" Linda's voice was unusually stern. She took his face in both hands. "If you think you can simply go back to your old patterns and behaviors, I am the one who's done! I will not live with that old man ever again! Are you hearing me?"

"Of course, but hey—"

"No buts, Chase. You go backward and you can back your way right out this home."

He removed her hands from his face. "I've never heard you like this. But listen, it's not what you think. I had—"

"And I've never heard you like this! Pull your mind together and embrace reality. I've gone through most of the same things you have, and I'm not standing here whining about it. The only illusion is your sudden belief that there is an illusion. Snap out of it!"

Chase reared back defensively. "You're serious."

"Of course I am. I need you, Chase. We need each other at this moment. Stay on course. We have to rescue our son."

Rescue! The word felt like a wake-up slap to his face. It indeed accurately described his own deliverance, Linda's victory over a tormenting relationship, and now Ryan's need for freedom from peer pressure. Rescue implied desperation. That was true of him, certainly of Linda, and perhaps of his son.

"You're right."

"Thank you."

"But let me ask you something, just out of curiosity. You'd actually have allowed me to walk out the door?"

"At that point, yes. I can't allow you to divorce yourself from reality."

"Okay, I'll work it out. Trust me."

Linda reached for his hands. "Let's do this together, Chase."

"I'm with you," he said, tightly squeezing her hands. "Hey, would you mind if I took some time alone? We can deal with Ryan later after he cools down."

"Sure."

Chase hurried to the humidor in his office, chose one of his Dominicans, stole a peek at Linda before grabbing a beer from the refrigerator, and walked hastily outside to his habitual place by the fountain. He hadn't noticed the back fence leaning awkwardly against one of the old maples. Assuming the wood might be deteriorating, he made a mental note to rescue the fence. He stopped when he realized the expense.

Isn't that the truth? Chase mused quietly. *There is indeed a cost to being rescued.* Pleased that Linda's ultimatum had roused him from his mental torpor, he was relieved that he could return to living his life with the lessons he'd learned regarding lies and truth. Chase now considered rescue's true price—a battle for one's soul, a relentless tug-of-war between reality and illusion, inner peace and disillusionment. But the alternative entered his mind. He pictured a man drowning at sea and rejecting a life-preserver tossed out to him. Then he pictured another man, frustrated with his slow progress, heaving his life-preserver aside to try swimming against the waves.

This must be his own precarious condition, still at sea, struggling to find land. Chase had assured himself of his own freedom, and he had beckoned others to join him on a newly discovered island of hope. Now he saw that the shoreline was still frustratingly far off, and he realized that he needed steady and determined patience merely to hold on. Could it possibly be worth the cost? Did the dividends outweigh the mental and emotional price? They had to, he decided. Rewards without cost, rescue without daunting challenges, must in fact minimize the miraculous gift.

Grumbling to himself that he forget to light his cigar, Chase torched the end and took a few satisfying puffs. Now where did he leave off? He couldn't remember.

His dad came to mind. Chase reflected on how he lacked a real father and resolved not to repeat his dad's mistakes. Life was interesting. On the one hand, how someone was raised made a difference; on the other hand, there was only so much a parent could do to influence children. Even those considered the best parents often found themselves burdened by the rebellious nature of their offspring, while others abandoned their children only to discover their incredible talent and success years later. So apparently the key wasn't so much what happened in a person's life but how he or she responded to what happened.

Chase recalled his grandmother Nattie telling him with a certain authority that God wouldn't let him die without accomplishing something good. Though he was uncertain about that, he knew he'd definitely progressed from where he began.

He wondered about eternity, thinking of his mom and dad, of Lane and Kathy. He found it interesting that the afterlife was typically an afterthought until someone close died. Then people hoped in the reality of it, discovering a sense of security in the possibility that life didn't end in the grave. But heaven and hell? Chase didn't understand much about them, simply concluding that if one existed the other must as well. However, who went where remained a mystery.

Chase took a few sips of beer and saw the ash on his cigar growing. What had he accomplished in his life of nearly forty-five years? Though he was content with his marriage and satisfied with his health and his finances, could those areas of success be good enough? And if so, good enough for whom? Most of his debilitating lies had been exposed and broken, and although this was a continual process, it led him ever closer to internal freedom. That had to count for something.

Or did any of it matter? Wasn't life simply about doing the best you can, enjoying it as much as possible, and treating others with respect and kindness? Or could there be something he had missed? Could there be a deeper meaning to it all that had somehow escaped him? The huge hand that rescued him from the spider web—could he one day identify it? The voice that spoke so clearly to him—would there ever be resolution to its source?

He finished his beer and tossed away the remaining cigar, feeling content at least to pursue difficult questions. Though left with no answers, only the solitude of an ocean of thought, Chase decided simply to enjoy his rescue.

BROKEN FORTUNE

F ollow the continued saga of Chase Macklin in *Broken Fortune* as he faces the challenges of morality, hypocrisy, temptation, and a newly discovered mindset and belief system. With half of the novel set in Brazil, you will travel from the jungles of the Amazon to the beaches of Rio de Janeiro, experiencing the beauty of the land and the people, as well as cross-cultural intricacies.

Broken Fortune provides the answers to Chase's inner turmoil regarding the source of his freedom from the spider web of lies, though not without reoccurring battles of the soul to maintain his freedom in order to live true to himself.

Printed in the United States
By Bookmasters